DREAMS, SCHEMES AND SPINY MACHINES
Book 3 of The Quillogy

I0609713

Joel Reeves

DREAMS, SCHEMES AND SPINY MACHINES
Book 3 of The Quillogy

DOUBLE DRAGON

A DOUBLE DRAGON PAPERBACK

© Copyright 2014
Joel Reeves

The right of Joel Reeves to be identified as author of this
work has been asserted in accordance with the
Copyright, Designs and Patents Act 1988

All Rights Reserved

No reproduction, copy or transmission of the publication
may be made without written permission. No paragraph
of this publication may be reproduced, copied or
transmitted save with the written permission of the
publisher, or in accordance with the provisions of the
Copyright Act 1956 (as amended).

Any person who does any unauthorised act in relation to
this publication may be liable to criminal prosecution
and civil claims for damages.

ISBN 978-1-78695-719-1

Double Dragon
is an imprint of
Fiction4All

This Edition Published 2022
Fiction4All
www.fiction4all.com

Cover art by Deron Douglas
www.derondouglas.ca

Introduction

The mobile fertilizing utility vehicle was clearly a design made for hedgehogs of the smaller variety, not humans. A stocky fellow sat inside the compact chariot, knees sticking up near his chin. He was mostly bald with just a small tuft of stubborn orange hair poking up a few inches above his bushy eyebrows. He steered the solar-powered cart through the network of gardens. The vehicle paused, a small rotary blade attachment digging a shallow hole in the black soil and depositing a delicate sapling. It continued on, rolling slowly through the green garden-all that remained of the once flourishing forests and jungles of Yurle Prime.

Odd Bob, known simply as just Bob to his good friends, had taken the off-world job gladly as it sounded like a welcome change from building large structures out of stone. Plus there was the added perk of being able to breathe fresh air; albeit, air artificially generated within a controlled environment inside of a refurbished super cruiser. Besides, no one really needed specialists to construct indomitable castles or walls fortified to withstand an assault by catapult or an angry giant with a bone to pick. Refusing to become obsolete, Bob enrolled forthwith in a training program through the Yurle Prime School of Sun Dome Technologies and Plant Care.

The brown patch on Bob's forest green uniform identified him as Senior Environmental Controls Officer. He liked being in charge after so many years of taking other people's orders. But, despite his newfound status, he'd promised himself that he would never treat his own workers as Baron Glauwer had once treated him.

His employees-fifty of the most dedicated and environmentally conscious hedgies anyone could ask for-were the true backbone of Real Plants in Space Enterprises. Many of these were aboriginal hedgehogs, and they had lived in the forests and jungles, witnessed their destruction first-hand, and brought an unequalled enthusiasm to the job of preserving what remained for generations to come.

The buggy Bob rode in whispered up to an elderly hedgehog. This fellow, also a recent graduate of the training program, regulated the water supply inside the complex. He adjusted a valve, which, in turn, pumped out a precise mixture of water and fertilizing agents through a series of hoses onto a bed of plants bearing beautiful and delicious-looking red and purple fruits.

Odd Bob stepped out of his vehicle and stretched.

"Those fruit look very healthy," Bob observed, licking his lips.

Harlix, former cemetery sexton, freedom fighter, and now senior plant manager, picked one of the fruits off and handed it to Bob. "Have one," he offered. "They're proven to delay senility, fight tooth decay, and they're only nineteen calories per serving."

Bob bit into the fruit hungrily. Juice rolled down and off his chin as he surveyed the interior of the impressive cruiser. The ship was, in fact, a

6

retired member of the Galactic University Defense and Research fleet that had been donated as a floating greenhouse. To Bob, the cruiser looked more like a satellite with its modifications. Although its guns had been removed in order to accommodate the installation of eight greenhouse domes, the ship was still equipped with two powerful engines capable of attaining near light speed for short intervals, as well as, a basic hyper-jump generator. Eight transparent reinforced corridors radiated out from the cruiser like the legs of a spider. Each corridor ended in a domed chamber of its own- burgeoning vegetation centers with independent maintenance modules and life support.. Bob could not imagine a situation in which the eight smaller vessels would need to separate from the mother ship. Still, if such an emergency materialized, it was comforting to know that the eight mini-stations would be self-sufficient for several months.

Bob swallowed the rest of the fruit and planted the woody pit inside the black soil.

Harlix nodded and smiled. "Thank you, sir, for recycling."

"Harlix, call me Bob," Odd Bob said, squeezing the aged hedgehog's shoulder warmly. "As far as I'm concerned, you do not work for me. We work together for one cause." He smiled fondly at the hedgie. "I'm Bob. That's an order."

Harlix saluted. "Yes, Bob!"

Bob chuckled and climbed back inside the mobile fertilizing utility vehicle. The buggy weaved onward, waddling up an adjacent corridor beneath a canopy of stars and into the artificial glow of Sun Dome Three.

Only Bob, Harlix, and a few other highly trained workers had clearance to enter this particular dome. The reason was pretty obvious: It housed several aggressive plants of the voracia carnivora family. The massive stalks of these towering plants were thick and thorny, almost tree-like. The heads were shaped like large melons with razor sharp teeth in mouths four to five feet in length--easily large enough to accommodate a young herding beast in a single gulp.

The pulpy purple head of one of the carnivorous plants poked over a wall of the transparent steel-glass enclosure. Its enormous maw opened and closed and it cocked its head to one side, curious. To the untrained eye, the plant really looked docile, almost friendly. But Bob knew better.

He got down from the vehicle and tripped the activator to begin the teleportation sequence. In mere seconds, a pair of moon cow calves materialized on the transporter. Bob pressed another button and the platform on which the two beefy animals stood lifted, coming to a stop just below the top of the wall.

The head of the carnivorous plant snapped up both animals, the quickness of its movement almost impossible to follow, and disappeared behind the wall. A moment later, another head appeared, waiting its turn, impatient.

Bob entered the code that would teleport another pair of the creatures from the well-stocked

Dinhari Moon Cow Farm Number Nine on Yurle Prime. He repeated the process eight more times until all of the plants within the enclosure had received their recommended daily allowance of meat.

He wasn't sure if it was possible to overfeed this particular species, but not giving them enough to eat could be very dangerous. He closed his eyes, trying not to think about the terrible accident that had occurred less than a year ago when an undertrained employee had entered the restricted area to retrieve a loose glass and fallen inside the enclosure. It had been Harlix who had discovered the platform, bloodied and still in the raised position.

Bob shut down and lowered the teleporter platform and hopped back on the little buggy tractor and shifted it into gear. He continued on his way through the giant greenhouse to finish his daily rounds.

Chapter One

Since his retirement as a commander in the Galactic University Space Force, Gamitof Pym-Larko's life had not lost much of its excitement. He glanced-for a glance was all he dared risk right now-at his distorted reflection in the tall glass bottle that stood before him on the little round table and frowned. His face was fuller these days-okay, fatter-and the soft curly brownish fur that covered his head had turned mostly white. The small black eyes, however, remained shiny and alert.

Twenty-seven years! Nearly three decades, he thought, since he and his crew members had driven Moleloch, the Dark Mistress and Empress of the mole race, from her subterranean lair. The disappearance of her major domo, Lord Butae, and the insidious device called Deep Thought, still worried him at times, but nothing had been heard from them in all this time and everyone believed both were lost somewhere in the void of space.

Unfortunately, in the end, the notorious demon hedgehog Walpole, more dangerous than both of them, had escaped.

"No, I can't believe we've seen the last of him," he muttered, lifting the nearly empty bottle to his lips to mask his words. Just thinking of Walpole was enough to send chills down his spine. Even after the mind-twisting hedgehog's existence had become little more than a memory, his dark legacy carried on.

Because of that, life for the retired captain and hero in the HHMW (Human Hedgehog Mole War) remained hectic. The pension from the Galactic University had been generous, but boredom and a fear of losing the full use of his faculties to old age had driven him to accepting a new occupation. Spy.

His new boss, Chief of Planet Security Oris Folpole, did not sugar coat the latest situation. "It involves running interference on a dangerous splinter group of known Walpole loyalists here on Yurle Prime. I must warn you, though. The job is very dangerous. A number of our best operatives have been killed in recent weeks."

Larko suspected that, if he didn't stay on his eight toes, he himself might be the next to die. It was hard to put a finger on exactly what had changed. But there was definitely something different in the air, a strange tenseness. Someone was planning something.

And it was in Grumpole's Hideaway-quiet, peaceful watering hole of the retiring sort-that he sensed was where to look for the next spot of trouble. He didn't have long to wait.

A tall, handsome and slender middle-aged man entered the inn. He was dressed in a Yurle Prime Space Force officer's uniform, his thick black hair slicked back with a shiny, gooey gel.

Jonathan Quintain, a face Larko had been familiar with since the man had been a squalling boy wrapped in the baronial towels of the House of Glauwer, adjusted the cap on his head and peered into the gloom of the smoky room. He spoke for a moment to Big Dale, the proprietor. The fat

11

bartender nodded in Larko's direction. Jonathan nodded and marched quickly across the room. He gave Larko a firm handshake, pulled up a chair, and sat down grinning.

"You, my friend, are a very hard fellow to track down," Jonathan stated.

Larko stared hard at the man. "Well, Jonny, what a surprise," he said. "It is you, isn't it?"

Jonathan chuckled. "I know, I know. I haven't had a chance to stop in to see you since the Day of the New Harvest Party at Bogo's place. They keep me busy, you know."

Larko nodded, sighing. "I realize that. It's not that I'm not delighted to see your face, my good fellow. It's just that things are a bit hot at the moment. And, I occasionally confuse one face with another. Must be the local ale."

Jonathan took off his pilot's hat and placed it on the table between them. He studied his old friend's face. It was lined with worry.

"I've heard about the rising heat. That's why I stopped in. Someone told me you were all alone on this case. Very foolish, even for Gamitof Pym, my resourceful mage."

"That someone was named Folpole, no doubt." Larko was about to shoo Jonathon away to safer places when his eyes darted toward the door. Two hooded figures dressed in gray robes entered the alehouse, paused in the doorway to survey its customers-the usual mix of human expatriates, Dinhari time spinners, and reformed moles-and sat down at the bar.

"I think it might be best if you left," Larko whispered. "For your own safety."

Jonathan noticed now that Larko had his back to the wall. His shining black eyes blinked, nervous. He suddenly had the feeling someone was watching them.

"Your chief was a bit vague," Jonathan stated, perplexed. "You wouldn't want to fill me in?"

"I forget you're not the little boy with the rather useless parents, wandering around that damp castle with only a silly rat mage for a friend," he said, then lowered his voice to a bare whisper. "The Crimson Quill Guild."

A hedgehog waitress, wearing a dress far too tight for her rather corpulent figure and staggering about in high heels that didn't remotely suit her little feet, weaved past carrying a tray of drinks. She stopped at a nearby table and began chatting with a group of ogling young pilots.

Neither Larko, who was Tandaran, nor Jonathon, a human being, were particularly attracted to hedgehogs, female or otherwise, so it was curious that certain of them were so intent on following human or outer Galactic fashions. The poor little waitress, Kookie, cute in her own hedgehog way, had clearly been torturing herself. Her legs were smooth, plucked clean of spines. Jonathon tried not to think about how much it must hurt to be *quilled*-a process that involved tweezers and daily molephine injections to prevent future growth. Happily, most of Grumpole's Hideaway clientele were hedgehogs, even the fliers from the nearby base. They certainly liked the waitress' new look.

"Big Dale must be really hard up to keep the clientele happy," Jonathon said.

Kookie finished telling a joke to amuse the pilots, then approached Larko's table.

"You gentlemen look really thirsty," she observed. "Can I get you something?"

Larko shook his head, still keeping an eye on the newcomers.

"No. Nothing for me. Doctor's orders." Larko smiled nervously at the waitress and then at Jonathan. "My friend is thirsty. Please bring him some of this inn's finest."

"Absolutely," she replied.

The waitress nodded and hurried off toward the bar. She returned moments later holding a tall mug of brownish liquid with a thick head of foam. She set the drink down in front of Jonathan, then hurried off to replenish the drinks at the fliers' table.

Jonathan took a sip of his drink. "You mentioned a certain Guild. Are we looking for anyone in particular?"

"They have their spies everywhere. They're definitely growing in numbers."

Jonathan nodded toward the beggar's table. "Him?"

Larko followed Jonathan's surreptitious gaze. A skinny human, dressed in a ragged trench coat, scraggly beard, and black glasses, hunched down in the shadows, almost out of sight. He appeared to be talking to a glass ball in the handle of his white cane.

Larko shrugged. "Looks like a blind, and admittedly, crazy beggar."

14

"Crazy, maybe," Jonathan conceded, "but not blind."

Larko studied the beggar some more, puzzled. "What do you mean?"

Jonathan grinned. "He seems to go in for the latest in hedgehog fashions. Or he just has a thing for high heels. He's definitely not blind."

Larko smiled. "I think you've spotted yourself a spy," he said. "So, he's not just making conversation with his cane. Well, that doesn't mean he's part of the Crimson Quills."

"So tell me," Jonathan urged. "How do we find these fellows, then?"

Larko took a deep breath. "It shouldn't be hard. The Crimson Quill Guild is looking for me," he said, trying hard to suppress the nervous tension in his voice. "They'd like me dead."

Jonathan quickly glanced about the room.

"What do they look like, these Guild fellows?"

The rat-man's nose quivered. "That's just it," he lamented. "It's not like old times when all of our enemies were moles. It was hard to hide that star-shaped nose. Our new enemy comes in all shapes and sizes. Well, hedgehog sizes. Being this is a hedgehog planet, they tend to be everywhere," he whispered, leaning toward Jonathan. "And they're getting close."

"Don't take this wrong," Jonathan replied. "But you sound a little paranoid."

Larko sat forward, his dark eyes glittering. "I wish the chief hadn't got you involved," he pleaded. "You can still leave. I'll get back to you later."

Jonathan stared at him, resolute.

"Tell me more about these...what do you call them?"

Larko sighed.

"The Crimson Quill Guild is an extremist hedgehog organization made up of thugs, cutthroats, and assassins," Larko explained. "They idolize Walpole and are determined to put him back in power one day."

Jonathan tried not to look too skeptical.

"It doesn't surprise me that the old hedgehog demon would still have some dedicated followers on this planet," Jonathan conceded. "You don't seriously believe, though, that the majority of Yurle Prime's citizens would ever want him back. Besides, no one's seen him for years. He's probably long dead."

Larko's eyebrows shot up.

"No, he's not. There's every indication Walpole is using the Guild to get a new claw-hold on this world. His efforts have been mainly covert."

"So covert no one knows if he's still around. I suppose the Guild could be..."

A burst of laughter drew Jonathan's attention to a nearby table.

Three red-spined hedgehogs-Dinhari, Jonathan surmised- played a game of Capture the Quill at a nearby table. It was a game of strategy that required a steady hand. The basic goal of the game, as Jonathan understood it, was to pull as many quills as possible from a tall pile without upsetting the whole stack.

Since the time of Walpole's fall from power and the death of the insidious mole empress, Moleloch, the Dinhari had become less insular. It gave Jonathan satisfaction knowing that he and his friends had played at least a small part in the mystically inclined sub-race of hedgehogs' emergence. He had never favored the Dinharis' decision to hide out inside the Great Storm. Despite their high level of mechanical expertise, it had left the sect cut off and unprepared to face the rise of Moleloch.

"The Yurle military will never let Walpole back," Jonathan pressed.

"The military has always been susceptible to the lure of a powerful leader," Larko said. "It's been nearly thirty years since there's been a major conflict on Yurle Prime. They are itching for action. That's why all the interest in the extra-solar colonization project, Fresh Start."

"Which reminds me."

Larko looked up inquiringly.

Jonathan took another sip of his liquor, a slow grin appearing on his face. "I wasn't just looking for you for Folpole. Fresh Start needs us."

Before Larko could respond, a drunken hedgehog, fat and boisterous, with a long mane of transparent spines that shimmered like diamonds, swaggered up to a piano atop a platform and started to play and sing. Several others joined in the dancing and stumbling about in intoxicated merriment.

Larko frowned. "What's on your mind, Jonathan?"

"We have to get the crew back together," Jonathan blurted. He hoped that hadn't sounded as desperate to Larko as it had to him. "Our world needs us."

Larko sat back in his chair, holding up one hand. "Whoa. Slow down. Our world needs us? Why?"

Jonathan wiped some foam off his upper lip.

"Operation Fresh Start is in serious jeopardy," he stated.

Larko sighed. Fresh Start-the joint government-military plan to seek out a new healthy planet upon which the dwindling populace of poor contaminated Yurle and Yurle Prime could settle now that they had effectively destroyed two worlds of their own. Frankly, he had a hard time mustering much sympathy for beings who repeatedly exhibited such irresponsible behavior.

"All the news has been good. Regular launches like clockwork," he urged. He saw Jonathan was impatient to continue. "Go ahead; I've gotten pretty good at listening and watching my back at the same time."

Jonathan took another drink, trying to relax.

"I don't need to tell you what a mess this planet is in. Space Force decided it was time to take action. Our military scientists have identified a planet not too far away that has a similar chemical composition and atmosphere to Yurle and Yurle Prime. Its name is Yurle Minor."

Larko leaned forward in his chair, interested.

"Ah, the hedgehogs, always full of original ideas. Since this discovery is not common knowledge, I take it there's a problem."

As Jonathan continued, Larko kept an eye on Big Dale, who seemed to be holding an extended conversation with the individuals dressed in gray robes at the bar. One glanced over his shoulder in Larko's direction and smirked. It was a hedgehog, a very large one, its snout quivering.

"Yurle Central is facing a big problem," Jonathan explained. "All of the missions they've sent out to colonize Yurle Minor have failed to return."

Larko grunted and gulped down the rest of his drink noisily. He made a satisfied sound. "That is a problem." He paused. "But it's *their* problem. Not mine. I'm retired. How is it your problem?"

Jonathan swallowed hard. This was going to be a tough sell.

"I've signed on to Fresh Start. Six missions have vanished and I want to know where they've gone. You know I've had some background in space flight, but not enough. They need your experience, sir. The brass has done a thorough post-analysis of the situation and decided that the crews they've sent, all hedgehog members, were just too green. They've ordered me to come to you because... " Jonathan stumbled, thinking, and then pulled out an official looking document folded up inside his uniform pocket. He opened it and read, "'We need a strong leader with experience, someone with true grit, someone who is resourceful, someone who does not know the meaning of failure, someone... '"

Larko waved at Jonathan to put away the note.

"I get the idea," he said, flattered. "But trust me, Jonathan. I'm not the guy they're looking for. I've got my hands really full right now. I'm sorry, but I'm going to have to respectfully decline."

Jonathan crumpled up the note. He felt as if the fate of the galaxy, if not the universe, hung in the balance.

"If you don't agree to lead the seventh mission everyone on this planet could die," Jonathan pleaded. "The scientists say this world is irrevocably damaged. They've poured poison into the water for too many years. There's a hole in our ozone layer as big as the moon and its increasing in size daily. Even the big storm has become erratic. The Dinhari have abandoned it pretty much altogether. Its course is bringing it several degrees closer to the capital and government buildings. Planetary officials are calling the situation urgent."

Larko took a deep breath. "I know all that." He sighed, tired. "Everyone does. But it's their own fault. They've done this to themselves."

Jonathan knew Larko believed that people should actually take responsibility for their actions. He took one last shot at his old commander.

"So the Tandarans and the Galactic University have written off the hedgehogs. Too far gone?"

"Retired means from the Galactic University, too," the old space explorer said. "I suspect, if you ask, that they probably have. Two dying worlds and now the hedgehogs are planning on going after a third. I don't know if I even approve of this mission."

Jonathan studied his old friend a moment. A thought leaped to his mind just as he was about to surrender to the inevitable.

"As an operative in Planet Security, you might be interested to know that there is some evidence to suggest that a powerful intelligence seems to have caused the failures on Yurle Minor," he blurted.

Larko's eyes grew wide. "You're sure? Is it possible? A powerful intelligence could be...Walpole."

"Space Force HQ received a few short messages from one of the missions once they reached Yurle Minor," Jonathan said. "One of the transmissions suggested the presence of hostile natives, and the clear worship of one called the Great Mind."

Larko cleared his throat. "The planet could be close enough for Walpole to instruct his people here by mental transmission. He might even be able to train them on this other world, then teleport them here. My stars, this might explain everything. The sudden rise of a well-organized cult, its diabolic efforts to destroy the old order, and to kill off those who thwarted Walpole the last time."

Jonathan tried not to look too eager.

"You think so? That would make Yurle Minor a dangerous place to colonize."

"But it must be done, if only to bring Walpole to justice and secure the safety of the galaxy. This might be just the thing to throw the Crimson Quill Guild off my tail. I doubt they'd expect me to fly right into Walpole Central."

"Whoa, where did she come from?"

Jonathan eyed a shapely woman in a black leather body suit. She had suddenly seemed to materialize in the gloom and was sharing a drink with one of the gray-robed figures at the bar.

"Part of the Crimson Guild."

"I'm not sure," Larko said. "Probably."

The room grew a little darker. The woman in the bodysuit and her two male friends in gray at the bar suddenly transformed into leering hedgehogs, their bodies covered in red spines. They pushed into the milling throng of patrons.

"Yep, Crimson Quill Guild. Better put off these travel plans for the moment," Larko whispered. "Things are about to get interesting."

The three hedgehogs pulled out weapons hidden beneath their robes-short clubs made of black wood with spikes in the end. They rushed toward Larko and Jonathan, snarling. A moment later, things went from bad to worse, as the friendly barkeep, Big Dale, also transformed into a slightly heavier set hedgehog and joined the attack.

"Well, I am disappointed in him," Larko said, snatching the heavy bottle in front in him.

The other patrons dodged out of the way, the menace in the Guild members eyes making it clear this wasn't just another bar room brawl.

Larko leaped up to defend himself, but Jonathan held his arm.

"Don't worry. We aren't alone."

Larko placed his hand under the tabletop, and taking a firm grip on one of the legs, flipped it over and into the path of the oncoming attackers. The first hedgehog slammed into the table head on, momentarily stunned. The other three were forced to take evasive action to avoid being hit by the table as it smashed against the front of the bar.

The hedgehogs quickly regrouped and closed in. They growled and bared their sharp yellow teeth, holding up their weapons, preparing to strike.

Suddenly, however, the large hedgehog pianist stopped playing, spun about on his stool, and leaped from the platform. He threw off his disguise of shimmering spines and it crashed to the floor like a suit of glass armor. The hairless, swollen mass of pale flesh lumbered across the floor. Jonathan recognized the man almost immediately. It was his former crew mate, the eunuch Bogo Grandmont. Apparently, Jonathan thought, the effects of the rejuvenator-that incredible technological wonder which had transformed the eunuch into a tall handsome man with thick black hair-had been only temporary.

At that same moment, the female hedgie waitress in heels stripped off her own head mask and coat of spines, revealing a striking woman of voluptuous proportions. Her fiery auburn curls fell out of the mask and over her shoulders.

"Emenine?" Jonathan whispered, stunned. She still looked gorgeous. It had to be molephine treatments.

A pair of colorful hard rubber balls suddenly appeared in her hands. She flung these with great force and exact precision, striking and knocking cold one of the surprised hedgies and dazing a second. The two remaining Guild members hesitated, confused, and were bowled over by the charging Bogo. They picked themselves up, and seeing that the odds were now stacked against them, fled out through the front doors of the inn.

"That was amazing," Jonathan stated, dumbfounded.

"I wanted to tell you I enlisted Bogo and Emenine as colleagues of mine," Larko stated. "But as they were undercover, I didn't want to take the chance of giving them away. You can see why."

"Impressive performance," Jonathan said, shaking hands with his old friends.

Suddenly the doors of the inn swung open. The two fleeing hedgehogs backed slowly into the room their hands in the air. An extremely short man with the delicate features of a ballerina entered, holding a laser rifle on the pair of surprised hedgehogs.

Jonathan cringed. "Lavolier!"

Lavolier nodded, never taking his eyes off the prisoners.

"Ugh, pretty boy Quintain," he said, "slumming down here with the common folk, are we? No precious rockets to pilot about, burning up the last of the world's fuel supply?"

If Lavolier had a middle name, it was Envy.

"I swore you were still in detention," Jonathan said. "Who did you sell out to get free this time?"

"I have devoted my talents to the betterment and protection of this world," the knight proclaimed to everyone in the place. "But, I'll regale you with my wondrous adventures later. What do I do with these scoundrels, old boy?"

Memories-most of them distasteful-suddenly besieged Jonathan. This obnoxious little man who in Jonathan's early youth had held a variety of titles-

24

the captain of the guard, Sir Lavolier, chief scout, and court majordomo-had what might best be described as a checkered past. He was an accomplished fighter with an unpredictable temperament. In the past, he had used his position as an excuse to mistreat the peasants who worked Baron Glauwer's fields. He also patronized the castle stonemason, Odd Bob, a talented and compassionate fellow for whom Jonathan had developed a profound respect and deep friendship. Moreover, Jonathan contemplated bitterly, Lavolier had never passed up an opportunity to ridicule Gamitof Pym-Larko, former court magician, and now, ironically, spaceship captain and Lavolier's superior.

Another of the dazed hedgehogs staggered to his feet. Lavolier eyed him wearily and pointed the laser rifle at him.

"Don't move a muscle you spiny devil," Lavolier growled. "I'm placing you and your anarchist cohorts under arrest."

Lavolier motioned with his head and began to march the hedgehogs out of the inn.

Jonathan called out to him. Lavolier stopped, glancing back.

"Don't leave just yet," Jonathan said, sensing a chance. "I have just been discussing a project with Commander Larko." He glanced at Bogo and Emenine, as well.

"I hardly think any project you would come up with is worth my time," Lavolier sneered.

"It might just make you famous. Shoot, it might make us all famous."

Lavolier stared at Jonathan. His eyes narrowed and shifted toward the hedgehog prisoners still standing nearby, hands raised. They looked, however, like they might bolt if given the least opportunity.

Lavolier squeezed the trigger on his laser rifle three times. A thin green ray shot out striking the hedgehogs; their bodies went suddenly rigid and they crumpled to the floor at his feet. "I stunned them," he said to Jonathan with casual satisfaction. "Now we can talk without being interrupted."

Jonathan motioned for the former crewmembers of the *Duweena's Courage* to sit down. They pulled up chairs to the table.

Jonathan glanced at Larko. The old commander nodded.

"Okay, you've heard of Fresh Start."

As Jonathan continued his pitch, the group of red-spined Dinhari, who had set up their table again and started another game of Capture the Quill, glanced over at Jonathan from time to time, listening. They completed their game and departed as the occupants of the other table rose and left, still arguing details.

Not long after, the place nearly emptied, the grizzled old beggar in the trench coat shook his head and stood up without the aid of his cane. He crossed his arms and shook his head.

"I could have killed Larko ten times tonight, and thrown in the rest for free," the man grumbled as he made his way to the door. "But no, the Guilders got to learn, he says. Just keep an eye on them, Verlag. It'll work out. Well, you got your troubles down, Walpole, my chum. Yes, you do."

The spy, Wenlock Verlag-aka Arg Strapper, cruel torturer, and Unger Fry, gourmet chef-walked toward the exit but stopped suddenly to study a poster hanging behind the bar. A wide grin formed on his pimpled face.

"Now, what's this?" He hadn't seen the poster before.

WANTED
Dead or Alive
(but mostly dead)
WALPOLE
(Aka The Sacred Hedgehog of Yurle)
100,000 ducats Reward

"A lovely likeness. Well, Verlag," he said. "At least until he makes a better offer."

He tore the poster off the wall and stuck it in his pocket just as the doors of the inn swung open.

Wenlock Verlag jumped, startled, as a striking gentleman dressed in a Space Force Special Forces uniform entered. Verlag adjusted his beard, nervous, and quickly leaned on his cane, hunching over a bit.

He stared hard at the officer. There was something familiar in the handsome face, he thought, an almost god-like aura. It was the vestiges of gills, barely visible, looking like pink tattoos on the man's muscular neck, that gave it away.

Yes, Verlag thought, *it was the son of Baron Glauwer's mistress. Lawson, his name was*. Not the Baron's son, however, but the offspring of some perverse union between that flirtatious juggler and a god. Verlag shuddered: by all the dark gods, that woman got around.

Lawson glanced about at the almost empty inn, the corners of his mouth turning down in disappointment. He eyed Verlag, perplexed.

"Where is everybody?" he groaned. "This is Tuesday, right? It's the all-you-can-drink tanagi fruit spritzer night."

"Family emergency," Verlag lied. "The owner's house caught on fire. Everybody went to watch... I mean help."

Lawson frowned. "Huh."

He spun smartly on one heel and marched out.

"Don't let the door hit you in your scaly behind, fish boy," Verlag mumbled. He pulled the poster out of his pocket and stared at Walpole's mug shot, smirking. "Just stay out of my way. I've got bigger... um... hedgehogs to fry."

He stuffed the poster back in his pocket, adjusted his beard, and hobbled out of the inn.

Chapter Two

"Lucky Seven," Bogo Grandmont stated, shaking hands with Larko. "That's what they're calling this mission."

Larko eyed the big eunuch, pondering his appearance sadly. That rejuvenator had worked wonders on Bogo years ago, giving him long dark hair, and a slender and strong-looking frame. But apparently the effects had been only temporary. Most of the dark hair had thinned or fallen out altogether. The pasty, bloated appearance had returned.

"I've done a little gambling in Grumpole's Hideaway," Larko stated. "Luck is everything when it comes to black jack and roulette wheels. We're not going to rely on luck on this mission, though, Bogo. That's why I've insisted on taking only the best crew with me. I was certainly surprised to see you all together with Jonathan."

"He's been working on a way to get you to join us," Bogo said with a wink. "When it looked like there might be an attack on you in that tavern, we all got together and set up an ambush."

"Well, it certainly saved me and some time," Larko smiled. "It's good to see everyone."

Jonathan burst through the door of the hangar, grinning proudly, accompanied by a hedgehog with a head full of closely cropped spines wearing a heavily decorated officer's uniform. They, in turn, were followed closely by Emenine and Lavolier and the three Dinhari who had been playing the quill game at the Hideaway.

"This is Major General Gerge Smeel Jagged, sir," Jonathan grinned proudly. "And, of course, the rest of your hand-picked crew."

"Well, someone's hand-picked crew, anyway," the old commander said. "I know Emenine, Lavolier and you, but who are these fellows?"

Jonathan snapped his fingers.

"Sorry, sir," he said, ushering the red-spined hedgies forward.

"This is Blip, Tagger-Streel, and Dorn. You may remember them from the tavern last night. They were designated to observe the situation and report to their Dinhari elders before making a final decision as to assisting us. But I'll let Blip explain their interest and role in all this."

Blip took one jogging step forward and saluted. "Blip is my name, member of the Dinhari techno-clan first class. My people have grown impatient with the Crimson Quill Guild impersonating us and committing their crimes against the people of this world. We are vilified and attacked physically. We will take part in the operation to bring Walpole and his dark followers to justice."

Larko remembered the great marching structures that the Dinhari had constructed to carry their people across the wastes left by the Great Storm, but he wasn't sure how that ability would apply to the present situation.

"I sense you are eager to help, but Walpole is a dangerous and devious creature. What can you bring to the fight?" He approached the oldest member of the trio, the one called Tagger-Streel, a strangely blue-eyed hedgie whose silver bracers gleamed from time to time beneath a black robe.

"I am Tagger-Streel of the Dinhari mystic clan. I am proficient in more than one hundred forms of hand-to-hand combat," Tagger offered, crossing his arms. "I have an acute sense of hearing and have never been surprised."

Lavolier shrugged, having given up trying to sneer the hedgehogs into submission. "You'll need a lot more than that on your resume to impress Captain Larko," he advised.

"I'm impressed," Larko said agreeably. "That's about ninety-eight more forms of combat than I know. And I find I'm constantly surprised."

The diminutive knight sighed contemptuously. "I know about that many but I'm not one to boast."

"That is much like us, sir," Tagger replied. "The Dinhari people do not boast about themselves. It is forbidden."

Lavolier rolled his eyes. "Never get anywhere that way. What about these other two? Do they have any skills or are they afraid they'll be boasting if they tell us?"

Larko firmly guided Lavolier out of the way. "I don't mean to embarrass you," he said, "but I must know every member of my crew and how they can be an asset to this mission. What about you two?"

"I, Blip, am a planetary biologist and botanist," Blip stated. "I also have a photographic memory."

The other hedgehog snapped to attention. "I am Dorn, a member of the Dinhari techno clan, probationary first class, pending my final examination on gear alignments. I am proficient in micro psycho-kinesis. I can move small objects with my mind and have the gift of delving."

"Delving?" Lavolier interrupted, smirking. "What's that? Sounds stupid."

"I can see things that are hidden to others," Dorn explained. "Concealed objects, buried treasure, invisible fault lines. Those sorts of things."

Emenine giggled. "Can you see under my clothes?"

The little hedgehog began coughing uncontrollably.

"I don't mind, I was just curious," the former jester said, patting the choking creature sympathetically, if lightly, on its spiky back. "I think they all sound perfectly useful. Let's leave Lavolier behind and take them."

"Maybe we should fight a duel," Lavolier said, turning red.

Before Larko could find the energy to bring his unruly crew under control Bogo, who had been eyeing the general's plethora of medals and awards attached to his uniform, interjected.

"And what does this one do?"

"Sorry, sir," Jonathan said. "General Jagged is here to give us any further assistance we may need before we start our journey.

"Ah, yes, good," Larko said. "I think we can use you," he told the Dinhari.

The Dinhari exchanged pleased glances, placed their hands together in congratulations, and hooted in excitement.

Lavolier frowned. "Don't need a lot of that."

"What about your son?" Larko said, turning to Emenine. "Lawson could be extremely useful."

"Actually, he volunteered to join us," Emenine said, pride in her eyes as she thought of her son. "However...the Yurle Space Force has already recruited him to lead an eighth mission. If they need one."

Larko turned to the general. "So that brings us back to you. It sounds as if you people expect us not to succeed," he said. "Perhaps you should just skip on to the eighth mission and we can go back to...whatever we were doing. Remind me to ask you all that some time."

Jagged cleared his throat. "Now Commander Larko, let's not read too much into future contingencies. Ensign Lawson is an asset we only intend to use once we learn what sort of...opposition...awaits us on Yurle Minor. You are vital to that purpose."

"So now we talk money?" Lavolier suggested.

Emenine leaned in. "Yes, that's an idea I can get behind. Juggling spies aren't usually high on the pension scale and I'm not getting any younger, although I'm sure it's hard to tell."

"You're quite divine, for a human, that is," Jagged said, bewildered. "I'm sure the financial end has already been settled, hasn't it, Captain? Anyway, I'm in charge of Operation Fresh Start. Now, let's get to the hard facts. You still insist on the refitting of your old exploration craft, the *Duweena's Courage*?"

Larko eyed him with suspicion. "I heard that she was purchased by your Space Patrol along with a lot of other old, retired GU ships, for civilian use and scrap. No one used my ship for scrap, did they, General? That would sort of bring this conversation to an end."

"Isn't Bob on one of those? Some sort of reseeding vessel, isn't it?" commented Bogo.

"Your ship was old, even before you crashed on old Yurle. It was underwater for decades," General Jagged pointed out. "Its components are out of date; the mainframe is obsolete by today's standards. The effort to refurbish it would be monumental."

Larko crossed his arms. "I thought I made myself clear on this point," he stated. "If the *Duweena's Courage* isn't going, then neither am I."

"I'm with you, Captain," Jonathan said, hiding a smile. "That ship still has plenty of life left in her."

The rest of the crew nodded in agreement, with the air of sharing a secret.

General Jagged grinned. "Well, the rumors about you are true, Commander Larko. You're stubborn, which will be important on this mission. Take a look at what we've got for you and try to tell me you aren't satisfied."

Jagged removed a remote from his pocket and pressed one of the buttons: A steel panel that divided the large building slid open with a click. Larko's eyes widened. A fully renovated *Duweena's Courage*, illuminated by several blazing floor lamps, rested atop a platform like a silvery jewel.

"Just look at her, Jonathan," Larko gasped. "She looks brand new."

"When people in ship maintenance heard you were coming out of retirement and wanted the old ship back," Jonathan said, "they bought her right out from under the scrapper's hammers."

"That sounds like the military all right," Emenine scoffed, shaking her head. "A bunch of sentimental puppies. Oooh, it is shiny, though."

Larko walked slowly toward the gleaming ship, his mouth open in amazement. He climbed a short set of stairs and stood on the platform gazing at the vessel like an old girlfriend. He took a step closer until he was standing just beneath the fuselage and then suddenly wrapped his arms around the extended arm that was one of four evenly spaced appendages of the landing gear.

After a moment, he stepped back, sniffed, and wiped his eye.

"She's beautiful," he whispered, voice trembling. "I hope, though, you haven't changed her too much."

"The boys rebuilt the engine, gave her a new paint job and changed out the decals and a few other superficial things," Jagged explained. "Inside, well, the layout is the same, controls, but you may have to get acquainted with the new AI."

"A new AI. Interesting," Larko said, feeling a slight foreboding.

"She certainly looks better than she did thirty years ago," Bogo stated, stunned.

"You never saw her when she first came off the line," Larko said. "The Tandaran shipyards never let one off the rack that wasn't just perfect. But, this is very nice."

Emenine spun about to smile at the eunuch. "Why thank you, Mr. Grandmont. And I didn't need an army of maintenance men to keep me that way."

Bogo looked confused for a moment, turned red, and then nodded graciously.

"Cosmetically, she may still be a little rough," General Jagged admitted. "But nothing has been left out to give you the optimum performance."

"We must test her out," Larko said. Jonathan was already walking past him and into the ship. "A new AI. Dear me."

The remaining crew members walked up the loading ramp and disappeared inside, as General Jagged stepped over to a protective viewing area.

Larko followed Lavolier through the opening in the side of the ship, and a door slid closed with a snap behind him nearly removing his tail.

"That may need adjusting."

The crew familiarized themselves with their places on the bridge while the three Dinhari were escorted to a passenger cabin and shown how to strap themselves in before the launch took place.

"We're not going to have the back-up people we had in the old days," Larko said. "I know you are all up for the challenge, but be sure you're clear on the operations before we proceed."

The others examined the controls before them, and then glanced at one another dubiously.

"They do seem the same," Jonathan said, seated at the back-up flight console. "Been awhile since I've flown anything this big."

"Have no concerns, crew of the *Duweena's Courage*. I have all operations under control."

Larko stared around at the others.

"Who said that?"

"I am Flyright Deluxe, your on-board controls system. I have plotted your course, initiated warm-up procedures and only await your order to begin lift-off countdown."

"You're the AI," the commander said. "May I ask you a question?"

"That's what I'm here for. All your questions will be answered."

"Good. Were others of your model used on the other missions to Yurle Minor?"

"I can proudly say they were, sir. All six missions incorporated my system model."

"And they all disappeared."

"Exactly right. You are well-informed. May I begin countdown?"

"I think we'll be switching to manual override, Flyright. While we're on our way you can begin a system overhaul and see if you can find any reason why all previous missions failed and if the AI installation had any part in those failures."

"But...oh, I see. Very astute. You think I may be a victim of some sort of sabotage. Why, I could even be the saboteur myself. Brilliant. I will begin search immediately and report to you upon completion. I am going to like working with you, sir."

The ship's controls went to green and Larko carefully checked each one to be sure he was in control.

"Very sharp thinking, indeed," Bogo said, resetting the navigation coordinates for their flight.

"Well, if we're going to fail, it may as well be our own fault rather than some sneaky trick of Walpole's," Larko admitted.

"This is an historic moment," Lavolier stated, spinning about from his place at the weapons station. "With your permission, Captain, I will proudly sing Yurle Prime's Inter-Galactic Anthem and then you may begin the countdown."

Larko made some adjustments to the bridge computer. He leaned toward Jonathan and whispered. "What do you think?"

Jonathan shrugged. "He's no Evan Owen, but I don't see any harm in letting him sing one verse."

Larko nodded. "Go ahead, Lavolier."

As the knight burst into a not unpleasant tenor, the commander settled his eyes on the last member of their old crew.

"Emenine, are you ready?"

The woman glanced up from her intense scrutiny of her console. "Yes, I think so. Hear ye, hear ye. Tonight's entertainment will be a film called *Return of the Hedgehog Avengers,* a gripping tale of heroic adventures, starring Avic Grudgepole and Suven Treemp. There will be snacks."

"Well, then, if Lavolier can finish that last note, I'd say we're ready to go."

General Jagged watched as *Duweena's Courage* lifted off. The ship climbed rapidly up and above the roof of the space port hangar. The roar of its loud quad engines sent a flock of ugly little gird-bats racing away from their hiding place under the hangar's eaves, then the sound rumbled out over the space port, a warning that Mission Seven was underway.

Bob and Harlix sat in the mess hall, surrounded by many of the other technicians and workers, as dinner was served by automatic dispensers. The meal usually consisted of tasty ingredients taken from the ship's own productive cells, and this one was no different.

"What's that?" Harlix asked, glancing out the helix-framed windows. Bob looked up to see a streak of light dart out from the distant planet and then fade as it headed out into deep space.

"Another of their stinking launches," he said. "Polluting the air, burning up the last of their fuel resources."

"Won't be long before they won't be able to do that," Harlix agreed.

Deeply engrossed with their flavorful meal, they failed to notice the light thud that could be just faintly detected by the ship's obstacle sensors. It was so light there was no alarm, as the great ship struck thousands of meteors each day, with no harm.

Deep Thought extended its own sophisticated array of sensors and inserted one of them into an external power unit fixture. It drew on the ship's resources so carefully that no indication was sensed that power was being stolen. When it had restored itself to full strength, it found the data hook-up used by workers that came outside on occasion on repair detail, and began loading itself into the ship's control computer. When it completed that, Deep

Thought released its old hulk back into space, and settled in to see just what it had found.

Chapter Three

"And so the seventh mission to the small mysterious world of Yurle Minor begins," Lavolier whispered into a device partially concealed in his hand. Unfortunately for the little knight, the acoustics in the command station were excellent.

Larko stopped fingering the keyboard of the recorder in front of him and stared at Lavolier.

"What are you doing?"

The golden-haired ex-scout stopped speaking into the device, startled.

"I'm recording incidents of interest relative to this mission for future generations. It's for my memoirs."

Larko leaned back in his seat.

"I'm keeping a log. You're free to access it any time. I'd rather you were concentrating on your duties."

"What is that thing, anyway?" Bogo asked, trying to get a look at the device as Lavolier tucked it out of sight in his jacket.

Lavolier took on a belligerent sneer.

"It's none of your business. You're not my commanding officer. I don't have to show you anything."

Bogo raised an eyebrow he'd drawn on his head a few minutes ago.

"That's suspicious. I think he's up to no good again. I'll bet he's reporting to someone."

"Who would I be reporting to, Baldy...the Crimson Quill Guild?" Noticing the questioning glances, he continued. "Well, I'm not. It's the latest in archival storage units, the Archivatron Deluxe. I can record five thousand hours of material before it needs a new storage wafer. And no, you can't touch it with your greasy fingers, Grandmont, so don't ask."

Bogo glared at Lavolier.

"Your memoirs. That'll be the greatest piece of fiction since the Merry Tales of Happy Henry, the Dyspeptic Hedgehog."

Emenine patted Lavolier on the shoulder. "That's all right. I liked that book. Lots of pictures and all Henry's adventures turned out happy. Am I in there?" She peered at the device as if she could see her face looking back out.

Lavolier put the recorder away again.

"Yes, you're all in there. I've saved your lives numerous times. I don't think the life of such a great personage should be lost. Especially when we are putting my life on the line again with this wild caper."

Larko sighed. "As long as it doesn't interfere with your duties. In fact, I think it's a laudable idea. Lavolier is finally showing a little positively motivated ambition."

The knight gave Bogo a curt nod. "I will take that as a compliment."

Bogo glared at the blond-haired crewman with contempt.

"Yeah, you're not up to anything. I'll be keeping my eyes on you."

"I don't want to interrupt this intellectual repartee," Jonathan said, "but I'm picking up something on the forward screen. I have it identified as the Armadon Rectangle. That mean anything to anyone?"

They all gathered around the viewer. Spreading slowly out before them was a glittering cloud streaked with the rainbow patterns one might see covering any of the oily puddles the hedgehogs called lakes back on Yurle Prime.

"Oh, I know. I know," Emenine said. "I saw it on that show...Magical Mysteries of Space."

Larko scratched his nose and brushed his whiskers thoughtfully.

"This is on our route to Yurle Minor?"

Jonathan nodded, calling up the information.

"According to the records of the previous missions, they all passed through the area, though the Rectangle varied in size and density each time, so the passage was different each time. There were no reported ill effects."

"That's not what they said on the show," Emenine cried, alarmed. "We need to stay light years away from that area. Lots of ships have gone in and never came out."

Larko glanced at Jonathan. "Well?"

"As much as I want to believe the Magical Mysteries show fact checks all their stories, there is no evidence of ships disappearing. In fact, hedgehogs haven't even been in space long enough to have reached the area until just recently. I wouldn't worry, Emenine."

"It could make navigation really tricky," Larko confirmed. "There is a chance we may be temporarily flying blind." He smiled at Bogo

"Fortunately, we have one of the best navigation officers right here with us."

Bogo patted his sweating forehead and found his seat.

"I'm ready when you are."

Larko fixed the coordinates of Yurle Minor into the main computer and nodded at Bogo. "Lock us in and then everyone but Bogo get to the stasis tubes. We'll ride this out there. The field will protect us from any effects of the Rectangle."

"I will stay with him," Lavolier volunteered. "I refuse to let it be said I ran and hid when a mere eunuch bravely faced the unknown."

"I don't want him here," Bogo said, his face coated in sweat, his overly loose flight suit spotted with perspiration. "He only wants to distract me. I still say he's a spy for someone."

Lavolier growled in anger, pulling a sidearm from a hidden holster inside his uniform. "I don't have to take that from this bloated monstrosity! I am behaving with the utmost honesty and he's decided to blacken my name."

"Don't pull that unless you intend to use it," Bogo sneered back, one eye on the spinning figures as the ship's computer calculated the trajectory of their approach to the rectangle.

Jonathan grabbed the gun from Lavolier. "Don't say stupid things like that. Of course he intended to use it. He's a pompous idiot, but in this case, I think he is just writing his memoirs."

The little knight tugged his uniform coat down and spun about derisively. "I'm going to the stasis tubes. Coming, Emenine?"

"If it will make everyone happy, I will," she said, dragging him more quickly as they left the command station.

"I'll store this in my locker," Jonathan said, pocketing the gun. "Some things never change, do they?"

"Hello. Anyone out there?"

The three remaining crew men looked about, startled.

"It's only me, Flyright Deluxe, your onboard computer AI. I have finished searching for evidence that I am sabotaging the missions to Yurle Minor. There was definitely something going on, tampering with my directional programming and targeting relays. I have corrected these problems and can assure I am in top shape once more. Shall I take over flight of the ship until after we pass through the Rectangle? That way, Mr. Grandmont may reside safely with the rest of you in the stasis field tubes."

"You may assist Mr. Grandmont, Flyright Deluxe," Larko said. "I think we need someone to make a living, visual record of the passage. If Bogo becomes incapacitated midway, then you may take over total control for the duration of this passage. Do you understand?"

"Yes, and obey. By the way, you may call me FD, for short."

"Come along Jonathan," Larko said. "We only have a couple minutes before entry."

Bogo sat at his station, feeling very lonely and somewhat apprehensive. "Well, there's not much more that can be done to my body. Not like I'm

45

saving myself for having kids." His thoughts ran back to Dame Littlefield, who had undergone the rejuvenation treatments at the same time as himself, but unlike his own relapse into grossness, she had remained lovely. She had wanted them to remain together, but he couldn't do it.

"I'll only hold you back, darling. You can't be the chief law officer of an entire planet and drag me around, too. No, I'll go back and see if there's anything doing with Larko and the old crew. You get yourself a fine young man and have some little more dames and sirs to carry on the Littlefield name." That had been many years ago, and not long ago, he'd heard she'd disappeared on a patrol deep in the southern wastes while pursuing the last members of the Over the Hump Gang. The search parties had turned up nothing.

The Armadon Rectangle was suddenly upon them, and Bogo felt *Duweena's Courage* slow as if sinking into a vat of molephine syrup. The windows began to streak with a strange organic substance that glittered as it flowed back over the ship.

"Temperature falling," FD reported.

"Falling? That goes against all physical laws. Friction should cause..."

"Shall I analyze the phenomena, sir?"

The ship lurched as if slewing sideways on a patch of ice. "No," Bogo said tensely. "No, just keep us on course." A loud whining noise began beating on the eunuch's senses and he felt light-headed. His eyes began to droop.

Bunched up in a cargo crate in the hold of the *Duweena's Courage* for seventeen hours straight, waiting for the launch, Verlag had to admit he was just beginning to feel the slightest discomfort. Using a listening device removed from the body of a hedgehog security officer who had crossed the old spy's path at just the right time (well, wrong time for the nosy hedgehog), Verlag listened while the crew argued over some stupid rectangle then went into stasis.

"Just the fat one left," Verlag said as he emerged into the dim light of the freezing hold. It had been a spur of the moment decision to hop ship with his old acquaintances, a decision to go after Walpole and the offered reward while pretending to pursue the old tyrant's agenda. Getting aboard was easy enough, even with the added security because of the first six failures. The hedgehogs had a weakness for uniforms and the more medals on one, the more blind obedience one could expect. Handcuff a briefcase to your wrist, whisper about "special orders" for the commander (no matter which commander) and he was on board and out of sight in a few minutes.

He climbed the ladder to the exit hatch into the main passage of the ship. It had been Walpole's plan to use the Guild to assassinate Larko and his old crew. Verlag was supposed to arrange the attack. That hadn't gone well. He could have accomplished the job in half the time, but Walpole wanted the kids to learn to do for themselves.

"If that's the way you want it, you bossy little pinhead, then I'll just leave the Guild to figure out that no one they're supposed to kill is still on the planet."

47

"Verlag! Verlag! Are you there? Answer me at once!" The nasty voice of his superior echoed around the hold. Startled, Verlag snatched out the clear orb from his pocket and quickly lowered the volume. It was the same orb he'd had fastened to the top of his white cane in the tavern, where he'd been keeping Walpole informed of the botched attack. "Thought I'd turned that blasted thing off."

He stared into the glass orb. A storm of static rolled about inside, then cleared. Walpole's impatient face stared back.

"What took you so long?" Walpole shouted. "I don't like to be kept in the dark."

"Really," the assassin muttered. "I've always seen you as the hands-off type of dictator."

"A joke?" The aging hedgehog glared out, his reddish eyes fiery pin-pricks.

"Sure, why not," Verlag said agreeably. For some reason, pompous hedgehogs struck him as funny. Even ones with the power to stretch him out like a rug and dance on his guts.

"Where are you now?" Walpole growled, his small sharp teeth flashing.

"I am embarked on a space voyage. We're all coming to see you."

"Who is coming?" Walpole said with quiet menace.

"Just who you feared. Larko and his gang of happy heroes. Keep your quills on. I'll see they don't make it all the way there. They've already decided to dive into the Rectangle. By the sounds of it, Bogo is having a psychotic episode. I want to get up there and see it. So, if there's anything else?"

If hedgehogs could fly, Walpole's rage would have lifted him into the stratosphere. After a long string of quite foreign expletives that Verlag would have to get translated later, he hissed a final warning.

"Larko and his crew must not reach the island. The Anointment draws near. I don't need them upsetting my plans. It's on your life, Verlag."

"Signing off, then." Verlag was sure to turn off the orb this time. He considered tossing it away, but he'd never been one to waste things. He might need Walpole later. Sticking the orb back in a secret pocket, Verlag's hand brushed against Walpole's wanted poster.

"We'll see whose life lasts the longest."

He stepped out into the main passage and crept along until he could peek into the nearest room. Three Dinhari hedgehogs slept an innocent sleep in their stasis tubes. Verlag had no idea who they were or why they were there, but he'd get to them later. No witnesses was the rule in his game.

A few steps more and he inspected the rest of the sleeping crew. "Larko. Jonathan Quintain. Emenine, lovely Emenine. Lavolier the pest. That leaves bouncing baby Bogo."

He switched on his penlight, unzipped a pocket in his special assassin's jacket, and dug out a packet that contained the blueprints of the *Duweena's Courage*, supplied to him by one of the Guild. He groaned. The directions were all written in hedgehog.

"This is going to be like trying to find the potty in the dark without a night light."

Finally memorizing the physical layout, he replaced the prints and removed a hand laser and continued to the command station. The annoying screech of the Rectangle's presence was familiar to him. He'd passed through it more than once on his trips back and forth from Yurle Minor to Yurle Prime, and had become immune to the soporific effect.

Leaning around the corner of the entry, he saw Bogo stretched out in his seat, slumbering along while a rather mechanical voice ran off a long series of coordinates, finally reporting that they would emerge from the Rectangle in three minutes.

"Time's a flying," Verlag muttered and slid open a panel beneath the door controls, exposing the emergency overrides. He cut the connections to the guidance and emergency landing back-ups, then slid a small cut-off timer chip into the new gaps. He replaced the panel then went into the control room.

"Just a few surprises in here to distract them from the real game."

"I do not see you on the ship's roster, sir," Flyright Deluxe said. It would have said more but Verlag casually shorted out the computer's communications with a steel pin and a half cup of cold beverage someone had left on the weapons console.

"It's the simple methods that bring one the most satisfaction," Verlag said, sniggering. "And now, the final step. One bundle of pure molephine dynamite-always use local products when possible." He shoved the bomb out of sight inside a niche under the navigation hub and smiled, pleased. "Old Bogo will get a kick out of that."

He turned to go and found three hedgehogs standing in the entryway, looking with a disturbing intensity.

"Did you see what I was doing?" he asked quietly.

The hedgehogs moved slowly toward him.

"Oh, looking for trouble, are we?" Verlag reached for his laser wand and was put out to find he'd zipped it snugly away. "Well, there's only three of you."

Verlag opened his eyes and found himself looking at several pairs of feet.

"Ah, I'd know those delicate tootsies anywhere. Is that you, Emenine?"

The assassin was hanging upside down in the command station, bound with some sort of material that the Dinhari had brought along with them amongst their supplies.

"What have you done to my ship?" Larko said, waving the disarmed molephine bomb under the spy's nose. "I mean, what else did you do to it?"

Verlag opened his mouth, then shut it again, tightly. If the Dinhari hadn't seen anything but the bomb, then for the time being, he had room to negotiate. It all depended on how long he'd been out and how far they were from Yurle Minor.

"He's just going to lie," Lavolier said. "Might as well space him now."

Mixing a few of the new Walpolian expletives into the response, Verlag told Lavolier how he felt about that idea.

"Oh my, someone gag him," Emenine said. "I am positively shocked."

Although the rest were a bit skeptical of that possibility, Jonathan stuck a sock in the assassin's mouth, and the crew set out to find out what Verlag had done to the ship.

The Dinharis' keen senses had felt Verlag's dark presence and they had gone out to investigate, but had only seen him short out the computer's communicator and place the bomb. Tagger-Streel had flattened the man with relative ease and then they'd gone and revived the crew, the ship having left the Rectangle behind.

"Can't find anything wrong with the controls, navigation, or the weapons," Larko said finally. "He's mucked up communications with FD, but it's running all right otherwise. Somehow, I think we're missing something."

"It would be hard to believe he would put himself in danger," Jonathan said. "There was an extra-vehicular suit in his pack. He might have intended to jump ship once he'd finished with his tricks."

"Let me talk to him," Lavolier said. "I'll find out everything he knows."

"I think the Dinhari caught him in time," Bogo said. "I was only out a minute or two, according to the records. He only had time to set the bomb."

Verlag's eyes widened. He had been sort of hoping Lavolier or one of the others would have threatened him a bit before he spilled about the chip in the emergency landing unit. With the gag, he could only gurgle and shake his head about. It didn't convey much.

"We'll be entering Yurle Minor orbit in less than an hour. I guess we'd better get ready," Larko said. "Oh, do be quiet, Verlag. You've caused enough trouble."

Chapter Four

Yurle Minor grew from a bright spot on the screen to a cloud-streaked world clearly dominated by sparkling blue water and dotted with large archipelagoes of islands, smoke streaming from hundreds, if not thousands of volcanoes.

"Clearly a world still young in its geological growth," Blip, the Dinhari scientist said. "Volcanic activity all over the planet, the islands a result of emergence from the sea in the last few thousand years. It was not long ago Yurle Minor was entirely an ocean world. There should not be any land-based life forms beyond whatever life might live on the shores."

"Yet, it was reported that the earlier missions were attacked by some sort of native force," Larko said. "Could there have been other colonization attempts we don't know about?"

Dorn, gifted with Deep Sight, opened his eyes. "It is very strange. I sense...hedgehog minds. Thousands of them. And all of them focused in concert on one thing...to serve the Great Mind."

"That sounds familiar," Jonathan said. "It has to be Walpole or someone just like him. He could have brought some of his followers here. This is going to be very dangerous. Maybe we should get more help."

"But thousands of hedgehogs," Bogo interjected. "He never had that many followers on Yurle Prime."

"However he did it, we can handle it. I'll just set the weapons for scorched earth and we'll dive in there," Lavolier suggested.

"I didn't know we had a scorched earth setting on that console or I'd never have let you handle the guns," Larko said. "No, we will investigate the situation and report what we find. I won't let it be said we ran just because things looked dicey."

"I'll set up an entry trajectory, then," Bogo said, turning to his console.

"Non-essential personnel buckle in," Larko said, setting the example.

"It'll be nice to see old Walpole again," Emenine said, settling into her seat. "I wondered where he made off to after the war. He hardly said good-bye."

"He didn't say good-bye, you tweedle-bumpkin," Lavolier muttered. "The Dinhari hiked him into space and he managed to land here; on all four feet and his tail, apparently."

"Entry in five minutes," Bogo announced.

"All crew secure yourselves and your personal belongings immediately!" screamed Flyright Deluxe. "This is not a drill. I repeat: This is not a drill! Time of impact: Two minutes, thirteen seconds. Prepare for splash down!"

"Splash down!" Lavolier shouted over the screaming engines. "I can't swim! Do something, Captain. I'm too young to die."

Bogo slapped Lavolier across the face. "No, you're not."

"You enjoyed that," the knight grimaced.

"Certainly. Shall I do it again?"

55

"What happened?" Jonathan shouted over the howling alarms.

"We have no control over the landing thrusters or the navigation system. It's as if someone cut the connections at the access panel in the hall," Bogo said. "Oh, yeah. Verlag."

The crew rushed about, stepping over each other as they did everything in their power to take control back. At the back of the cabin, Verlag swung about like a pendulum, making a giggling sound.

"Next time I think we should let Sir Lavolier interrogate Verlag," Emenine said, trying to force an inflatable boat over her head like a life preserver.

The interior lights blinked on and then went off. Jonathan wrapped his arms around a nearby bulkhead. The ship spun, dipped, whirled, and then plummeted. He watched his fellow crew members banged about, the lucky ones clinging to any stationary object they could find.

The computer warning stopped. "I think you get the idea."

The ship began to spin and there was the horrific sound of metal tearing loose.

"Atmospheric stabilizers no longer functioning," FD stated. "As a matter of fact they've departed entirely. Ship is no longer space worthy, but I don't think that's a problem anymore."

"Shut up, FD," Larko shouted. "Unless you can land this thing safely, just shut up."

Discouragingly, the computer made no such claim. Something else tore free and the ship finally stopped spinning.

"That was fun," Emenine said. "I think I choked on my tongue but that kept the vomit down."

Jonathan watched as the sensors reported the rising heat as the shields on *Duweena's Courage* began to glow orange, first dull and then brighter and brighter. Jonathan said nothing but was sure the vessel would catch fire and they would all burn up inside her. Not a great way to go.

Suddenly they dove into a pendulous gray cloud layer and the heat sizzled away as freezing rain cooled the shields. Plunging out of the lowest layers of cloud, they saw that below them stretched a vast blue sea.

"Fifteen seconds to impact. Ten... Nine... Eight... "

"Thrusters functioning," FD said flatly. "Initiating-."

"Thrust! Thrust!" the whole crew screamed in unison.

The thrusters burst into life, just in time to reduce the impact from utter disintegration to brick wall. The impact of the collision with the sea jarred everyone loose, leaving them in a heap at the entry where Verlag lay unconscious, his bonds snapped.

"We're going to sink fast," Larko said, straightening his commander's cap on his head backwards and brushing his whiskers back in place. "I remember this drill, too. Everyone should don life preservers and proceed to the emergency exit."

"I think he's bumped his head," Jonathan said, lifting his commander to his feet.

"Sounds all right to me," Lavolier muttered. "Did I mention I can't swim?"

"Yes. That's a shame," Bogo growled sarcastically. "I guess you're going to drown."

The little knight jumped to his feet and ran out of the room in the direction of the emergency exit.

"He's going to open the door before we get there," Bogo shouted. "The little runt will kill us all. Jonathan, you had his gun. Shoot him."

Larko saluted the wall next to the entry way, and then spun around with surprising skill.

"Bogo, grab Emenine and escort her to the exit. Jonathan, grip Verlag by his heels and drag him in a rough manner along with us. Lavolier, don't forget the emergency supplies. We may be at sea for some time. I know I'm forgetting something but it will come to me. Off we go."

They started out, but Larko halted them. "Oh, and no shooting. The head librarian will see you and we'll get demerits."

"Yeah, he's fine," Bogo said, helping Emenine as she tried to inflate the boat still dangling around her neck.

"Good thing I had this," she said. "We'd have never found it in all the mess."

"Yes, you did good," Bogo agreed.

Lavolier stood mid-way down the hall, swinging helplessly on the crank that manually opened the emergency escape lock.

"Need...more...weight," he grunted. "Come here, Bogo."

The eunuch pushed the knight aside and wrenched the crank around. Smoke and sparks began pouring down the passage.

"Help, help," the computer AI screamed. "Do not abandon me. I'm not waterproof."

Jonathan felt guilty, but there was nothing to do. "Sorry, FD. We're sort of in a situation here. Do the best you can."

"Do the what?" the computer howled, then there was a loud bang and a steady hiss of static.

The hatch suddenly flew open and the crew barely had time to take cover as large bolts-used to seal the exterior hatch under high pressure-sprang out in all directions, pinging off the metal interior of the ship.

Jonathan heard Emenine scream as black sea water burst through the opening, slamming into everyone and pouring down the sloping passage of the sinking craft.

"How does this thing open?" she said, waving the inflatable boat in the air, her head just above the incoming water.

Larko perched on Bogo's shoulders.

"Step one. Remove protective--."

"Pull the big tab!" Bogo shouted. "Not in here, out there."

Emenine ducked into the rising tide of water and pushed out into the open. The boat opened with a loud pop and began drifting away. The others forced their way out into the open sea, dragging Verlag behind them and climbed into the boat as Emenine held it against the side of the quickly sinking ship. As they pushed away, the Duweena's Courage slipped under the sea.

"That was close," Lavolier said. "Good thing I kept my head and got that lock door open."

"Oh, my gods, what about the Dinhari," Jonathan cried. "They were sleeping in the stasis pods."

"The poor devils," Bogo said. "Never had a chance."

Suddenly, the water began to swell upward near the spot the ship sank and a huge bubble of air burst into view. Inside sat the three Dinhari, the one called Dorn clearly using his psycho-kinetic powers to create the bubble.

"Help them onboard," shouted Jonathan, using his arms to splash the boat in their direction. The bubble collapsed and the small hedgehogs climbed on board.

"Any landing you bob away from," Lavolier muttered.

"We sensed the crashing ship and prepared to escape ourselves, Dorn sensing that you would not have time to save us yourselves," Blip reported. "We are not angry, just a bit disappointed."

A quick search revealed a set of long oars and they were placed in the locks.

"We have food, water and medicine," Jonathan said. " Blankets and a large cloth for making an awning so the sun won't kill us right away."

"Maybe our Dinhari friends can tell us which way to row," Bogo said.

"The ship sure sank fast, didn't it?" Larko said sadly.

"Feeling better, dear?," Emenine said, stroking his shoulder sympathetically.

"Well, not really. My ship is at the bottom of the ocean. Again."

Lavolier, standing up in the bow, shaded his eyes. "Yeah, I noticed you have a track record in that direction. I don't see any land. What about it, Deep Sight Dorn? Any ideas?"

The little knight was suddenly elevated in the air and dropped overboard.

"His tone is not respectful," Tagger-Streel said. "That's going to happen a lot if he doesn't show some to Dorn."

"Man overboard," Bogo said half-heartedly, slapping at the knight's bobbing head with an oar. "I'll save you. Just don't move."

There was a scream of pain and then Lavolier's hands appeared on the sides of the boat. His head popped into view. "So, did we get a direction?"

Dorn's abilities were a bit vague at long distances, but he finally decided on a direction, and the oars were put in the hands of Bogo and Jonathan, the two most likely to try to maintain a steady course.

Larko, his head bandaged by Emenine so that it seemed he wore a turban, still remained bleak. "She's gone forever."

"Well, the *Courage* got us here, more or less in one piece," Jonathon said as he rowed. "Better than ending up in a salvage yard, being cut up to make park benches."

"Even after all Verlag must have done to her, she still got us down," Bogo said agreeably. "Speaking of which, how is he doing? Anybody see any movement yet?"

Emenine, who had been rummaging among the supplies, climbed up on the stern and peered behind the boat, where the assassin floated alone on a large raft made of empty bailing jugs and canvas.

"He's sitting up. He's waving and trying to say something. Maybe we should have removed the gag."

"Not ready to exchange pleasantries with that rat yet," Larko said, twitching his nose in anger. "He's got his pack and a jug of water. He'll survive a while."

"Unless something big comes up out of the sea and eats him," Lavolier said. "Do you think that could happen?"

"As likely as something big coming up and eating us," Larko said. "Blip seems to think the sea life is largely benign."

"I hope that means it's edible," Emenine said. Amongst the emergency supplies, she had found a fishing pole and a package of artificial worms. "Guaranteed to catch aquatic life forms on any world. If you starve, call Tandara 880-96000."

She handed the items to Lavolier.

"You're not serious," he said, insulted. "A man of my position and rank does not fish like a common peasant."

Emenine stared at him, disgusted. "Well, you won't row and you won't bail and you won't rub my feet, so this will give you something to do until we get rescued or make it to shore."

The knight sniffed, scratched a salty patch off his forehead, and looked miserable.

"I got all wet and my clothes are ruined. Don't I deserve a little sympathy?"

The silence was complete. He snatched the pole out of Emenine's hands, baited the hook, and cast the line off the back of the boat.

Commander Larko, rubbing the bump on his head and wincing in pain, slid along the side of the boat and sat down beside the sulking knight-fisherman.

"Have you given any thought to weapons, Lavolier," Larko said. "You are the weapons officer."

"I'm apparently reduced to this," the knight said. "Fishing."

"Well, it's your duty to put your mind to our situation in regard to defenses. We all have the utmost confidence in you when it comes to that sort of thing, you know."

Lavolier swallowed hard, then smiled faintly. "Well, there's the canvas and lots of those elastic ties you use to hold things down in a wind storm. You could fill the empty jugs with sea water and use them as cannon balls. We could make a great big catapult and when the enemy approaches--."

"Good, work out the details in your head. Hopefully, we won't need to fight any sea monsters, pirates or such, and if we make shore there should be more materials for making weapons."

Larko moved over to sit next to Jonathan.

"Nicely done," he said, whispering in the Tandaran's ear.

"It's a small boat and his feelings are easily bruised. A little flattery goes a long ways," Larko said. "Oh, by the way, you're doing a wonderful job of rowing."

Jonathan laughed. "Doing it for my health. A man pushing forty needs to stay in shape. Right, Bogo?"

"Speak for yourself, old man," the eunuch said. "I'm still in the bright summer of my life. I just keep telling myself this is a pleasant morning jaunt, just like in the old days on a Queen's Day outing."

The fishing line whipped past Bogo's head.

"Hey, watch it, you maniac," the eunuch howled as the hook barely missed his eye.

Lavolier reeled the line in thoughtfully.

"Just calculating trajectories. What's your problem?"

Taking a break, they let the boat drift on for a few hours. Emenine watched the Dinhari as they sat engrossed in their quill pick-up game. A thick layer of fog began to settle over the sea in all directions.

Lavolier sat at the back of the boat, talking to himself bitterly, catching not a single fish, but managing to hook Bogo twice in the back of the neck. The Dinhari Dorn, rising from the game to let Emenine play, went over and sat down beside the grumbling knight.

Lavolier glared down at the Dinhari, annoyed. Dorn ignored him. Instead, he peered into the water, his forehead wrinkled in concentration.

"There!" He pointed at a spot very close to the boat. "Quickly, cast your line over there."

"Oh, sure, what was I thinking?" Lavolier scoffed. "I've got news for you. I've been fishing for hours and not one bite. I'm pretty sure there's not a fish in this entire sea."

Dorn extended his short arm.

64

"Give me the pole, Sir Disrespectful."

"Better do it," Bogo said, opening one eye as he lounged against the stern, trying to sleep.

Lavolier glared at the red-spined hedgie.

"It's my pole," he said, and made a short cast in the direction indicated.

After a few moments, the colorful bobber-actually one of the balls Emenine used for juggling converted by Blip into a hard rubber flotation device-bounced up and down on the now still surface of the water. Lavolier's eyes grew wide. His hands trembled. He yanked on the pole, snapping the sea creature out of the water and into the bottom of the boat. It was streamlined like a fish, but where its fins would be, stringy tentacles coiled and stretched.

"Ew," Emenine said. "Not eating that."

Lavolier ignored her, instead patting Dorn gingerly on the creature's spiny back.

"We caught a fish," he boasted. "Team work, that's the way, eh Dornie?"

The hedgehog rolled its eyes, but couldn't hide a pleased look.

"Your quick wrists did the trick. There are many more out there."

"Good place for them," Emenine said, eating a hard cracker with decisive finality.

Bogo frowned, brushing water off his face.

"I'd like it better if you'd sit back down before you tip over this boat. Someone is going to have to test the fish, see if it's edible. Should probably be the one who caught it."

Lavolier stared at the now limp creature.

"Well, we do have enough to eat for now without it. Let's just put this down to experience. We know we can catch...whatever that is, right?"

"A wise decision," Larko agreed, carefully unhooking the fish-like beast and dropping it overboard.

"After all, we can't be that far from land," Jonathan said. "If Emenine cuts down on her daily meals from six to three, we should have enough to make it."

The jester replaced the tall stack of crackers in their storage case. "I was just counting them." She drew out three of her juggling balls from a pouch at her belt and began tossing them into the air.

After another hour, Jonathan and Bogo again took to the oars. The boat was surrounded in fog, the rope leading to Verlag's raft seeming to hang in mid-air, occasionally bobbing up and down as if the assassin was rolling around, trying to get loose.

Jonathan glanced over at Bogo, who was puffing slightly with each drag on the oar, sweat runneling down the sides of his face.

"Can I ask you a question?" Jonathan asked. "I mean, it's sort of personal."

Bogo shrugged. "It only looks like I'm having a heart attack. I'm tougher than I look."

"No, it's not that," Jonathan assured him, "but it sort of revolves around that. What happened...you were tall and strong and handsome for a long time, then suddenly, back to the old Bogo."

Bogo stared dreamily ahead.

"I was a living doll, wasn't I? Well, obviously, the effects were only temporary. I think my chemical make-up, as Commander Larko would call it, was too altered by my decades of eunuch-hood to maintain the maleness. Who knows, maybe secretly I missed the old me. Mind over matter."

"So, whatever happened to you and Dame Littlefield?" Jonathan pressed. "I mean, she got the regenerator treatment, too, right? I thought maybe you two might... "

Bogo snorted, amused. "They must have kept you out in the field for a long time," he said. "You missed the great, on again, off again romance that will go down the ages of hedgehog lore. It mostly consisted of running gun fights across the wilds of Yurle Prime. No, it didn't work out," he explained. "Actually, we did put aside our old conflicts and struck up a really nice business relationship. Until I returned to my old form, that is. Then, I just let her get on with her life and I hooked up with Larko and his investigation of Walpole's evil Guild."

"You know where she is?" Jonathan queried, curious.

Bogo shook his head. "That's the thing," he said. "She was taking her own interest in Walpole and his cohorts on Yurle Prime. Last I heard, she was on a mission to find the access point where the dirty little tyrant was teleporting in his henchmen. She disappeared."

"Do you think...," Jonathan began but Bogo put a finger to his thick lips.

"I do," he whispered. "It's the main reason I'm here. I think Walpole has kidnapped Dame Littlefield. He always hated law enforcement types and she was a constant thorn in his side. I think

67

we'll find her wherever Walpole is hiding. I only hope we're in time to save her."

Jonathan looked worried. "She's tough," he said tentatively, remembering how she had fought bravely, even with a broken arm on a bloody field in the king's realm. "If Walpole has her, she'll stand up to him."

The eunuch sighed. "That's what I'm afraid of."

The boat grew quiet as the other castaways found places to sleep. The pair continued their rhythmic dipping of the oars, nearly asleep themselves.

Jonathan jerked with a start, having dozed off. Bogo sat with head hanging down, breathing regularly. There was movement at the stern and he saw the sharp-eyed hedgie, Dorn, sitting there, peering into the dark.

"See something?" Jonathan asked.

Dorn raised his head. "I've been watching a strange light for some time now. It's hard to tell how far away it is in this fog. I'm not sure what it is," he explained, puzzled.

Jonathan looked in the direction Dorn pointed. "I don't see anything," he said. But, then he did see something very disturbing. The tow rope was dangling in the water.

"Where did Verlag go?"

Dorn reached down and pulled up the rope. The end had been neatly severed.

"That's a bad sign. Verlag with something sharp." Jonathan nudged Bogo awake.

"We've lost our prisoner," he said lowly.

Bogo rubbed his eyes and squinted into the dark, misty air. "No, I don't think so. Unfortunately, I think he's just thumbing his grubby nose at us. Listen."

The sound of a heated argument drifted over the water.

"What's he up to," Jonathan said. "Can we sort of back track and see if we can find him."

The eunuch clucked his tongue. "Not my first thought, but why not?"

While Dorn crept forward to awaken the others, Jonathan and Bogo brought the boat to a halt and then slowly back-paddled until a tiny flickering light could be seen, then the makeshift raft appeared out of the mist.

Verlag had rid himself of his bindings and gag, and had somehow affected a wardrobe change, as well. He was dressed in a long white robe and a tall white conical-shaped miter cap covered his head. His slender pimply nose and sly little mouth stuck out through a thick white mustache and beard.

"Okay, that's a new look," Bogo said. "How much stuff has he got in that backpack of his, anyway?"

A pair of binoculars rested on the seat beside Verlag. He lifted them and looked toward the approaching boat.

"Yes, the fog seems to be clearing. I can see them well now. I may have to take action to defend myself." He spoke into a glass ball in the end of a white staff. Jonathan now recognized it as the one the blind beggar carried at the tavern.

"So, that was Verlag, the little sneak. Hey, aren't those our binoculars."

At the sound of Jonathan's voice, Verlag lowered the binoculars and stared at the nearby boat.

"Oh, there you are. Why am I'm dressed like this and talking into a silly stick? Long story, best save it for another day. So, I take it you've repented your extreme behavior toward me and have come to apologize."

"My god, and I thought Lavolier was delusional," Bogo muttered.

"I'm awake, fat boy," the knight said, holding the fishing pole like a rapier.

There was a buzzing sound coming from the glass ball. Verlag rolled his eyes.

"No, I don't see how they could have survived," he whined. "They live charmed lives. I will talk to you later. Company's arrived."

Larko stood awkwardly in the bow of the boat. "What do you have to say for yourself, miscreant? You have wrecked my beautiful space ship and left us floating lost on this seemingly endless sea."

"Why are you dressed like that?" Emenine said, leaning over the gunwale to get a closer look. "It's very disturbing. Who do you *think* you are?"

"Ah, the juggling concubine," Verlag sneered. "I can think of so many reasons they brought you along on this mission and none of them I can repeat in decent company. Wait, what decent company. Shall I go on?"

The woman brushed back her curls and shrugged. "Such a nasty creature, but clearly the ramblings of a disordered mind. Lavolier, run him through with that fishing pole."

Reaching up to his upper lip, Verlag reattached a bit of white hair that was coming free. "Blasted water everywhere. Loosens the glue. If you must know, I am the High Priest of Walpole's latest brainstorm, the Great Mind. Since we're nearly to the island, I thought I might as well prepare myself for my devoted followers."

"You mean Walpole's followers, right?" Bogo asked.

"Well, you know," Verlag said non-committedly.

"Did he say we're nearly to an island," Jonathan wondered. "Which way, you viperous traitor. You're still our prisoner, you know."

"Actually, it might be in your best interest to be mine. The locals aren't partial to strangers."

Larko removed his head bandage and tossed it aside.

"You're still our prisoner. It's clear he's been here before, though, and has revealed that Walpole is at the bottom of the failed missions. We must be prepared for great danger."

"You must address me as High Priest Pliffle, Voice of the Great Mind," Verlag directed. The assassin carefully covered the glass ball at the top of his cane and stuck it ball down in his pack. "Now, before any of us go off half-quilled, as they say in these parts, if you're willing to be reasonable, I have a proposition."

Bogo snorted. "There are just too many ways to interpret that. Be careful, Verlag, there are ladies present."

"I'll keep you in mind," the assassin retorted. "Now, you know Walpole's worth a fortune in rewards back on Yurle Prime. If we work together, we can capture him, take him back, and make enough to come back here in a new ship and lay claim to one of the archipelagoes. I have a nice one in mind."

"You sabotaged my ship," Larko complained. "If you wanted to cooperate, wouldn't it have been easier to just make yourself known before we crashed?"

"Walpole would have been suspicious and, say what you will about the nasty little runt, he's got some mean powers. He's been turning people inside out lately. Spoils dinner to no end."

"Land ho," shouted Dorn, perched on the bow and pointing toward the horizon where thin tendrils of smoke rose toward the sky.

"So, what do we expect when we land," Larko said, "if we decide to throw in with you?"

For a moment, everyone thought the assassin looked very unscrupulous and deceitful, but it could have been the strange light.

"Well, there are some dangers, of course, besides Walpole. They're a bit hard to describe. It'd be better if you just saw them for yourselves."

"Sounds like famous last words," Bogo grumbled.

Emenine whistled loudly.

"Yes, but whose? How about it, little hedgehogs. What do you sense about all this?"

Dorn rubbed his bristly head.

"There are many of our brethren on the island ahead. There are dark forces afoot. And a restaurant that serves shakes and spiny curls at a reasonable price." The Dinhari seer shook his head as if trying to get a bug out of his ear. "I picked up a commercial frequency. It was in hedgehog, though."

Blip and Tagger-Streel conferred between themselves.

"When we land Blip and I should go ahead and do some recon before any of the rest of you go any further than the beach," Tagger said.

"A good idea," Emenine said. "Is it just me or can anyone smell fried food? Mush balls or, my goodness, spiny curls."

Although Verlag argued that he should go ahead and clear the way for the others, he was convinced that the others were not going to trust him out of their sight for some time. The island, a long, low silhouette, rose on the horizon. Tall trees, surrounded by heavy brush, were set back several yards from the beach, a bright white sand littered with wreckage.

There was no movement as Bogo and Jonathan oared them the final distance and pushed them up on shore between the ruins of missions Two and Three. The sun had climbed up the sky, burning off the remaining mist, and the shipwrecked crew could see in the far distance a towering volcano, silent and ominous, the slopes up to its peak naked rock.

Blip and Tagger-Streel leapt to the sand, armed with home-made slings.

"Use one of the ships for cover," Tagger said, "and stay low. If we're not back in an hour, I'm afraid you're on your own."

The two hedgehogs scurried across the sand, appeared to discover a path through the bushes, and disappeared.

Verlag pushed his raft ashore, straightened his white robes, reapplied his facial hair, and then smiled.

"Well, now that the dynamic Dinhari duo are out of our hair, who wants lunch on me? I have my discount card. It's my restaurant, after all."

"We're supposed to stay here," Jonathan said. The smell of cooking food made his stomach growl. "Do they do take out?"

"I'm not complaining," the chief administrator of Real Plants in Space Enterprises said. "It's just that we'd like to know why your units have suddenly become twenty-eight per cent more efficient in the last week, Bob."

"I have a great crew, sir. Never a complaint, even when one of them gets chewed up a bit by the special plant research subjects. As to the greater efficiency, I can only attribute it to that."

Bob loved talking to the boss. For some reason, his vocabulary got all official and smart sounding. Before his conversations had mostly been with himself and concerned the general upkeep of mortar and stone.

"Well, whatever it is, keep up the good work. There's been some concern down here that the

74

expense of the project might outweigh the benefits of preservation of our biosphere. Now, I think we can assure our stockholders that there will be a positive outcome."

The post-communication buzz was so happy that it took Bob several moments to notice Harlix's viewer blinking in emergency mode.

"Yes, Harlix, what's up?"

"Bob, we have a little problem here. The navigation people have told me that no matter what they do to reset the course, we keep turning toward the Rectangle and that little planet they've called Yurle Minor, which by the way, is just way too confusing."

"I'll head down to the command center. Probably just some water in the wiring."

Deep Thought liked subtlety, lived by it, really, so far. He'd hoped the minute course changes would not be noticed by what he had gleaned were a bunch of farmers with fancy titles. However, the old computers were being recalcitrant, so DeepThought would have to be more assertive.

Alarms began screaming as the great ship began to heave around and head away from its orbit around Yurle Prime. A few million miles away, the Rectangle was a mere foggy patch in the void. Deep Thought turned the ship's communications array about and began to speak to it.

Chapter Five

The island had clearly been the final destination for all of the previous Space Force missions. Beyond Number Two was One and Six, to the other side of Three was Four and Five. Several had made rough landings, their hulls smashed in or cracked open, but Two and Six appeared nearly intact, their landing gear down, though it was bent and nearly collapsed, as if the touchdown had been almost uncontrolled. Hatches on all the ships swung loosely, the locks wide open to the outside air.

An old space helmet stuck out of the sand near Jonathan's foot. Water ran into the helmet through a hole in the face shield. The helmet was dented and muddy, but the Yurle Prime Space Force insignia was still visible.

Jonathan's appetite suddenly disappeared. He smelled death in the air.

"They put up a fight, at least some of them," he said. "If there are survivors, we have to find them. Who knows what Walpole is doing to them."

Verlag tugged his raft onto shore and shouldered his pack.

"Well, I'll just go and get us something to eat."

Lavolier appeared from around the rear of the nearest wreck.

"Not so fast. You can leave your pack here. We want you coming back."

"I need my pack," Verlag protested.

"He's most likely to vanish," Lavolier said. "That wouldn't be a bad idea, but he's been here before and knows the layout. We need to know all we can about Walpole and his forces before we can do anything."

"And, it looks like he has forces," Larko said, his hat sitting high on his head so as not to rub the sore spot. "What kind I don't know."

Dorn, the Dinhari who had remained behind, had been edging along the sand, stooping to sniff at bits of wreckage.

"I sense dark things."

Emenine, staring into the sun, looked around.

"He said that before. Should we be worried?"

The trees were thick with foliage, the upper limbs heavy with large bright yellow objects that could have been fruit or nuts, the ground covered in tall ferns with black, spiky fronds and clumps of small crimson berry-like orbs. A pair of fluttery creatures with bright gold plumage ran into view, squawking, then vanished back into the dense growth before anyone could react.

"We'll keep the pack, Verlag," Jonathan said. "While you're gone, perhaps we can determine if any of those...whatever they are...are edible." He pointed at the berries. "The feathered things seem to like them."

Verlag dropped his pack with a grumble. "I've locked it, so no snooping if you know what's good for you." Dressed in his white robes and hat, the former assassin looked like some large bird himself as he flapped his way down the beach and disappeared around a sharp curve of the shoreline.

"I feel better already," Sir Lavolier said.

Dorn kneeled suddenly, motioning for the others to come close. He peered down at one of the footprints left in the sand. There was a small object near the heel of the impression. He dug down with small pointy fingers and pulled out a cheap necklace. A plastic locket hung from the crude chain.

Brushing the sand away, Dorn pried open the locket.

He glanced up at Jonathan. "I think this explains a lot."

The familiar face inside one side of the locket leered out at him. A hologram in three dimensions with terrible red eyes that blinked and burned straight through to the soul, the head covered in white spines, and a mouth filled with sharp yellow teeth.

Larko squinted at the picture.

"That's Walpole all right. What's it say? The Great Mind Who Knows All."

Bogo snickered. "He must like that picture. It's the same one that's on Verlag's wanted poster. And look who is his most loyal subject."

Emenine spelled out the words slowly. "Bishop Pliffle, Archbishop of the Church of the Great Mind. That sure looks a lot like Verlag."

"It is Verlag," Lavolier sighed. "They're right back at their old games. God and his chief follower. No wonder Walpole knows when the missions are coming. Verlag was reporting right to him."

"Do you think he really wants to help us capture that spiny rat?" Bogo asked. "Or have we just walked into a trick of the, and I use the term with reservation, Great Mind?"

"The crews of the first six missions were mostly hedgehog, with a few specialists, all human, I think," Jonathan said.

Larko held the necklace with the winking Walpole locket, looking at it from different angles as if hoping the face would change.

"He's been teleporting his own people up here for decades. I remember hearing about disappearances nearly every week for a while. Even investigated a few of them. I knew Walpole was strong and getting stronger when we overthrew him, but this is more than anyone could have guessed."

"The hedgehogs he brought here," Bogo began, "were they already loyal to him or is his Great Mind controlling them?"

Jonathan shuddered. "What was the name of that scientist that vanished from the maximum security prison, the one that wanted to implant mind control devices in his enemies? If he fell into Walpole's paws, who knows what we may come across."

Emenine sat next to Jonathan on the ground, stacking odd little, squarish sea shells in pyramids around her feet.

"Science Master Kresgan. Lawson first captured him. I wish Verlag would get back with the food. Or Blip. He could tell us if those big seeds are any good to eat."

The sun was setting behind the volcano's peak, and the sea breeze was turning cold.

"Do you think the crews are all dead?" Jonathan asked. "I mean, why would Walpole kill everyone. He could have controlled them, used them for some weird project."

"I'm sure we'll find out soon," Lavolier said, putting the final touches on a bow. He dragged several thin, pliable branches from the brush, along with several twists of vines. He began peeling the bark from slender reeds he intended to use as shafts for the arrows.

"Why do you say that?" Bogo asked.

"Everything bad happens when it gets dark," the knight said, picking through several golden feathers he'd found at the edge of the woods. "Shouldn't someone start a fire?"

Larko groaned with pain and held his head.

"Is it worse?" Jonathan asked. "It could be a concussion. You hit your head awfully hard."

Emenine examined Larko's injury. "It's a closed wound. If only we hadn't lost our medical diagnostic scanner on the ship.

"There's a long list of things I wish we hadn't lost," Larko said. "Is there any more of the pain medicine?"

"Not much. Here, take another tablet."

"When Blip gets back, he will be able to find something natural to use for pain," Dorn said. "If it is more serious, we may have to find a better location to rest."

"Perhaps one of the wrecks would still have a working scanner," Bogo said. He rose and headed toward the nearest ship, number Three, its main hatch looking like a dark mouth waiting to swallow anything that came too near.

Suddenly, there was the sound of movement in the nearby brush and Blip and Tagger-Streel appeared. Tagger carried two of the golden-feathered fliers and a large blue and yellow striped gourd.

"They're back," Emenine said, adding sheepishly, "as you can all see. Is that dinner?"

"Finished skulking out in the woods," Lavolier said. "Let me have some of those feathers for the arrows," he added, snatching at the golden feathers. Tagger held them out of his reach and walked past without acknowledging him.

Blip handed the gourd to Emenine. "This is edible. Tastes good, too, which is a nice surprise. The creatures are something I've never seen before, but their chemical make-up is not poisonous. I'd try cooking them."

"Again, that means starting a fire," Lavolier said, sneaking up behind Emenine, who was distastefully plucking one of the winged creatures and catching the feathers as they flew in the air.

"A fire will attract attention, but we must do it, I suppose," Larko said, sitting down and leaning back against the side of Number Two. "Jonathan, I believe there were fire starters in the emergency pack. If not, go through Verlag's bag. He has everything else in there."

The wind off the sea became colder and colder, and the others moved quickly to gather up whatever looked combustible to use for the fire. Verlag's raft was dismembered quickly and stacked in a sheltered spot near Larko.

"Lots of fire starters. A little smoke might not be a bad idea. Have any of you been smelling, well, spoiled meat?"

"Now that you mention it," Bogo said. He'd been assisting Emenine in dissecting the pseudo-fowls and slicing the gourd into equal parts. "Only since the sun set."

Lavolier twanged his newly made bow.

"Told you so. Bad things happen after dark."

The fire blazed into life, Jonathan leaping back to avoid having his hair singed.

Tagger-Streel raised his hand.

"Blip has run tests on several of the seed-bearing plants and many slips of bark from the trees. "There are abundant materials for natural pain killers and antibiotics. However, it would be best to wait until first light before trying to collect anything."

Lavolier snorted. "I noticed you Dinhari got back before dark. Afraid the ghosties will get you? Maybe that's why you hid out inside some big storm for hundreds of years while old Grumpole and Empress Moleloch imprisoned or killed thousands on Yurle Prime? That's why you know so much. Lots of time to study when you're hiding...oof."

Tagger-Streel had been little more than a black streak as Lavolier spouted off, and the knight found himself on his back in the sand, one of his arrows pushed partly up his nose.

"Are you calling us cowards?" Tagger growled, the quills on his back prickling and turning a deep

82

shade of red. He poked the arrow a bit further. "On behalf of my people, I demand an apology, or I will be forced to-"

"Stop this at once," Larko shouted, holding his head in pain. "Lavolier, why do you insist on antagonizing our friends? Now, apologize to Tagger at once or no doubt we'll need twice the pain medicine tomorrow."

Bogo dropped a piece of a creature on a square metal plate he'd pulled from one of the wrecks. It sizzled enticingly.

"Please don't stop Tagger just yet, Captain," he pleaded. "I've always been curious if you'd strike anything if you poked around in that skull of Lavolier's."

"I was just wondering why we weren't trying to help Commander Larko now," Lavolier said, sounding rather nasal.

Blip waved Tagger off the knight. "Because it would be dangerous to try to distinguish the right ingredients in the dark."

Nearly everyone noticed that Lavolier hadn't apologized.

"It could have been explained to me without the rough-housing," he grumbled, shaking sand out of his trousers. "Fast little spine-ball."

"It is clear I'm not up to the rigors of command," Larko said, still holding his head. "At least, while we are on the island, someone else must lead the search."

Sir Lavolier straightened his uniform jacket significantly.

"Jonathan, you're second in rank," Larko said, "you'll take over the hunt. I would suggest we eat, get some rest, hope that Verlag returns so that his knowledge of the area can be put into effect, then we'll begin our investigation of the island."

As Lavolier threw up his arms in exasperation, Jonathan leaned down beside his commander and nodded.

"I forget you're no longer that insecure young boy of more than thirty years ago," Larko whispered. "You're a competent, experienced officer and a friend I know I can trust to stick to the mission."

"I thought you'd notice eventually," Jonathan smiled. "I'd have never lived to see this day without you standing behind me, sir. We'll get to the bottom of this."

Emenine lifted the smoking carcass of one of the gold-feathered creatures.

"Dinner is served."

The gourd was refreshing and removed most of the bad aftertaste of the meat. Divided among them all, and supplemented with crackers and whatever else was left in the emergency supplies, there was just enough to tide them over for the night.

"We're going to need at least more of those gourds," Jonathan said, watching Bogo add more fuel to the fire.

"It looked as if they'd been well-picked over," Blip said. "We are clearly not the only ones on this island that need that sort of nourishment."

The members of the crew glanced around them, eyeing the dark edge of the woods, and the shadows encircling the wrecked ships added even more menace to the situation.

"Maybe we'd be safer inside one of the wrecks," Bogo said. "These two are still in pretty solid condition. Only one door to defend in case Walpole decides to rush us with his little possessed helpers."

Jonathan was about to suggest that Bogo and Tagger take a closer look at Number Three, when a low moan caught their attention. It was difficult to tell where it was coming from, though Jonathan thought it had come from down the beach, where other of the wrecks lay.

"What was that?" Emenine said, moving to crouch behind Bogo's great bulk.

"Bet there's a lot of noises we wouldn't recognize," Jonathan said. "Isn't that right, sir?"

Larko nodded slightly. "Yes, though it certainly sounded like a human moan. Perhaps someone is hurt."

"We'd better take a look," Jonathan decided. "Emenine, please stay with Commander Larko. You too, Dorn. The rest of us will check it out. I think it came from the end wreck, Number Six."

Leaving the circle of the fire, only the stars gave a light as the party moved cautiously down the beach. With Jonathan at point, the crew advanced toward the Mission Six vessel. Sea water had left a tidewater mark on the ship's steel frame. Thick, slimy brown algae clung to its twisted landing gear in long tangled strands. Small scuttling creatures headed for the water, hundreds of clicking claws marking their flight, their forms black in the dark.

There was no sign of movement around the wreck. The main lock hatch appeared to be open a few inches. Jonathan grasped the handle on the outside of the door. He gave it a hard tug but it appeared frozen, the water having corroded the metal.

"Whew," he said, backing away as a foul smell seemed to roll from the narrow opening in the entrance. The air around him became suddenly icy and the wind began to increase. It became even darker as the stars slipped behind the sudden arrivals of heavy clouds.

"Look!" Blip shouted.

Jonathan glanced in the direction that the Dinhari pointed. It was Verlag, still dressed in his role as Bishop Pliffle. He stood at the edge of the jungle, arms spread wide, white staff raised.

"How did he get his hands on that," Lavolier said. "He's got his pack. The nasty thief has stolen his own...he's good."

The ball in the handle of the staff-formerly a clear transparent globe-glowed an eerie red and something swirled black and ominous inside.

Rain began to pour down, then lightning lit up the sky. Thunder crashed, drowning out any words they tried to voice. Jonathan squinted and held up his hand, trying to shield his face from the sand and debris driven by the unnatural wind.

Suddenly the door of the Mission Six vessel crashed open with a screech that overcame even the thunderous rage of the storm.

Jonathan jumped back, startled, as something that appeared to have once been human, crawled out of the opening. It rose slowly to its feet and peered at him with empty eye sockets, sneering through rotted lips. He threw up his arms as the creature, growling like a rabid animal, and with what seemed to Jonathan an unnatural ability, leapt across the space between them and drove him to the ground. Pinning Jonathan's arms beneath its knees, the creature seized his throat in its dirty, clawed hands and squeezed. Helpless, he choked, eyes bulging as spots formed before them.

There was a bright flash as something exploded above the struggling pair and the clutching hands fell away. Jonathan saw Bogo straddled over him, staring in amazement at the attacking creature's head in his hands, smoke and sparks pouring from its neck.

"That was not what I expected," the eunuch said, tossing away the head and dragging the rest of the creature off of the other man. "More, you know, some sort of disgusting yellow-greenish ichor. I guess we should be grateful for small favors."

"Robotic zombies?" Jonathan wondered aloud. Screams all around them told him they were not through yet.

Two more of the fake zombies-dressed in ragged and dirty Space Force uniforms-leaped from the craft, attacking the others. Blip, lifted from his feet by one of the monsters, beat at the thing's face with clenched paws, but had no effect. Suddenly, Tagger-Streel, spinning through one of his forms of attack, lashed out with his foot. The powerful swift strike hit the creature at waist level with deadly force. His foot sunk into the zombie's midsection and burst out his back, effectively cutting the creature in half in a burst of crackling electricity and flying transistors.

Another of the high-tech undead, eyes blinking mechanically like cameras recording the unfolding situation, charged Jonathan. The creature had the form of a female with long tangles of yellow hair that fell across one side of her face and down her bony white shoulder. As he grappled with it, Jonathan had to remind himself that what he saw-the rotting flesh covered in black flies crawling in one nostril and out of a cavity in her broken cheekbone-was all just for show: rubber, electronics, and special effects.

"Probably courtesy of Walpole and his mind tricks."

And just like that, the horrific zombie effects vanished and Jonathan found himself battling a spindly robot, crudely made and spewing smoke and sparks as it struggled against him.

Despite the sudden exposure of the creature's real appearance, the danger was no less real. All around him the others fought. He wondered what they saw.

Suddenly, the world seemed to waver, and Jonathan was again battling a zombie. He shouted in horror, trying to shake her off, but she clung to him, snarling through clenched teeth. Her long slender arms wrapped like a vice around his neck, squeezing and choking him. He felt her claws cut into his cheek. Her mouth opened, inches from his face. He breathed in the stench of her breath-*nice touch, an olfactory trigger*-strangely cold against his face and smelling of grave worms long dead.

He squirmed, twisted, and then swung about throwing himself backwards, smashing her against the side of the ship. Her grip loosened just for a moment, and he tore her arms from around his neck. He cringed, shaking off bits of the zombie's sticky flesh that clung like globs of old gravy to his fingers.

He snatched up a bar of metal sheared from the nearest ship and swung. The blow flung the creature backwards against the ship, impaling it on a jagged spear-like protrusion. The zombie shook and tried to pull free but was snagged. A smear of some dark green chemical sprayed from a rupture inside its chest cavity, staining the silver metal exterior of the moldy vessel. The female ghoul blinked, its flesh-eating fury slipping suddenly away, its eyes calm.

Jonathan looked into the creature's face, a face he recognized as an old friend he had trained with years ago.

"Walker?" Jonathan whispered, horrified, then relaxed. He had left his old companion back on Yurle Prime, serving in the Requisition Department.

Again, it was the frail robot dangling there.

"They're robots," Jonathan shouted, glancing around at the others, who had overcome the rest of the attackers.

Bogo shook his head. "You mean gru-worms from the deep swamps of Old Yurle."

"No, wind demons of the Outer Wastes," Blip and Tagger-Streel insisted.

"One of my mothers-in-law," Sir Lavolier said as he stomped again on the creature at his feet. "One of the real nasty ones."

"It's a mind trick of Walpole's," Jonathan said, then turned toward where the slowly backing away figure of Verlag-Pliffle was just visible. "And his. Get him Tagger, Lavolier!"

Verlag, tripping over his robes, waved his staff toward the sky. The storm doubled in its fury, hail now streaking down in sheets that stung and blinded the others. Lavolier slipped and fell in the sand, but Tagger continued. With a shout, Verlag dropped his staff and fled into the trees. The Dinhari hedgehog halted as there was the sound of some sort of machine starting up, and then a needle-like object streaked away across the island toward the volcano.

"He was planning to betray us all along," Bogo said as the storm began to disperse and they once again stood up against the falling wind. Tagger returned, carrying Verlag's staff and the pack he'd restolen.

"That might be of interest," Jonathan said. Tagger held it up and they examined it closely for the first time.

The warrior hedgehog turned the staff over in his hands. He peered closely at the end of the device. He gripped it and twisted the end counterclockwise. The others watched, fascinated, as Tagger unscrewed the end of the staff, revealing a peculiar looking electronic dial inside. Luminous greenish letters-glowing in the falling dark-were spaced evenly around the circumference of the dial's interior. A tiny notch in the staff appeared to act as a pointer.

"Some sort of compass or weird clock?" Lavolier muttered, brushing sand from his uniform.

"Maybe," Jonathan said. "If so, it's like nothing I've ever seen before. The letters are probably abbreviations."

He examined the sets of letters trying to make sense of them. The notch currently pointed at ActZb.

"That's probably how Verlag had it set just before the zombies attacked," Bogo interjected. "It might be the abbreviation for Activate Zombies. They didn't seem to work very well."

"I think the fear factor was the real weapon," Blip said. "I was nearly paralyzed with fear, seeing the most dangerous of Dinhari enemies coming out of the old ships. It was so totally unexpected. I think we were meant to be so afraid we couldn't defend ourselves."

"Luckily, the illusion wasn't completely successful. Either we're not entirely susceptible to Walpole's mind or there are other factors working against him."

"I knew my mind was too powerful for him," Lavolier said. "My mothers-in-law. I was never afraid of them. Well, maybe one of them. Actually, there was something quite satisfying about that fight."

"Yes," Jonathan said, trying not to be distracted by the knight's personal speculations.

Tagger peered at the controller.

"I think it's a very good guess. I wonder if TPort might be transport or teleport. Could RecZb be recall zombies? And maybe Wet-Contr might be short for weather control."

"That's very good," Jonathan stated. "It would be nice if it still worked."

Bogo shuddered. "Teleport us where. Into the middle of the volcano? Out in the middle of the sea. I think we'd better not start playing around with it. Remember, it's one of Walpole's creations, I bet."

Jonathan read the groups of letters aloud beginning once more with the current setting: RecZb, TPort, TransI, ActZb, ActRb, RecRb, VComm, ActA-Lift, Wet-Contr, ML1, and ML2.

Bogo was right. There was too much unknown information and both Verlag and Walpole had dangerous and devious minds. Using the wrong setting might cause the staff to explode or worse.

Lavolier tried to snatch the staff out of Tagger's hands impatiently. He was coolly rebuffed by the little hedgehog.

"All of you are just making wild guesses," Lavolier growled arrogantly. "As a knight, I have expert training that I can put to use here. Give me the staff and I'll have the secret message worked out by morning."

"I think we should let Commander Larko take a look at it. It may be some sort of old Galactic University technology," Blip suggested.

They all turned toward the distant ship where they'd left Larko, Emenine and Dorn.

"It's been rather quiet over there, hasn't it?" Bogo said. "Normally, Emenine's screams would have given me a headache."

Kicking sand to all sides, they raced back to the base camp. The trio they'd left behind was gone.

"It's no use," Bob said, faithfully recording the message to his superiors, though the sending array had not worked for several hours. "We are still advancing on the Armadon Rectangle and have already entered the outer dust envelope. The ship will not respond to our commands and we've been forced to boost all the artificial lighting to maintain sufficient illumination so that the plants are not injured. Our sun is no longer providing enough radiation now that the dust is blocking its rays."

Bob turned off the recorder and looked at Harlix. The hedgehog was watching the technicians disassembling the navigation boards. He extended one of his diminutive digits and poked at a loose connection.

"Maybe we should eject the pods from the engine module. Put them in a trajectory to orbit the sun."

They went to the observation window and watched the dim orb that had been their bright sun only a short time ago. It seemed to fade another magnitude as they penetrated deeper into the Rectangle.

"Do you think it will let us?" Bob wondered.

Harlix started nervously. "You feel it, too?"

They looked at the flashing warning lights and the frozen navigation screens that displayed their illicit path into the nebula. Something was controlling their wonderful ship.

Bob walked to the main computer bank and sat down. He pulled out the manual keyboard and typed slowly a short message.

"Hello in there."

Deep Thought allowed part of its consciousness to consider the attempt at communication from the crew of its ship. The rest of the AI's attention focused on the medium now surrounding it.

"Hello out there," it said, in a code somewhat dissimilar from that used by Odd Bob.

Chapter Six

As the others trudged down the beach, Emenine turned back to the little fire. Larko sat nearby, his back against the shell of the downed spacecraft. His head slumped forward, as if he was dozing. Nearby, Dorn sat, buried in a deep thought trance.

"No one to talk to," she said mournfully. Aside from the strange moan coming from down the beach, the night was almost silent. Waves shushed softly onto the shore. The fire crackled reassuringly. Occasionally, night insects and other flying creatures with long, sharp beaks and flashing eyes flew in and out of the light.

Bored, Emenine found five pieces of dried driftwood the others had collected for the fire and lit the ends of each stick. Expertly, she tossed first one and then another of the burning sticks into the air, until she had all of them in motion above her head. The flaming sticks crackled and sparked in the night sky. Emenine caught one behind her back and then balanced one of the brands on her forehead, while still managing to keep the others aloft.

As Emenine entertained herself, the fire crackled and sent wisps of ash and smoke up into the night sky. There were shouts far down the beach where the others had gone. She caught the sticks and tossed them back into the fire. She took several steps forward, trying to see in the dim light.

Behind her, the fire blazed and a shape took form; a squat, spiny figure whose blazing eyes even outshone the fire around them. Walpole looked about for his important servant.

"*Verlag! Verlag!*" the hedgehog hissed telepathically. "*Where are you?*"

Walpole's eyes settled on the shapely back of the juggler.

"*I'd know that posterior anywhere. So, Verlag has failed to eliminate them. I shall do it and get a great deal of fun out of it.*"The demon hedgehog focused all of his attention on the jester.

Come to me! he commanded.

Startled, Emenine jumped, and looked about, searching for the source of the voice, but saw only darkness and the dying fire. Distracted from the growing fight, she walked slowly back to the fire. Walpole's form faded into the flames. The evil creature's powerful consciousness drifted out over the sand and paused.

"*As I feared. She and her gang of misfits have developed a kind of immunity to my mental powers over the years. Well, there's more than one way to catch that cartwheeling courtesan. Just need to poke around in that brain full of puns, doggerel and dirty limericks and see what would entice her to climb into a stranger's carriage.*

The hedgehog's probing powers searched Emenine's mind. She stood still, as if listening to distant music, her eyes blank.

A large, familiar figure rose to the forefront. *That's interesting*, Walpole smiled slyly. "*Still have a soft spot for him, have we? I can put that to very good use.*"

"Emenine, what's wrong?" Larko looked up at the woman. Dorn glanced over distractedly.

Walpole hissed to himself. *Forgot about you two.* A quick stab at Larko's mind found it fogged, the images sometimes doubling as if looking at something cross-eyed. A Tandaran brain was complicated and Gamitof Pym Larko's had been subjected to many strange influences and experiences over the long years.

The sounds of shouting and fighting from down the beach were dying away. Time was growing short if he was to break up his enemies' forces. Walpole all but lifted Larko to his feet.

"Come along, Dorn. I believe I've calculated where *Duweena's Courage* has washed up on shore. It's only a short way down the beach."

"But shouldn't we wait for the others," the little Dinhari said, shaking sand from his quills. "I have been looking into the future and..."

Larko was already stumbling down the beach in the opposite direction the others had gone. "Can't let her be lost. Can't let her be lost again."

Dorn looked at Emenine, who still stared off into the dark of the woods, then hurried after the Commander.

"Wait, sir. You're in no shape to be running around. I'm coming."

Walpole gasped with laughter. *That was easy. Now, have to get the Jiggling Jester on her way before they come back.*

In the distance Walpole sensed the others had gotten their hands on the powerful wand he'd let Verlag use. *That idiot will pay for his incompetence.*

With a single thought Walpole broke all connection between the object and himself, then turned to Emenine.

"You are talented in so many ways."

Emenine swung about. Her mouth opened, stunned.

A man-tall, dark, and handsome with the crooked smile of a scoundrel-stepped from the shadows at the edge of the wood.

"Randall?" Emenine gasped in disbelief. "Is that you?"

"There's no time. Come with me, my lovely jester. I have a hideaway where we can become reacquainted."

Emenine felt her feet begin taking the steps that would approach the impossible apparition. On the other hand, her mind struggled against the betrayal of her body. Baron Randall Glauwer had been dead for a long time, killed at the battle before the walls of his castle.

"I've never known Emenine to be afraid of anything," the baron said, tauntingly, as was his usual manner. "I will explain everything, in time. But, let's go. The others will spoil our reunion. Hurry."

The woman broke into a run and slid her hand into the one the man stretched out before him. They vanished into the trees.

Jonathan scanned the empty campsite. There was no way to tell, in all the confusion of the sand, which way anyone had gone.

"They couldn't be any more than a few minutes away," Bogo said. "We weren't gone that long."

They began shouting into the falling darkness. Blip tossed more wood on the fire, and soon the edge of the forest gleamed back at them, but there was still no evidence of where Larko, Emenine and Dorn had gone.

Lavolier joined the group, furiously shaking the staff they'd found.

"It's gone dead. Somebody's shut off the power."

"Never mind that," Bogo said in annoyance. "Emenine and the others are gone."

The knight took in the sight. "Well, I figured she'd run off sometime. Just thought she might say good-bye. So, who has a charger? We need this staff to work."

Jonathan came back to the fire.

"It's too dark to search now. We'll have to wait until daylight and then go after them."

"Dorn would never go without leaving some of message for us," Blip said. "Unless he was under some sort of control." Tagger-Streel nodded in agreement.

The five remaining crew members sat down around the fire, tried to make themselves comfortable, and waited for the dawn.

Emenine walked along beside Glauwer as they wound their way through the dark, overhanging woods. A small light, drifting before them like a fairy, seemed to be acting as their guide.

"Jonathan looks a bit like you now," she said. "He's got his mother's brains, and of course, he's really Evan Owen's son, but there's something about the way he carries himself, the way he wears his clothes. Well, you were his superficial father. I suppose the superficial traits rubbed off on him."

"Yes, Jonathan. Never mind him. He's gone his own way, I suppose. Now, as you can see, I'm still your faithful companion and devoted lover, Baron Randall Glauwer. Well, there's been some changes."

"You mean you're actually faithful and devoted now?" she quipped.

"You saucy little...!" the illusory Glauwer growled, the voice of Walpole slightly coming through. He laughed nervously. "You always had a delightful sense of humor. Now, you must believe that people change."

Emenine held up her hand to shield her eyes against the baron, who was definitely shimmering in the gloom.

"I guess you have changed in one way," she conceded. "You admit you need to be a different man than you were."

Randall's glow faded.

"I've been transformed," he explained. "I was dead, Emenine. I've discovered the...ah...undiscovered country. I've walked amongst those who can see without eyes and speak without mouths and hear without ears. I've descended into the blackest night, entered the city of lost souls, held audience with its undead lord, and come out the other side."

Randall struck a pose that would have been familiar to a vast horde of hedgehogs, past, present and future. He lowered his head and smiled benevolently at the woman.

Emenine glared at him. That sounded like the old Baron Glauwer. A lot of fancy words with very little meaning.

"Don't screw with me Randall," she warned. "Tell me what all of that jibber-jabber you just said means."

"It's complicated," he insisted, perturbed. "When I died, my soul passed into the realm of the dead."

"You have a soul," she said scornfully. "That doesn't say much for the gods, does it? You cheated on me," Emenine said, eyes flashing in accusation as she recalled their long past together. "I was young and naive and I trusted you."

The Baron looked at her and grinned. "Now who's throwing around the jibber-jabber? When we met, I believe, you were the lead act in a rag-tag troop of half-starved sideshow performers. I remember a cute little snakeskin outfit that changed color when you stood on your head. I fell in love right then."

He smiled his most winning smile, the one that had melted many a young damsel's resistance, if not their hearts. His twinkling blue eyes and scoundrel mouth began to cast their spell. She felt her legs grow weak. She'd forgotten about the snakeskin jumper.

"How did you remember that?"

Glauwer shrugged. "It must have been important. Being dead gives you time to go back over your past deeds and repent that you didn't do things differently.

"My dearest Emenine," he said, placing his hand on her shoulder. "My time in the realm of the dead was filled with torment and torture," he said, his face filled with pain. "Even now I cannot bring myself to talk of it. I just want to do things to better the world, to make amends to those I've hurt. Will you give me a chance?"

She pushed his hand away, though its warmth brought back a rush of feelings that made her blush.

"I refuse to feel sorry for you," she snapped. "You were a master at playing on the emotions of others. You did mine."

Again, Glauwer emitted a strange hiss and the glimmer around him illuminated the dripping bushes lining the trail. For a moment, Emenine thought he looked just a little spiny, but dismissed it as her imagination.

"Please be patient with me, Emenine. You'll see, I'm dedicated to trying to be better. You're absolutely right. I deserve your scorn. I only ask that you give me one more chance." He blinked and a silvery tear made its way down his shining cheek.

Emenine stopped suddenly, searching the eyes of Glauwer, seeking a glimpse into his newly discovered soul. She had the oddest feeling that, although the face was familiar, it was another person she was seeing.

"Fine, I've come this far with you" she sighed, skeptical. "Prove yourself, my old darling."

Randall bowed, as if acknowledging her approval of his great performance.

"There is much you don't know about this planet, even this very island and its dangerous inhabitants."

Emenine suddenly realized she'd left her companions behind. She was about to turn back, but something drew her on down the path as Glauwer led the way toward a distant red light just perceivable in the dark.

"The natives on this island are very dangerous, cruel, and crafty," he warned. "Look at the spaceships wrecked along the beach. Those poor explorers arrived on this shore alive and well, but they were lured to their deaths by demon creatures who assume the form of hedgehogs."

"Walpole and the Crimson Quill Guild," she nodded. "Commander Larko figured as much."

In his far away lair, Walpole slumped back in his seat, disgusted.

"They always blame me first." The tall illusion produced by the demon hedgehog rapidly shook its head in the negative. "No," he said quickly. "Not Walpole. The Crimson Quill Guild is not involved either. In fact, the Great Mind is working very hard to make this a paradise for everyone. It is someone else entirely."

"Walpole making a paradise? That'll be the day." she smirked. "So, if it wasn't that little spiny bug-snapper who brought down those exploration ships, then who did? We must tell Commander Larko."

"Funny, I don't remember that old rat-mage throwing around so much authority in the old days," Glauwer said. "Maybe I should keep a closer eye on him." He saw Emenine staring at him. "Because it would be awful if something should happen to him before he can achieve his dream of bringing Walpole to justice. Where, I'm sure, a jury of his peers will find him quite guiltless of any real crimes. I mean, if being the best you can be is a crime, then who among us...never mind."

Emenine was peering into the dark, trying to make out what the red light signified. Glauwer urged her onward.

"They call themselves the Raiders of the Ceramic Underground, I believe," he explained. "They are anarchist artists, very temperamental fellows, with one goal. To overthrow the good leader of this island and place him and his people in shackles."

Emenine thought a moment, perplexed. "Anarchist artists? Don't sound all that dangerous. What do they do? Paint threatening murals? Write taunting poems?"

She felt a hand on her shoulder and stopped.

"No," the Baron ordered, his voice suddenly hard. "I know your friends are brave, but they are no match for the Ceramic Underground. Just by sheer numbers they are unstoppable." He stopped, clearly thinking hard. "Oh, and its leader is a cannibal."

"Cannibal?" Emenine cried, her pretty mouth hanging open. "That's incredible. Why do islands always have cannibals? No wonder the crews of the other ships vanished."

"Yes, that's it. The cannibal artists ate them. I knew you'd understand, Emenine. You always were so understanding. Now, come to my headquarters and we'll lay out a plan to defeat the evil Underground and bring peace to this world."

The baron gleamed like a fiery star in the sky, taking the form of his most youthful, vigorous self, the one that had captured Emenine's heart so long ago.

"I will go with you Baron Glauwer," she decided. "I think that..."

"My sweet Emenine, let me do the thinking for a while."

Before them stood a dark, shapeless form nearly lost in a blanket of vines and branches.

"We're here. My modest little home."

The door opened, a sliding affair that rose out of sight, revealing a red light beyond. Emenine and the Baron disappeared inside, the door dropping down behind them like a trapper's cage.

When the light of the rising sun finally came, the form of Glauwer's home was revealed to be that of Walpole, smirking arrogantly across the woodland. In his gnarled paws he crushed a planet.

Deep Thought brought the large seed ship to a halt, resting in the densest portion of the dust cloud. All around the ship, a kind of static electricity seemed to dance and leap, often running along its contours. The AI read the messages conveyed in the flashing streaks of cosmic fire.

"Waiting. Alone. So near to...birth. A little more."

Deep Thought interpreted the attached data, the universal mathematics that described and explained the universe, and found the message clear. The Armadon Rectangle was alive, but trapped by its own vastness, the material of its existence scattered over too much space. It needed more mass. Deep Thought wondered at the possibility of a new life form, much like himself as to its singleness and youth, and contemplated its options.

Time passed and millions of calculations were made. The AI sent out a warm response.

"I can help. I shall take you to a place where you may grow and emerge to take your place in the universe."

The entity that was called the Armadon Rectangle by astronomers on distant worlds (and who would soon wonder where the object had gone) had obtained curiosity over the vast time it had existed, and it agreed.

Deep Thought looked back the way it'd come, and saw that no planet was as near as the one that lay at the far side of the Rectangle. It was small, but dense with vital elements that would set its prodigy quickly toward independent life. Flashing through the data banks of the ship, it came up with a name for the planetary midwife to his adopted child.

"Yurle Minor."

"I think we have got control of the engines again," a technician shouted to Odd Bob, who had been wringing his hands, stared out into the blinding haze. The ship had stopped altogether and nothing they had done so far had enabled them to start up again. The solar power generators were failing and he feared the growing portions of the ship would begin to die off.

106

"And we'll freeze, too," he muttered. "That's not good either."

He was about to order the crew to get them underway when the ship lurched, throwing those on their feet to the floor.

"Thrusters have come on," Harlix said, who had been seated at the navigation station eating a sandwich. "All of them."

"Main engine firing," the technician said.

"Good work," Bob said, climbing to his feet.

"I didn't do it. It's working on its own, sir. We're going forward, out of the main cloud, but we're taking on a spin. It's going to get...unpleasant."

Bob was about to ask why, then he got the message without explanation. They were spinning, around and around, while moving forward at the same time. Without any control of their own, they could only hang on.

From a distance, the great seed ship with its many attached pods, emerged from the dust, moving on a trajectory toward the distant world of Yurle Minor. The spin, ever quickening as it went, began drawing a tail of dust out of the cloud. It grew and thickened until the strand stretched along behind the ship like a stream of dirty water drawn down a drain. The Armadon Rectangle was on the move.

Chapter Seven

Commander Larko stumbled and fell to his knees in the wet sand. The hedgehog Dorn halted some steps behind.

"I do not yet see the ship," the Dinhari said, trying to sound hopeful.

Larko pushed the bandage back off his head and dropped it to the ground.

"I was so sure. It was like...a vision. The *Duweena's Courage* resting on the shore, damaged here and there, but it looked almost ready to fly again."

Dorn patted the Tindaran on the shoulder with a tiny paw.

"I think we have been tricked by Walpole. He clearly wants to split us up. We should return to the others."

Larko looked off toward the sea, sparkling in the starlight, the waves lapping nearly up to his feet.

"Maybe so. I think I'll just lie back a moment and rest, all right?"

The hedgehog looked around but could see no immediate threat.

"All right."

He turned and walked a few feet back down the beach. The sounds of the others had long faded and the curve of the shore blocked any sight of the wrecks. Their own trek had been slow so he didn't think they were too far away.

The interior's heavy foliage had continued down the beach and Dorn had intermittently scanned it for danger. This time, as he peered into the gloom, something lighter than the shadows moved into his sight. A tiny flicker of flame winked into view, then vanished.

"Who's there?" Dorn said. At the words, Larko raised his head and looked wearily at the hedgehog.

"Trouble?"

The Dinhari was about to suggest they return to the wrecks when several more tiny lights, smaller than the candle flames on a birthday cake, sparked into existence.

As their eyes adjusted, each flame slowly illuminated a face behind it. Clearly browned by the sun, the faces were fat and round, the wide-set eyes pale as if washed too often in the sea. Moving down in his examination, Dorn detected thin necks that seemed too weak to hold up a load as big as the creatures' heads, and they protruded from gray, smock-like garments that had clearly seen better days. The garments hung raggedly to their knobby knees, and the whole form stood braced on broad three-toed feet.

"No doubt good for paddling about," Dorn said thoughtfully. "They look...possibly...harmless."

The creatures stepped into view, and Dorn could see they varied in height from three to five or five and a half feet, and all were on the thin side, aside from their heads, of course. The lights were nothing more than twigs with bits of rag tied to the tops, then set afire. Each, however, carried an unpleasant looking spear, with jagged teeth inset at the blade end.

The group huddled together as they scrutinized Dorn and Larko.

"Not fish," one finally said. "One isn't a hedgehog, either."

"So, which category are they in?" another said, the voices smooth and light, with just a bit of petulance. "A new culinary sensation. Or a subject providing a fresh perspective of artistic enlightenment to the eyes of the Ceramics."

"Eat or paint, that is the question," another said, in a voice that seemed feminine, although with the garments they wore, it was difficult to tell.

"Paint, blah. That outmoded medium. I say perhaps sculpted from sneel-wood, using only the toes."

"Sneel-wood? Where would you get sneel-wood, now that that foul tyrannical hedgehog has confiscated it all for his own vile statues?"

"Hah, that is why we are at war," the first one said. "To save our sneel-wood."

"And free the people," another reminded.

"Yes, of course. The patrons. I always forget the patrons. Where would we be without them?"

They stopped the discussion and all looked at Larko and Dorn.

"Are you patrons?"

Larko rubbed his sore head.

"I guess so. Where would you be without us?"

"New patrons. Fresh eyes to see, to sense the genius that is the Ceramic vision."

Dorn smiled, showing his hedgehog teeth.

"Having trouble with a large, cruel hedgehog, are we?"

110

"We are the Ceramic Free Art Brigade, the true native voice of our dear isle of Ceramia, nestled in the sea of Gentle Azuria, who sends the warm, sultry breezes to our fair shore and the tender and delicious packs of dunnel-fols for our nourishment."

Larko glanced at Dorn.

"Are you getting this down somewhere? I think we've made contact with the natives."

"As patrons you are welcome," the largest said, bowing slightly. "I am Devello, Master of the Shaping Sticks. This is my squad, all fine artists in their own right, but presently embroiled in a dire conflict with a foul army of interloping hedgehogs and their mad leader who calls himself the Great Mind." He glanced at Dorn. "Please excuse the language if he is a friend of yours."

Dorn's eyes winked in surprise. "Oh, by the Great Storm, no. Please hate him all you like."

"Let us take you to our Grandmaster. He will be just finishing his composing for the night. We are forced to create under the cloak of darkness and defend our dwindling territory during the day. Very exhausting."

"We will be glad to help," Commander Larko said, "but we should inform the rest of our party."

"I will send someone. Where are they?"

"At the wrecks down the beach," Dorn said, pointing in the direction from which they'd come.

"Oh, I see. You are more of the explorers. I am sorry we could not free them from the Great Mind's clutches. He has done terrible things to them, I don't doubt."

While one of the Ceramics trudged off down the beach, Larko and Dorn followed the others into the forest, hitting a narrow trail. Along the way, the natives gathered up bags of what they'd called dunnel-fols, which turned out to be the butterfly-like fliers they'd first seen on their arrival. They also picked the ripest of a round pink fruit from a bush they referred to as the broler.

"Good for keeping the insides moving," Devello stated, "and makes a fine bright dye as well."

They'd traveled some distance, crossing wide clearings by crawling on their bellies to avoid being spotted by hedgehog patrols, and using shallow streams for paths to hide their footprints. A narrow, circular cave entrance marked the end of their expedition. Larko and Dorn followed the others inside.

The cave ceiling lifted away over fifty feet in height, and the cave itself opened out into a huge cavern. Nearly every foot was filled with statuary, finished or in progress, walls covered with artwork of what someone might suggest was a primitive abstract style, and in a far corner, a group of natives seemed to be tuning up for a concert.

"This is the Gallery," Devello said, waving his hands theatrically. "Poetry reading is at noon."

Jonathan woke first to discover the dawn already breaking over the sea. The distant sun cast a greenish light over the waves, some sort of precursor to a change in the weather. Thunder grumbled far off, and the horizon flickered with lightning.

112

"Get up," he said, suddenly recalling the events of the night before. "We have to find Emenine and the others."

Bogo rolled over, his bulk leaving a substantial depression in the sand.

"Morning already? I assume we weren't all killed by robot zombies in the night, which is a step in the right direction. I was thinking I could have used those in the battle at Krelpuk Castle. Would have added just the right level of shock to the initial assault. Always leave your enemy feeling they should shower after every assault."

"What is he babbling on about?" Sir Lavolier whined, rubbing sand from the side of his face. He snatched up the defunct staff and shook it again. "Rats, I thought it might automatically recharge overnight." He strolled to the shore. "Anyone want to carry this thing?"

No one volunteered. The knight spun about and tossed the glass ball-topped staff out into the ocean, where it bobbed half-submerged in the salty water.

Blip and Tagger-Streel made widening circles in the sand, searching for evidence of the missing crew members' direction of departure. Suddenly Tagger-Streel stopped, pointed down at something for his companion to see, and then shouted for the others to come over to a spot near the jungle's edge.

"A single set of footprints, light and narrow, like your friend Emenine," Tagger-Streel said, pointing out the trail leading into the foliage. "She went this way."

"No sign that the others were with her?" Jonathan asked. The hedgehogs shook their heads.

"Well, we must follow someone, I suppose," Bogo said. "Might as well be her."

Lavolier snorted. "Really? Why? She probably just met someone that caught her rather easy fancy."

Jonathan, in a quandary about following the woman or looking further for sign of Larko and Dorn, suddenly felt an overwhelming urge to violently confront the knight.

"What do you mean by that?"

"It would be just like that fickle female," Lavolier said with a sneer. For a reason he could not even fathom, the need to deride Emenine was overwhelming. "The jester has run off again, what a shock. On this island, I doubt it was even with a human being. Revolting."

Jonathan stepped forward, fists clenched, jaw rigid.

"You've always disliked Emenine," he shouted. "But I'm not going to have you talking behind her back."

"That's right," Lavolier sneered. "Go ahead and defend her. Everyone knows she's a tramp and runs off with every man she sees. By the gods, her only child is half fish."

"You sneaky little backstabber." Jonathan lunged at Lavolier, socking him squarely in the nose. Bogo watched a moment, pleased, and then, as if battling the instinct to leap into the fray as another combatant, he stepped reluctantly forward and dragged Jonathan off the other man. He struggled, flailing his fists about, then suddenly dropped his arms.

Tagger and Blip held Sir Lavolier steady as he wiped at the trickle of blood running from his nose.

"I would cut you up in little pieces," the knight said as he brushed off the restraining paws. "But, I must admit it, I was asking for it. And I don't have the foggiest notion why."

Jonathan realized the overwhelming anger he'd been feeling was utterly gone.

Bogo laughed. "Well, I guess we know who is still about."

Lavolier and Jonathan stared at each other.

"Walpole."

"And that's how he lured off the others. Emenine must have seen someone she knew. Larko and Dorn were tricked the same way," Bogo explained to the Dinhari. "If you see us acting out again, remind us of that, will you?"

Blip tucked some botanical samples in his pack, then scratched his head through the quills.

"Very complicated. Plants don't suffer mind control, thank the Great Storm. Shall we go?"

The group gathered what few belongings they had and trailed into the jungle.

Far up the side of the volcano, a strange structure had been thrown up, with a sort of rushed ingenuity that was crude and fascinating. The face of a sneering hedgehog appeared everywhere, carved from the mounds of red rubble or molded from a greenish clay and used as part of the building material. The area was busy with hedgehog workers and soldiers, strengthening the main structure or adding to it, lines of figures hauling supplies inside. One large group, which included many native slaves, hauled tubs of water to a deep depression that had been hollowed from the volcanic rock. The fluid was poured in, creating both a reservoir of drinking water and a partial moat defending one corner of the castle from attack.

Walpole stared down from a window in the topmost pinnacle of his retreat, still giggling over the fight he'd instigated with Jonathan and his companions.

"The fortress is nearly completed, Kresgan. You're sure the volcano is not going to explode and bury everything? I would be very angry if that happened."

Another hedgehog, stooped and mangy with age, limped from the shadows, wringing his paws together nervously.

"I am sure, Great Mind," Kresgan lisped, his wide-set eyes winking with nervousness. "It is in a settled phase now. What did you wish for me to do, master?"

Walpole turned and eyed the scientist.

"You will see that the swarm of fliers is finished before my anointment. We will be spreading the word of my coming to the other islands and nothing makes a better first impression than bombing their quaint little fishing villages into dust before dropping in to say hello."

The scientist sniggered unpleasantly at the thought.

"They are nearly done. The power units are tricky, but some of the explorers actually have good ideas as to fixing that problem."

The Great Mind scurried back to his throne and climbed up to the seat.

"I was wise to preserve them. After all, what bother is it to hold them in the security cells? They eat surprisingly little and show a desire to be useful, rather than some nonsensical need to martyrdom."

"Exactly," Kresgan said, then limped out of the room to the elevator and disappeared into the caverns under the castle.

A loud yawn caught Walpole's attention.

"What is on your mind, Pliffle...Verlag...you make up all these names to confuse me, don't you?"

Verlag, dressed in fresh robes and looking bored, rose from his own, much less impressive throne in an alcove at one wall of the chamber.

"What shall we do about Quintain, Fat Grandmont, and Sir Bragalot?"

"Those you failed to eliminate before they got to the island, you mean?" Walpole said with an almost visible menace in his voice. The archbishop of the Great Mind nodded.

"If any of us were perfect, we'd still be on Old Yurle, making the peasants dance, wouldn't we? Yes, that bunch."

"I gave you a powerful weapon in my Staff of Control, and you managed to lose it."

"That was a bit irresponsible on my part, I agree, but look who you're dealing with. I've been given one chance after another to mend my ways and I keep on turning to evil at the most inopportune moments. But, since you've shut it down, it's no threat to our plans."

117

"You will go and fetch it back. I dislike my zombie machines lying about rusting. But first, place two squads of my shock forces in a position to intercept the wanderers and bring them in. I may as well torture them to death as a prelude to my anointment. It always pays to put on a good show for my loyal followers."

Verlag bowed out, almost avoiding letting a bit of insolence ooze out as he went. As he skipped happily down the dark hall, he took another look at the reward poster. He calculated his cut of the take should he have to split the loot several ways with members of Larko's group. He frowned, disgruntled. He just wasn't a team player and generally did not play well with others. No, he decided, he would never be satisfied unless he bagged the bullying hedgehog tyrant and took home the entire reward himself.

Tagger-Streel cut through the creepers and hacked at vines, and it was not long before they came upon more evidence of Walpole's presence: a thick multi-segmented pole, standing some twelve feet in height. The four sections of approximately three foot lengths each was carved with the head of a leering hedgehog, each facing in opposite directions like sentinels.

Lavolier surveyed the pole with disdain.

"I would recognize that ugly puss anywhere. After that little face down we had back at the beach, I'm remembering that he has some nasty skills. Maybe we should just find a way to get off this planet and go back and warn General Jagged and his well-trained armed forces."

Wiping sweat from his broad face, Bogo leaned against the post.

"Not really a bad idea, if we had any way of getting off the planet."

"We need to find Emenine and the others," Jonathan insisted. "Anyway, I think our best bet for getting away is to find Walpole's hideout and make him return us."

"I don't think I want him teleporting me anywhere," Bogo said. "That's a good way to end up riding a comet to nowhere."

Jonathan groaned. "We travel halfway across the solar system and manage to end up on the same planet with that wretched creature."

"Well, that's what you get when you let a bunch of soft-hearted Dinhari hand out the punishments," Lavolier suggested, a hint of a smirk on his face. "Maybe this time they'll be a bit more useful."

Tagger-Streel rose from where he'd been examining the dimly marked trail.

"I forget, Sir Lavolier. Which side were you on in the last war? I seem to remember a lot of crying for forgiveness and requests for one's mother."

"I was a victim of Walpole's psychic powers," the little knight said flatly, as if by rote.

"Our friends the Dinhari have been greatly helpful," Jonathan said, "and will be this time as well. You saw they were not affected by that tyrant's mind games."

Blip scurried into view.

"There's something big ahead. Come on."

The jungle fell away, revealing a broken land of rough hills and tumbles of volcanic stone, in some

119

cases huge boulders that had clearly been tossed from the distant smoking cone. Pale yellow and green grass struggled to cover the bare places where dirt had been pushed into view, and a trail, much more visible in the open, if grimy air, led into the ruinous wilderness. Where the trail began, a huge sculpture in red stone that seemed to almost bleed into the earth around it stood; another homage to the Great Mind, Walpole. An entrance had been carved into its lower region, a stone door standing open in sinister invitation.

"Mistress Emenine's footprints lead up to the door," Tagger-Streel reported, Blip nodding in agreement.

"Then I guess we'd better take a look," Jonathan said, finding the situation very suspicious.

They marched up to the great sculpture, making sure no one was hiding behind it or any of the other dozens of excellent locations that could be used for cover. The interior was dark, the faint path of light from outside only illuminating the first few feet. Jonathan motioned to the others to stay outside and watch for trouble as he entered, flicking on his lantern and holding it high over his head.

The interior was perhaps twenty feet around, the area hollowed out above and a set of narrow steps carved in the side so one could climb to a platform in the head and peer out the eyeholes in Walpole's sneering image. No one was up there at the moment. There was no one anywhere in sight. But, there had been a fight.

"Bogo!" He shouted for the eunuch, who appeared immediately.

"Have you found her?" Bogo's huge form threw a shadow over the entry as he entered. "Oh, I see."

There had been a table and benches, a water barrel and some crockery. Everything was smashed, and someone had been injured. Together they examined the small bloody hand print on the wall near the steps.

"She tried to get up the stairs to get away," Bogo said. "Get to the high ground. Smart lady. But, they, whoever they might be, were too much for her. Drag marks, heels digging in, go to...where?"

They hunted for a secret door or passage, but found nothing.

"Walpole must have teleported her away after she was subdued," Jonathan said, hopeful it wasn't Emenine's blood on the wall.

"Yeah, the little monster wouldn't take any chances of getting hurt himself," Bogo said.

A shadow appeared in the doorway.

"The wee hedgehogs think they've found something else," Lavolier said. "Busy little bees, poking around all the time. I warned them they might find something."

Jonathan and Bogo went back out, reporting what they'd found.

"So, she's out of our hands," Lavolier said. "May as well go back and see if we can find Larko and the other one. What's his name?"

"Dorn," Jonathan said.

Tagger-Streel looked edgy.

"We're being watched. From the jungle."

"Oh, yeah, they mentioned that," Lavolier said. "I don't see anything."

Turning back to the jungle trail they'd just traveled, they could only see the heavy foliage hanging down, throwing shadows and revealing sudden patches of light over the wet ground. Suddenly there was movement, the sound of a twig snapping, and a figure stepped just into view.

A humanoid-a skinny, spindly creature with a large head, wearing an artist smock that hung open revealing a strange bone structure-crouched behind a nearby bush and waved at the crew urgently, and then disappeared.

Lavolier scratched his nose. "Okay, I saw that. Not a hedgehog."

"One of the natives, I guess," Jonathan suggested. "He seemed to want something."

"Decent clothes," Lavolier said. "Or maybe a couple pints of my blood or my liver. He looked dangerous to me."

"He did not," Jonathan countered impatiently. "What, there he is again."

The creature appeared again, waving more anxiously. Its head twisted violently about, the strange eyes bulging with fear, then it darted out of sight.

Horns began sounding all about them. The crew of the seventh mission turned in several directions, trying to tell where the sounds were coming from, and it was only a moment before they found out to their consternation. Huge hedgehogs stood drawn up along the rise of the nearby hills, mounted on thick-bodied, black-haired steeds whose origin

122

could have only started with a very angry and constipated warthog. The foul smell reached the party well before the enemy force began its approach. More of the riders approached from the edges of the jungle in both directions, cutting off their retreat.

"Run," Jonathan shouted, heading for a maze-like field of boulders and broken ground where he hoped their attackers would be unable to follow on their mounts.

Bogo groaned as he trudged after the others.

"Not the plan I'd have gone with. My feet won't take this for long." He squeezed between two boulders just as the first of the pursuers arrived, and he caught the stench of their breath as the massive jaws of the riding beasts snapped at his backside.

The others had scattered, the hedgehogs flicking in and out of view as they dodged into a zigzagging crevice in the ground, capped with slabs of stone overturned in a past eruption. Lavolier struggled to draw his hand laser and, scrambling to the top of a boulder, took aim at the nearest rider, an immense hedgehog outfitted in bright leathers that the knight suspected indicated some sort of rank.

The hedgehog leader's eyes flashed as it took in Lavolier's own attack, and streaks of red fire stabbed across the distance and struck the knight's weapon. The material of the laser gun flared with a blasting heat and the knight threw it wildly away, his hand badly scorched.

"They aren't living creatures," he screamed as he struggled to find a gap in the stones. "They're like the zombies, some kind of machine." Behind him, he could hear the sound of cold, cunning laughter. Their pursuers worked their way into the maze of stone after them.

A spear clanged over Jonathan's head and fell to the ground. He snatched it up and deflected the heavy wire net that spun over him. He'd emerged from a small canyon into a worked over area in the center of which was what he could only describe as a garden. Tall plants of an unknown variety towered over him, laid out in precise plots with paths winding between. Different growths filled huge pots of clay or metal, and a riot of color topped rock-bordered beds filled with strange flowers.

There was a noise behind him and he spun to find Tagger-Streel and Blip at his sides, gasping for breath.

"They hunt for the knight and the big one in the stones," Blip said. "What is this wonderful place?" His tiny paws reached out to cup one of the strange flowers. "I don't recognize this species."

"Don't be distracted, brother," Tagger-Streel said. "We must set up a defense. Our lasers are of little use. You have a spear. Good."

Jonathan waved it feebly.

"Not really trained in spear," he said.

"Give it to me. Avoid their nets. They wish to capture us, I think." The Dinhari warrior spun the spear about and headed back toward the entrance to the garden. "I will try to surprise them."

As he hurried away, Jonathan and Blip found a place among the large pots of fern-like plants to hide. "What did Lavolier mean, they aren't alive?" Jonathan wondered.

"It is the work of that mad scientist, Kresgan," Blip explained. "He was always trying to replace the living with his machines. An army of robots cannot be corrupted he said. After the initial cost, no expenses for food or housing. Just stand them in a warehouse until you need them."

"If their commander is corrupt, how is it different?" Jonathan asked. "If Walpole commands them, their original purpose hardly matters."

"Exactly what our leaders said. Kresgan was very unhappy and planned some very bad things to happen but he was locked away. Until he disappeared. Now we know where."

"Walpole has an eye for talent, no matter how wicked," Jonathan admitted. "It's clear now why the other missions were overcome so easily. Walpole knew exactly what our plans were and was ready for us. Robot hedgehogs, how terrible."

"I wonder if their mounts are machines as well," Blip considered. "It would be strange to make a robot smell bad."

There was a terrible howl at the entrance to the garden. They peeked through the ferns and saw one of the huge riding beasts flinging itself sideways to the ground, the spear Jonathan had given Tagger-Streel protruding from its chest. The rider, another of the robotic hedgehogs, had tumbled to the ground and the Dinhari was on its back, bashing away at the thing's head with a jagged stone. With a sudden puff of oily smoke, the robot's head fell off and rolled into a flower bed. More oil squirted out like a fountain and the whole body shuddered and collapsed.

125

"That's one," Tagger-Streel shouted.

Lavolier appeared at a full run, leaping over Tagger-Streel and diving into a stand of bamboo-like stalks.

"Good one. Get the rest, will you? I'm bushed."

Behind him appeared three more of the riders, several others working their way out of the stone field close by, dragging Bogo in a net at their heels.

Tagger-Streel rose, empty-handed, and made a rush for the spear protruding from the dead mount. Nets flew expertly over him, dragging him down to the ground. The riders entered the garden and dismounted, adding to their numbers until they made up a line that covered the entire width at one side.

A gap was made and another rider entered, a smaller hedgehog than the others, his face red with exertion, the jowls dripping slobber, the eyes bloodshot. He remained mounted, drawing a bottle and taking a long swig from it.

"Not a robot," Blip said, edging to the wall of the garden nearest to him, feeling it for weaknesses. It was very solid.

"Invaders of the realm of the Great Mind," the hedgehog announced pompously, "surrender and I shall let you walk to your fate before the Great Mind. Fight me and you shall be dragged like this fat one, which will be painful. Or so I've been told many times."

"Who are you," Lavolier shouted, backing deeper into the stalks.

"I am High Commander Towdle, general of these forces, the Red Legion. The army of the Great

Mind, the gift of his most cunning servant, the Wise Kresgan."

"Gee, sorry I asked," Lavolier said flatly.

Jonathan snorted with laughter. "You have to hand it to Lavolier. When all is lost, he keeps his sense of humor." He looked around but Blip had disappeared.

"We'll never surrender," the knight suddenly screamed, and burst from the reeds with an end of one of the stalks in his hands, the dirt-encrusted root swinging like a club.

One of the robots turned and its eyes flashed out. Lavolier was knocked over like he'd been hit by a lightning bolt. He lay sprawled there, his limbs jerking feebly.

Jonathan leapt to his feet and charged out, drawing his laser. He fired, apparently catching the robot in recharge mode, as his laser found its mark and opened a black hole in the thing's chest. It burst into flame and fell over. Before he could fire again, he was knocked over like Lavolier; the last thing he remembered was seeing Blip's little quilled butt vanishing over the garden wall.

Chapter Eight

Emenine found Randall's company absolutely delightful and had quite forgotten about the plight of her companions for some time. She sat at an ebony table with her dinner host, staring into his eyes. After a while she examined the meal and found a magnificent spread before her: all her favorite foods, even down to a few secret delights she had never told anyone about before.

"It's almost as if you could read my mind," she said, sipping at a fine purple wine. "You can't, can you?"

Randall downed his own drink hastily. "Would that be so bad? Catering to your every whim even before you have to voice it?"

"Well, it wouldn't be bad, I guess," the former jester said thoughtfully. "Although, I do have some thoughts...." She smiled slyly. "A girl must have her secrets."

"Is this the sort of life you'd like, Emenine? If it is, I can give it to you in an instant. Just say you'll give up those conniving troublemakers you've been traveling with and come away with me."

"But, I thought you were going to help us beat that awful Walpole."

Glauwer chewed carefully. "Of course I said that, my dear. But, how well do you know old Walpole. Certainly, his methods can be...abrupt...and...violent...at times, but really, once you get to know him."

Emenine smelled trouble.

"I have no intention of meeting that spiky gangster unless it's with a sword at his fat little throat."

"No need for personal insults," Randall said, his voice taking on a sharp hiss. "Hmm, now it's like this. The Dinhari sent me...him...to this world against his will. Do you think he was just going to sit around in a dirty hole somewhere and live out the remaining years of his life like some common slug?"

Standing up slowly, Emenine shook her head against a fog that suddenly was seeping in all around her. The ebony table vanished and a crudely made one stood before them, covered with old crockery filled with raw nuts and berries. Something wriggled from one and fell to the floor. The goblet she'd held was nothing more than another old piece of pottery, partly filled with dirty water.

"Randall doesn't really exist, does he?" she said, seeing the place for what it was now, a watch tower with a narrow set of stairs leading up to a platform where the dim light from outside threw spots of illumination on the far wall.

The door slammed open behind her and a massive hedgehog stood there, its eyes glittering red, its paws clutching a pair of manacles. She spun to protest to Randall but the room was empty.

Another, smaller hedgehog edged inside, smiling that sneaky smile that was so common among the Walpole crowd.

"The Crimson Quill Guild has arrived."

"You'll never take me," she said, backing toward the steps to the upper platform.

"Oh, we have no intention of taking you anywhere. The Great Mind will bring you into his presence. We are only here to make sure you are safely subdued before the encounter."

Emenine ran for the steps, but the small hedgehog was fast and grabbed her from behind before she could ascend more than a step or two. She slammed her elbow into his nose, and blood splattered onto her hands as they rolled back down to the main floor. She struggled to her feet again and tried for the entrance, but the great hedgehog gripped her hair and lifted her against the wall. The other hedgehog, wiping his nose, clenched his paws to strike her, but then simply hissed and slapped the manacles over her wrists. Backing away, he seemed to fall into a trance.

The jester/acrobat snarled and kicked the huge hedgehog in what were for most hedgehogs its most tender spots, but the creature seemed to have none. She took a deep breath and prepared to scream. The room around her vanished.

Emenine found herself looking up at a chandelier that cast glimmering reflections of diamond-shaped lights across the ceiling. Her eyes fell until they rested on the familiar features of Walpole leering at her from a throne at least five sizes too large for him. She swore it had rockers.

"Where did you find a chandelier around here?" she asked as she shook her manacles to test their strength.

The demon hedgehog's eyes narrowed until they were intense little slits.

"The jester speaks, and always it is with the most immediate relevancy. No 'oh my, don't ravage me' or 'what an amazing way to travel.' No, it's about the chandelier. Considering swinging from it already?"

"You're smaller than I remember."

Walpole smiled malignantly. "Not for long, pumpkin. With each day I regain my godhood. Soon I will be the invincible menace you remember."

"I don't think we define invincible the same way," she quipped, slowly taking up a hand stand position before the throne. "Do you find this disrespectful, wormeater?"

"You always were a lot of fun. I think I have pictures around here somewhere. Anyway, I believe you are tastelessly referring to my last setback on Yurle Prime. You will find I learn from my mistakes. I intend to kill all my enemies immediately, then they won't have time to plan things. That's why I'm about to kill your friends Jonathan, Fatty Grandmont, Sir Bragalot, and a couple of those Dinhari pests, who I really don't like, by the way."

"You'll have to catch them first," she said, then cringed when it was clear Walpole was ahead of her on that point.

"My robot hedgehog soldiers are taking them to the place of execution as we speak. I like to combine revenge with object lessons for the folks down in the ranks. I was going to offer to make you my concubine rather than face an awful death, but I did find that handstand offensive."

"A concubine? What would a hedgehog do with a human concubine?"

A figure stepped from the shadows at one side of the throne room.

"A good question," Verlag said. "I was going to suggest she be made a thank you gift to me. For all the work I've done, you see, to get your enemies into a position where they were no threat."

"Verlag, where are those sandwiches we sent you out for," Emenine said, sitting down at Walpole's feet, her back to him.

"Where's my staff?" he countered.

"I think Lavolier was picking something with it. You wanted that back?"

"Funny. So what do you say, great one, can I torture her? You can watch."

"No. You seem to think that we of the hedgehog race lack the ability to come up with truly nasty ways to kill people."

"I think it's the tiny paws," Verlag sniggered.

"Really? Making fun of a tyrannical ruler with the mind power to turn you inside out?

Emenine looked from one speaker to the other. "You know I'm here, right? Don't I get a say in how I'm to be disposed of. I was thinking the Verlag concubine thing was probably your best offer."

"There is the one thing," Verlag said, winking at Walpole.

The hedgehog wrinkled his nose. "You mean...no, that is too much. The woman is only a nuisance. The very level of overkill would not reflect well on...there she goes!"

Emenine knocked Verlag over and sprinted for the door, unable to refrain from a somersault and a pair of cartwheels along the way.

Walpole rolled his beady eyes and tapped a button on the arm of his throne. A bright wall of light appeared in the path of the jester. She tried to slide to a stop, but the floor was suddenly as smooth as glass. She vanished with a faint popping noise.

Verlag rose, brushing himself off. "Which one was that?"

Walpole glanced down. "The light's bad in here. Either the blue one, which sends her to the fields where she can lend a hand in the harvesting, or maybe the purple one, which would send her to the worm mines. Ha, hope she's not squeamish."

"Not the black one," Verlag said, hopefully.

The tyrannical beast ran his longest digit down the panel.

"Black, black, black. That would be awful, wouldn't it? Couldn't call it a fate worse than death, because I'm quite sure death is in the mix. Still, I wouldn't want to end up there."

Verlag walked to the door. "I'm going for the staff. Too many of the natives know what it can do if it's activated."

"I have no intention of activating it again," Walpole said, sliding off his throne and waddling to a table laden with tasty tidbits a servant had just laid out.

"You may change your mind. You're not quite like the Dinhari with their ability to predict future outcomes by reading the clouds or wind or something."

"Go away," Walpole said, thoughtfully chewing.

"Yes, Great Mind." Verlag bowed out and the hedgehog could hear his whistling as he strutted off down a hallway.

The Gallery was a busy place, what with the Ceramics' preoccupations with various art projects and their proper display for patrons, and the training of those that still felt the need to oppose the tyrannical rule of Walpole. In addition, the basic necessities of life were prepared here: cooking, sewing, and poetry readings. Commander Larko had some difficulty finding the true leader of the resistance among all the Masters and Grandmasters and Masters Emeriti who insisted they had some part in what was important.

Devello finally was able to find the true leader of the Brigade, a sturdy (by Ceramic standards) fellow named Virago, who led a group he called the Raiders. It was from him that Larko got the history of Walpole's arrival on the island of Ceramic.

"The world you call Yurle Minor, which I might add, seems a bit presumptuous," he instructed, "we have long called Potalis, named after the goddess of art and civilization, whose aspects we hold dear."

Larko glanced around the cave.

"Civilization."

"We had quite as much as we wanted before this Walpole showed up. It was clear to us from the beginning he was nothing but a bully and a

134

troublemaker. Some of us tried to make him a patron and even chose to serve him as artists and designers, but that didn't last long. We make art, Commander Larko, not propaganda. When we protested, we died, terribly."

"That sounds like Walpole," Larko said. "So now you fight him."

"We do. We were not a militaristic people, sir," Virago said flatly. "We lived simply, but for the complexities of our artistic natures. But, artists are creative, sir, and we have put that to use, believe me. The Great Mind, as he so preposterously calls himself, will rue the day he invaded our fair island."

"What about the other islands?" Dorn asked.

Virago eyed him suspiciously. "You resemble the tyrant a bit. Are you sure you're not a spy. We've had trouble with spies."

"Dorn is a Dinhari hedgehog, and so an enemy of Walpole," Larko quickly explained. "His own culture was threatened by him and his people fought back and were the ones who sent him here after his defeat."

"Thank you very much," Virago quipped. "The other islands are distant and inhabited by talentless scribblers and dabblers in the arts. We could not depend on them for loyal support. At least not until the Great Mind decides to expand. Then it will be too late."

"We did not know your world was inhabited," Dorn apologized. "We are here to help you now."

The leader of the Ceramic forces shrugged. "Help we need. Our numbers are dwindling despite our successes in thwarting Walpole's plans. He keeps finding more and more hedgehog troops. Big, nasty ones. And then there are the walkers. Some of them resemble what you call human beings; others are like you, others different."

"They may be members of the crew whose ships Walpole made to crash on the shore of your island. Do you know if they are alive?"

"These were not. When we attacked them, they acted like automatons, inhuman things, with oil for blood, bits of wire and glass for brains."

"Robots," Larko said, staring at Dorn. "Could Walpole be building robots as his soldiers?"

"A mad scientist, a hedgehog named Kresgan, was a great designer of such things," Dorn said. "He has lately vanished from the cell he'd been locked up in. I guess it is clear where he's come to rest."

"As if our problems weren't bad enough," Larko said.

"Your problems," Virago muttered. He clenched his three-fingered hands in rage. "If that terrible creature focuses on us, we will not have the resources to stop his assault. Our way of life will be lost and that nasty creature's awful artistic tastes will spread over our beautiful land and across the seas."

"We will do whatever we can to help. Perhaps our weapons, our experience will be of service. We must collect our friends and they will have ideas, I'm sure."

There was a commotion at the entrance to the Gallery and the young male who had gone to find Jonathan and the others appeared. He trotted over to Virago and beat the side of his head with a fist.

136

"Salutations, Mior. What is it?"

"I went to the camp of the strangers. It was deserted. I followed their tracks into the Fringe and discovered them just as they were taken by High Commander Twodle and his shock troops at the old Garden of Plotis. I tried to warn them but there was a golden-haired one that kept making fun of everything I did and by the time anyone paid attention it was too late."

"What will this Twodle do to them?" Larko asked nervously.

Virago played absently with a paint brush he'd taken from a holster on his belt.

"It's hard to say. If Walpole wanted them dead, Mior would have seen that. I think he wants to do something awful instead."

"Worse than killing them?" Dorn gasped.

"Oh, we pray he only kills our captured comrades," Virago said. "What he does to them when he's in the mood is quite unpaintable. We've tried. All we can do is try to intercept the High Commander's troops before he gets them to Walpole's impregnable stronghold on the side of Aweegeepop."

"Aweegeepop?" Larko asked.

"The volcano."

"They'll stop at Prickley's first," Mior said. "They always stop there. Lazy brutes."

"What is Prickley's?" Dorn didn't like the sound of that at all.

"It's a lot of things," Virago said. "Rest area, food collection center, dance hall. Before Walpole

137

came along, it wasn't a bad spot for a drink. Now, he's turned it into a den for his troops."

"We must act immediately," Larko said.

Virago pulled a small horn from his belt and blew three well-modulated notes. His troops began to assemble.

The four crew members-Jonathan, Lavolier, Bogo and Tagger-Streel-swung uncomfortably above the floor of a very cold house. Around them a variety of frost-covered sea animals-a weird array of beasts of the deep- hung from the ceiling on similar meat hooks.

There was a loud ripping noise and Bogo fell to the floor.

"Ha, there is an advantage to being so fat," he said, standing up and pulling his ripped clothing back into place. "The hook tore right through my lovely, tailored space togs. Remember you all saw that it happened in the line of duty so when I submit the chit..."

"Shut up and get us down," Lavolier ordered, his short legs scrambling in thin air. "I'll catch my death in here."

Jonathan stilled his chattering teeth.

"Not so loud. You'll have the guard in here and I don't think he's the sort to be reasoned with. Did you see the size of those robot hedgehogs?"

Bogo did the same, rubbing his hands together, breath visible in the frigid air of the big freezer.

Bogo lifted his second-in-command down and cut through the bonds with a meat saw someone had left embedded in a side of a turtle-like creature. Tagger-Streel followed, with the fuming knight last.

"Now what," Lavolier said. "We can't get past the guards, even if we could unlock the locker doors. Maybe there's a back door."

"In a meat locker?" Jonathan glanced around, just in case. "No, I don't think so."

They had been brought into what was clearly some sort of company town, all the store names including the title Prickley's in them: *Prickley's Dry Goods, Cafe Prickley, Prickley's Meat Storage, Prickley's Storage Elevators, Museum of the Prickley Historical Society.* The robotic hedgehogs had taken up sentry positions all along the streets, while several smaller hedgehogs, clearly members of the Crimson Quill Guild, gave orders and lounged about, eating, drinking and sight-seeing.

"Is Walpole calling himself Prickley or just using an old local name?" Bogo wondered. " If this Prickley is a separate guy and still around, he might be the sort of muscle we need. He can't be happy with the hedgehog legion stomping around his premises."

Jonathan walked over to the main door, rubbed a small square of frost from a tiny window, and peered out. He eyed what appeared to be a vast warehouse filled with fresh produce, including strange looking fruits and vegetables, leaf wrapped loaves of something bread-like, sacks of other unidentified foodstuffs as well as fresh supplies of items that would appeal to the hedgehog palate: wormy insectoids, grubs, and stringy clumps of roots or wispy vines.

Four of the huge robotic hedgehogs stood guard, poised like statues before the locker entrance.

Beyond, at the exit far across the large warehouse, two more stood at attention. Their steeds could be seen beyond that milling in a corral across the street.

"None of the dirty little ones," Jonathan said. "Just the big immovable ones."

"I wonder how long they intend to keep us here," Tagger-Streel said.

"Until we are frozen solid," Bogo said, knowing he was likely the last one to enter that state.

Tagger-Streel dumped a pile of the locker's tools at their feet.

"We are not without resources. Besides the meat hooks, which look very similar to the ones the zombies were using at the wreck site, we have two large cleavers, the meat saw, a mallet, and a good deal of salt."

"Salt? Are we going to season them before or after we attack them?" Lavolier sneered.

"In the eyes of the living ones," Tagger said simply. "As for the big ones, I think I demonstrated quite clearly that they are not invincible. Their heads come off quite easily if you find the proper leverage."

"And avoid their stun rays," Jonathan recalled. "It was nice of Walpole to include a stun ray."

"Sounds more like Kresgan to me," Tagger-Streel said. "That mad thing would have included every possible device in his creations, just to see if they'd work."

"Well," Bogo interrupted, "this is all interesting but how do we get this door open and the drop on

140

those things? I'm all for decapitating them, but I have to get to them first."

"I have no doubt Walpole has given his Guild boys the okay to burn us down if we are in danger of escaping," Jonathan said, "I don't think he's going to give us his life story before the execution. So no holds barred."

"If Dorn were here, he could do something to lure the robots inside," Tagger-Streel offered. "I suppose we must wait until they come to take us on to whatever fate awaits us."

"Then we attack," Jonathan said. For once, all heads nodded in agreement.

Virago had organizational skills, there was no doubt of that. Larko and Dorn watched as the Raiders were assembled. The large headed creatures with the thin necks and three-digited hands began slipping into a strange array of armor. It was clearly hand-made, probably by the user himself or herself, with lots of ornamental flourishes that probably didn't add much to the combat-readiness of the suits.

"If I were one of Walpole's troopers, I wouldn't have a clue what they were up to," Larko said. "It'd be like the approach of a Liberation Day parade crossed with the annual fashion show."

Dorn winked in amazement. "Yet, it does seem functional. They have braced their necks with heavy guards and the helms are sturdy as well. What the extra eye holes are for, I don't know."

Virago came over, holding his helm under one long arm.

"We leave the legs as free as possible so we can run away in haste. We have no trouble with the ones called the Crimson Quill Guild, but the huge ones with their rays have caused many casualties."

"Your suits are...colorful," Larko said hesitantly.

"Each warrior has expressed his artistic taste to the fullest. If one is to die a horrible painful death, at least he may die surrounded by that which he finds tasteful."

"Yes, that goes without saying. And such a wide range of expressions," Dorn agreed. "Are you ready to go?"

"Yes," the commander of the Ceramic force said. "We will begin moving out in squads and meet on the outskirts of the Prickley compound. You will come with us. Do you wish to add something artistic to your garb, or are you...umm...satisfied?"

Larko looked at his drab suit and shrugged. "Better go with what we're familiar with, I suppose. You ready, my friend?"

Dorn closed his eyes and slipped into a quick trance. His eyes snapped open.

"Best we hurry. The forces of our enemies are about to go into motion."

The Ceramic forces and their two allies broke cover and headed for their appointed destinies.

Jonathan and his companions worked steadily to loosen the great door of wood and metal from its fastenings, but it had apparently been intended not only for meat storage, but as a final defense against some foe imagined by the Prickley organization. It wouldn't budge.

Hours had passed, and a good amount of the time was spent leaping about and exercising to keep from freezing.

"What is taking them so long," second-in-command Jonathan said. "They can't just intend to freeze us to death. It's so unlike Walpole."

"I think our captors have forgotten us," Bogo said. "They seem to be enjoying a good deal of revelry out there. I think I saw sack races."

"Madness," Sir Lavolier screamed. "Robots and zombies and a hedgehog party town. We should have stuck it to that rotten Walpole when we had him. But, everyone was so full of forgiveness and understanding and that garbage."

Bogo snorted. "If we hadn't been, you'd have been stuck too along with Walpole, Lavolier."

"Let's not go back over that again," Jonathan said, fearing another mind control attack by the demon hedgehog. "We have to stick together."

The small knight grew red in the face, but then seemed to crumble onto the frost-covered floor. "I give up. No one knows what it's like, being so multi-talented, so attractive, so full of fine dreams and hopes. Every day I have to stop and say, no Teilhard, don't let your light too far out from under the basket. Don't let them see into the light of your soul to the wonder that is Sir Lavolier. Jealousy, hatred, confusion. I've tried, really I have."

Bogo snorted. "Did he say 'Teilhard?' I haven't heard such self-pitying..."

Jonathan grabbed his arm and shook his head in warning.

"I think its breakthrough time."

"Imagine working for that numbskull Glauwer," Lavolier reflected. "With his tawdry womanizing, his tiny dream of holding that crumbling fort against all comers. So I join Walpole. Sure, he's a blood-thirsty, tyrannical psychopathic hedgehog responsible for the deaths of thousands. But, you know, he was the only one who really appreciated my...gifts. But, deep down, I knew he was only using me, and I didn't want to be evil. Not really. I was just trying to live life to the fullest of my abilities. By the gods, I feel tired."

Lavolier rolled over and hunched up into a ball, his back to the rest of them. The others waited for a moment, then decided the speech was over.

"Locked in a freezer with him," Bogo sighed. "I wonder if they're torturing Emenine now. I'd trade places with her in an instant."

Larko and Dorn crawled to the top of the rise and looked down into the place called Prickley's Compound. Hedgehogs were everywhere, many passed out in the street or draped over benches up on the walkways along the shop fronts.

"I didn't know hedgehogs could get drunk," Larko said.

Dorn scratched his quill-covered head with a tiny paw.

"I'm a hedgehog and I didn't know it. They must feel safe, with those big ones standing guard. They don't look drunk at all."

The Dinhari closed his eyes a moment and when they opened again, he groaned.

"The big ones are not living creatures. Those are the ones the mad scientist Kresgan has built as part of Walpole's army."

"I wonder which building they're in?" Larko asked.

Dorn concentrated but shook his head. "Too many possibilities, too many lives down there with mixed destinies."

Larko was about to suggest the trial and error method when he noticed something odd. A bush was moving across the main street, halting and changing direction as drunken soldiers passed by.

"Strange types of plants on this world," he said, pointing out the plant to Dorn.

"Walking bush. Unique. If only Blip were here."

"Well, that might be a problem, because that's him down there," Larko said. The botanist Dinhari's head rose into view, then ducked out of sight as a rider and beast galloped past, sending him and his bush tumbling across the street and against the raised walkway on the other side.

"So, he's escaped," Dorn said. "He may know where the others are held."

"Or he's wandering around lost. Still, we can get closer."

They edged down the hill and took up positions behind a water tank. The bush with Dinhari legs had moved some more and was in front of a place called *Prickley's Meat Storage*.

"My guess is that's the place," Dorn said.

"Should we wait for Virago and his Raiders?"

The Dinhari gave Larko a skeptical look.

"Do you really think so?"

The Tindaran commander sighed. "Let's see if there's a back door."

The compound had once been a neatly kept area, but since Walpole's hedgehogs had taken over, the grounds were cluttered with emptied barrels, crates and piles of garbage that stank terribly. In places, the jungle's fringe snaked its way down to the outskirts of the town, and heavy vines and bushes filled the once empty places. Larko and Dorn used the cover to reach the back of the meat storage building. The smell of rotten food was heavy.

"The storage part still works," Dorn said. "But the Crimson Quill Guild tosses all their leftovers out back here. It's lucky they aren't all sick with some disease."

"Duck, someone's coming," Larko said and they slunk behind some barrels overflowing with stinking rubbish. A bush appeared, rolling along steadily. It turned the corner and halted before a back door.

"Blip," Dorn hissed in a loud whisper. The bush tumbled over and the other Dinhari tumbled into view. The others joined him quickly.

"Are the others inside?" Larko asked while Blip shook himself free of the rest of the plant.

"Yes, they're in a meat locker. I followed as closely as I could. A few minutes more and I'd have had them free, I'm sure."

The other two rescuers nodded. "Certainly. Still, perhaps we can help," Dorn added.

Larko forced a narrow tool from his pack into a small rear door and levered it open. A narrow dark hall ran alongside the meat containment room. Beyond the main warehouse could be seen, light streaming from an open outer door across the way.

They crept up the hall to the opening. Four robotic hedgehogs stood at attention before the door of the locker. Near the far door were others, including members of the Guild who weaved drunkenly in and out, shouting curses at those trapped in the locker.

"Tricky spot," Larko said. "Any ideas?"

"Move the big ones away," Dorn said.

"If Virago was about, he could start a diversion outside, and we could get to the door."

The Dinhari went into trance mode again.

"They are some way off yet. A problem with color coordination in the ranks, I believe. I will act unilaterally."

"My guess is that those fruits and vegetables are domesticated varieties," Blip said.

The others paused. "So...."

"Just an observation. Sign of a well-developed society."

"We'll keep that in mind," Larko said as Dorn positioned himself.

Raising a paw before him, Dorn stared out into the room. Larko felt a prickle of electricity in the air. Heaps of food supplies sat in bins and barrels all over. Suddenly, a large oval-shaped red fruit danced into the air and swooped over the heads of the robot guards. Their heads swiveled upward, red eyes following the movement of the fruit.

147

"Don't let it escape," one of the machines said loudly, and the guards at the outer door slammed the sliding panel shut. The room grew dim, but still was lit by open slots high up on the walls.

The fruit made a sharp turn and slammed into the face of one of the robots, splattering gooey matter across its eye-sensors. The robot backed away, its short appendages unable to reach its eyes as it scrabbled to clean the lens. There was a hiss and then narrow beams of red light snapped into view.

"Bit of a design flaw in the basic construction," Dorn said. "Real hedgehogs can at least wipe their eyes."

"Visual sensors clear," the robot said. "Heat of rays burn away residue."

"Course we don't have the ray option," Dorn added regretfully.

The other robots seemed to nod in approval, but they were immediately distracted by more of the fruits spinning into the air.

"Aggressive action," one of the robots, apparently the leader, announced. "Defend at all costs."

Red beams went out, crisscrossing the open spaces of the warehouse, blasting fruit from the sky as it swooped past. Larko watched Dorn, both paws now out before him, moving as if he were directing the movements of some game.

"Watch now," he whispered. One of the fruit dove at a robot. Before it could fire, the one next to it did so, fixed on the movement of the fruit and not the area behind it. Concentrated red light blasted through the side of its nearest neighbor's head. There was a flash and the patter of metal and other debris and it toppled over.

Jonathan leapt to his feet and ran to the window.

"What's going on out there? Bogo, look. They're shooting each other. Or at fruit. Both at the same time."

Bogo's large head pushed up beside the other man's.

"What's making them do that?"

Tagger-Streel laughed. "It's Dorn. We are saved."

Larko slipped up behind the last of the robots, still occupied with burning a recent barrage of goo off its lens, and knocked its head off with a handle taken from one of the pushcarts scattered around the room. Dorn hurried over and lifted the heavy latches from the meat locker door and the rest of the crew tumbled free, Blip and Tagger-Streel half-dragging, half-leading Lavolier between them.

"We could have done that," the knight muttered as he vaguely took in the ruins of their enemy.

"What happened to him?" Larko asked.

Jonathan glanced at the knight, who seemed to be slowly recovering his aplomb.

"Not good in enclosed spaces, I think. Good to see you again, sir."

"Likewise. Now, if our Ceramic friends can throw the rest of Walpole's forces into some sort of disarray, we can get out of here."

"Ceramic?"

Larko described their meeting with the local natives.

"I think we saw one of them just before we were captured. He tried to warn us, but things were a bit rushed at the moment. We've lost Emenine. I think Walpole has her."

"Then that is our next task," Larko said. "Free her and take Walpole into custody."

"Can your new friends help us there?" Jonathan asked. "They must know how to get to the demon hedgehog's stronghold."

Dorn approached the pair. "They are about to attack. Virago and his raiders are on the rise overlooking this area. They await some signal from you."

They moved to the front door of the warehouse and peeked outside. The hedgehogs appeared unaware of any battle that had taken place inside, but it was clear they were beginning to form up again into their squad. The large riding beasts were being saddled and High Commander Twodle appeared from a nearby building, strutting along as he straightened his rows of medals.

"They're coming this way," Jonathan said.

"Over here," Bogo shouted, motioning to a side door that had been hidden behind a stack of barrels. They all ran over and found, standing in the alley between the warehouse and the next building, a large wagon with a heavy wooden box wrapped with thick metal bands constructed over the bed. A dozing hedgehog sat on the seat in front, holding the reins leading to a pair of elderly looking beasts similar to the ones the hedgehog soldiers rode.

"Our mode of conveyance to the place of execution," Bogo said. "Might as well put it to use."

Tagger-Streel leapt to the driver's seat and dragged the befuddled driver down. They pulled him inside and tossed him in the meat locker. Going back to the wagon, Larko, Bogo, Jonathan and Blip climbed inside, while Tagger-Streel took the reins and Dorn and Sir Lavolier climbed to the roof of the mobile prison, loaded with baskets of hard-shelled nuts or fruit the size of a man's fist.

"Should raise a lump or two," Dorn said. Sir Lavolier hefted one of them, menace in his eyes, clearly looking for revenge.

"Let's get out of here," Tagger-Streel said and he lashed the beasts with the reins. With strange hoots the animals lunged forward and drew the wagon out into the street. Cries of anger and surprise rose from the hedgehog troopers as the heavy contraption knocked aside anyone too slow to move out of the way.

High Commander Twodle tried to leap into the saddle of his own riding beast, but the animal, startled by the loud rumble as the wagon passed by, threw him into the dust of the street.

"That's going to make him angry," Jonathan said. "I think we can plan on a persistent pursuit in the near future."

"Maybe not," Larko said, poking his hand through the front window of the cell. Down the hillside came Virago's raiders, a flurry of spears arching through the sky and scattering the already confused hedgehog defenders.

"Stop," Larko shouted as they rumbled past Virago, who stood at the side of the trail and watched in wonder as the panicked beasts dragged the heavy wagon past him.

"Would like to," Tagger-Streel said. "Have to wait till they tire out, I think."

The wagon vanished in a trail of dust over the rise, heading down along the twisting trail toward the badlands surrounding the distant volcano.

To Deep Thought, Yurle Minor was already a cold world with tiny dots of heat lying in clusters along lines that indicated a network of rifts and ridges that knitted the continents together deep beneath the ocean. Magma pushed its way out and up, and where it emerged, chains of islands formed, each centered around a volcanic heart.

Like a dusty stream pooling behind a newly fallen obstruction, the Armadon Rectangle spread out in a cloud that to observers on the planet below appeared to be a fog spreading across the stars and dimming the sun. The temperature fell ever so slightly. At first.

"Adjust all environmental levels," Odd Bob said, examining the scrolling read-outs that told him that the solar power his ship vitally depended on was falling off steadily. "Activate the fusion generators."

"Storage?" Harlix asked.

"Yeah, we'll have to tap into the batteries pretty soon unless we can get control of the ship again and get out of this cloud."

The other hedgehogs, listening to the exchange, ducked their heads sheepishly as Odd Bob looked

152

around at them. Despite days of overhaul, they had not found a way to get around the blocks Deep Thought had placed on their controls. Each time a way opened, a shield seemed to drop over the circuits. Bob didn't blame them. He had figured out by now that something far superior in intellect had decided his seeding ship was going to serve a purpose other than its true mission.

"I think it's time to go to manual release and get the pods out of here. I want our staff to draw lots for each of them. They'll go on the pods and maintain them until we figure this out," Bob decided.

"Maybe once it is only the main body of the ship, we can do something to take it back," Harlix said.

"Maybe." Odd Bob had his doubts.

A tiny silver ship, dubbed the Meteor, hardly larger than a repair probe, emerged from the tail end of the Rectangle as it drew itself up and around Yurle Minor. Floating in an emersion tank, safe from the terrific g-forces that had propelled him to his destination at speeds that would have killed a normal passenger, Special Agent Lawson closed his gills and rose. Drying himself off, he edged his way around the computer installation that filled most of the ship and directed the special engines, he flopped down in a seat before the view port and took his first close look at Yurle Minor.

"Coming, Mother."

Chapter Nine

"This does not look like any harem I've ever read about," Emenine observed. "Granted, I'm not a big reader. It does look like a place Verlag would find arousing."

Emenine found herself in a damp, dark passage, a volcanic tube left empty after the passing of a lava flow. Its walls were streaked with yellow, the smell very reminiscent of a hedgehog gathering place. A singed wooden sign stuck out of a pile of broken stone.

TURN BACK NOW!

YOU HAVE ENTERED THE LAIR OF THE MONSTER WRATHGOG

ALL TRESPASSERS WILL BE TORTURED, EATEN, INTERROGATED, AND EATEN. BY ORDER OF THE GREAT MIND (aka Walpole). HAVE A NICE DAY.

"Well, still on the same planet," the jester said, as she backed way. The warning was quite explicit and she just wasn't in the mood to face a monster in a dark corridor.

"Even though it's probably just Verlag in a costume, as if he needed one," she shouted defiantly. Turning around, she took a step, and found herself at the edge of a precipice. Far below the incandescent glow of magma was visible. A blast of heat made her skip back. A sign stood leaning at the edge.

TURN BACK NOW!

YOU HAVE REACHED THE END OF THE PASSAGE. BEYOND IS THE FIERY BOWELS OF THE VOLCANO, IMPASSABLE SEAS OF LAVA AND SMOULDERING BRIMSTONE. ANYONE TRESPASSING BEYOND THIS POINT IS EITHER VERY STUPID OR HAS A BIAS AGAINST BEING EATEN. THIS WARNING BROUGHT TO YOU BY THE GREAT MIND (aka Walpole). HAVE A NICE DAY.

"How can I be a trespasser if there's only one way out," she muttered as she stalked up the smooth passage. Away from the glowing crevice, the corridor grew dark and cold, her hands groping along, becoming coated with the yellowish, chalky material that covered everything.

With danger and darkness her only companions, Emenine's thoughts grew morbid.

Never see Lawson again. Never enjoy the sunshine on my face. And, I'll never get to play the center ring of the Yurle National Circus. And I had a good chance at that. Face it, hedgehogs don't make good acrobats and their sense of humor is limited. All those 'where are you hiding the worm' jokes.

She stopped short. Something had scurried away into the dark.

"Not a monster. Definitely too small."

What would a monster named Wrathgog look like? The vision of a creature of enormous proportions with skin like armor, a mouth full of razor sharp teeth, long pointed fangs and flesh tearing claws, with yellow malignant eyes took shape before her imagination. As she stood there, the vision altered into a fat little hedgehog in a top hat with a placard around its neck that said "Boo."

"Yeah, that's more likely. Walpole and his nasty mind games. He can conjure up anything in my head if I let him. That Glauwer deal was a really dirty trick. I will make it a point to pay him back some day. A woman's thoughts are her own, you smelly little pin cushion."

Still, the atmosphere was getting eerier. A chilly breeze rose before Emenine, brushing her sweating locks, strange smells mixing with the sulfur and damp ones already prevalent. Trembling, she pushed on down the corridor and suddenly, turning a corner, found a large chamber. A bubble of volcanic gas had welled up here, then collapsed, creating a nearly perfect half-shell overhead. There was a glittering effect that gave some indication of the room's size, though the light was minimal. It would have been stunning, if there had been any true light, and if Emenine hadn't felt something crunch beneath her feet.

She peered downward and gasped.

The floor around her was strewn with bones. Humanoid bones. A few fully intact skeletons leaned against the walls, as if someone had carefully placed them there. It was hard to tell, but Emenine didn't think they'd been gnawed.

"This Wrathgog at least has good table manners," she muttered, drawn to a corner where a pile of what must have been the victims' belongings were piled.

The hoard-for lack of a better word to describe what seemed to be Wrathgog's plunder-was made up of bent and twisted swords, splintered shields, a dented suit of metal armor and, shockingly, a torn space suit, clearly marked with the insignia of the Yurle Prime Space Force, Mission One.

Emenine tried to recall the names of those on that first mission but it had been some time ago and although she could remember the faces as the crew marched to their ship and on to their doom, individual names escaped her.

"What a terrible way to go," the jester commiserated. "Eaten by a monster. Beastly, simply beastly." She poked through some white robes speckled with hardened clay and flakes of paint, boots and a mixture of odds and ends: a toy necklace of pretty beads, a copper ring, several mud-covered playing pieces for a board game popular for those on long cruises (or space flights), and a locket inscribed to *Alko from Tiert, on the day of her first showing.*

Emenine opened the locket. Inside, instead of two lovers' faces, were engravings of some sort of ornament or statue.

"The local idea of romance, I guess," she said, slipping it into a pocket of her tunic. She was overjoyed to find the spacesuit's utility belt lying nearby. Still attached in place was a light rod, with half a charge left. She flicked it on and was immediately surrounded by the sparkle of uncountable stars. The chamber's natural beauty was revealed even as Emenine felt a chill run up her spine. She doubted if the former owner of the light had had a chance to enjoy the spectacle.

Emenine returned to the space suit, hoping its pockets might conceal other useful items. A large hairy spider climbed out of the collar onto her arm. She examined its glittering amber eyes, wondered if it liked being down in this natural dungeon, then brushed it off. It skittered across the stone floor and disappeared beneath the heap of discarded garments.

Something else glittered in the illumination of the light rod. Lifting a sturdy tunic from the pile of old clothes, Emenine found attached to the breast pocket what appeared to be a battered badge of some sort-a star, its silver edges showing signs of rust. She squinted trying to read a word engraved in the metal.

"Littlefield?"

"Sheriff Dame Littlefield?" Emenine recalled the story Bogo had told them about the rejuvenated sheriff who had once chased the eunuch army across Old Yurle, how she'd come to Yurle Prime with the others and after defeating Walpole, joined with her old rival, Bogo, to fight crime on that world. "He said she'd disappeared a while back. That terrible Walpole struck out against her first in his thirst for revenge."

The jester looked into the dark recesses of the large chamber and saw other exits, natural fissures where lava had once flowed. "She was so beautiful once she'd been rejuvenated. Poor Bogo, I could tell he missed her, even though he said he was over her after he reverted back to his larger self. I must get out of here and tell him what happened. She didn't just abandon him, that's for sure."

One of the passages looked more used than the others, rubbish pushed aside and the ground brushed clean, as if some large body had heaved its way through that tunnel on a regular basis.

"Interesting. Should probably not take that one," she said, pocketing the badge to return to Bogo at a later date. Picking another of the passages, Emenine shined the flashlight into the darkness. Nothing moved. She started ahead, glancing back once more at the final resting place of so many, hoping her own bones would not be soon joining them. In a few moments, she was right back in the same chamber again. The passage had doubled back on her. Further exploration showed that, except for the suspiciously clean one, all the passages returned to the large chamber. She had no other choice. She would have to take the very one she didn't want to.

Before she could act, she heard the approach of footsteps, strangely seeming to come from overhead. Emenine shut off the flashlight and laid flat against the cold stone wall, holding her breath. She heard the sound of stone grating against stone. A large square of light was thrown onto the floor at the center of the chamber.

"Don't know why we got to feed it," a voice with hedgehog accents growled. "Ain't that huge ugly jester woman enough for it today?"

Emenine yearned to show the owner of that voice who was huge but she remained quiet. There was the sound of several wet thuds as something was dumped into the chamber from the feeding door above.

"Don't even know if it's still alive," grumbled another hedgehog voice. "Ain't seen it for a long time. Thing was so vicious probably beat itself to death. Glad old GM ain't so ready to toss people in here for every little mistake nowadays. At the beginning, after he created it, I thought everyone was going to end up down here."

"Well, keep talking and he'll be sure to think of reviving that project. Close up and let's get to our own chow. I hear the worms is...."

The trap door slammed shut.

Emenine stepped out and looked up. There was no sign of the door. It fit perfectly into the ceiling.

"First bit of good designing the nasty little beggars have managed, naturally." She went over and checked the meal deposited there. She quickly wished she hadn't. It was a noisome pile of animal quarters, some beast she didn't recognize. At least there didn't seem to be anything intelligent about it. "Local fodder," she decided. "No wonder Wrathgog prefers fresher victims. Like me."

She made for the last passage.

"Just have to hope I find the way out before it finds me."

No offense, Wrathgog, Emenine thought, *but I would prefer not to make your acquaintance. Anything Walpole has created can't be pleasant.*

At Tagger-Streel's urging, the great beasts pulled the prison wagon over the rise and down the other side. He drew them up beside a large mound of volcanic dust, held in place by yellow, thorny weeds.

"Have to give the animals rest or they'll not be ready for a fast escape," the Dinhari warrior said when Jonathan asked why they'd stopped.

"Where are we going?" Sir Lavolier brushed away the grayish dust from his already badly stained space suit. The powdery material had risen in a constant cloud as they had traveled the rutted trail. "Is the plan to head straight for Walpole and be destroyed quickly or are we going to dash around a bit more and see if picking us off one by one is more fun?"

"Well, he's feeling better," Bogo muttered, spitting out the same nasty dust.

Commander Larko had been sitting quietly the whole time.

"I have been considering our situation," he said. "We still do not know exactly what sort of arrangement Walpole has up in his stronghold. Virago and his band have faced him several times, and although they've not had a good deal of success, have not been utterly beaten. I think we should once more team up with them and use their knowledge of the terrain to approach our objective."

Jonathan sat down next to his commander.

"Our objectives, I'm thinking, include freeing Emenine and anyone else that he may still be holding, help the Ceramics, as you call them, break Walpole's hold on them, and generally liberate the island and make the planet safe for truth and justice."

161

"Which means packing up the idea of making it a new hedgehog haven," Bogo said. "If the place is already inhabited by an intelligent race, it would be awful to inflict the hedgehogs on them."

Larko glanced around. Blip was staring at him questioningly, and Dorn's head appeared in the window above.

"I think we must learn if the whole planet is in use. Perhaps arrangements could be made. Anyway, we will probably all be killed, so no sense worrying about things we may never have to face."

"Good thinking," Sir Lavolier said, pushing Dorn aside to look down at the others, a position he seemed to relish. "I have a question."

"Yes, your hair looks fine," Bogo said, rolling his large eyes.

"Good," Sir Lavolier said, "but that's not it. If this is a beast drawn wagon, why is there an engine compartment on the back of it?"

Everyone piled out and hurried around to the rear of the vehicle. Lavolier was right. There was an engine and it was clear the wagon was self-propelled.

"Weird," Jonathan said, closing the fuel cap. "Smells like some sort of sea-weed extract. This could be one of Walpole's little secrets he doesn't want to share. Yurle Minor has fuel-producing potential."

"The natives could refine the extract themselves and the Galactic University could help them set up a trading network," Larko said. "They could be very well off, very soon. Organic fuels are still highly sought after on many of the worlds of the University."

Tagger-Streel finished unfastening the beasts and the creatures ambled happily away, heading back the way they'd come.

"There's a control box under the seat that pulls out and lifts into position. Simple rudder stick and throttle control."

"I wonder who else knows about this machine and the fuel it runs on," Bogo said. "Do his underlings know?"

"I wouldn't tell Verlag, that's for sure," Jonathan said. He glanced at Sir Lavolier, who'd become very quiet since they'd begun their discussion. The little knight seemed to be calculating something, using all his fingers.

"I say we go find our Ceramic friends and make our plans," Larko said, climbing back inside the wagon box. "Anyone else coming?"

The rest climbed aboard. Tagger-Streel hit the starter and a cloud of smoke poured from a grill in the side of the undercarriage. The smell of rotten seaweed filled the air.

"Ah, smells like home," Dorn said. "Shipping that extract off planet would be a good idea."

Tagger-Streel quickly had the feel of the rudder, though they'd nearly plunged into a ravine or two before he really settled in. A fork in the road halted them a moment, but a sign indicating that Walpole's stronghold, and the volcano behind it, lay ahead, inspired them to take the other route, toward a place called the Tuber Fields.

"Perhaps it will be green at least," Blip said, looking to replenish his botanical specimens. "I would like to get back to that garden where all the flowers and other strange plants were growing."

"I wonder if that was one of Walpole's creations, too," Jonathan said, "or if it belonged to Commander Larko's new friends."

Larko wished he'd left a message with Virago before they started off on this new exploration.

"The Ceramics don't seem the agricultural type, though I suppose someone must take an interest in such things, or they wouldn't be so numerous and well-nourished."

The wagon lumbered over several hardened lava fields. In the distance they could see thin streams of steam or smoke rising from the ground, and geysers of boiling water burst into the air. Yet, as they descended along the curving roadway, new growth of droopy-limbed trees spread around them, almost bound together in a solid mass by vines and wildly growing bushes. Soon they were beyond the most recent volcanic influences, and a wide, slowly sloping area appeared. Tagger-Streel brought the vehicle to a halt at a point that served as an overlook to the activity below. Wide fields were being cultivated and planted, by a variety of methods that spoke volumes as to the nature of the tyrannical creature in charge.

"Those are some of Virago's people," Larko said, pointing to a straggling line of the spindly creatures moving behind a multi-toothed digger being pulled by a wagon similar to the one they were in. Behind the Ceramic natives, several of the large, robotic hedgehogs whipped them along as they planted tubers in the newly turned soil. Each slave dragged a huge bag of the lumpy seed through the rich, black dirt.

"That little beast could have created an automatic planter," Bogo said, wincing as one of the workers was struck by a robot for moving too slow. "Those ugly robots could do the work in half the time."

Jonathan had to agree. "He just wants to hurt someone, no matter how pointless the action."

Larko climbed to the ground.

"I think we should step in and stop this brutality."

"I could run those robots over," Tagger offered. "They're not as tough as they look."

Sir Lavolier tossed away the pit of one of the fruits he'd filched from the warehouse, wiped his mouth, and nodded. "We use the wagon for cover...odd, does anyone hear music?"

The others paused in their planning and listened. There was clearly the sound of pipe music. A few yards further up the road, a cleared area, landscaped into a park, with many of the loveliest of the flowers Jonathan and the others had seen in the other garden, were planted to their best effect. A band, made up of Ceramic natives, was playing lively music while, at tables near a babbling stream, people sat eating and drinking. Their voices rose occasionally in song and the words sounded familiar if unclear.

The crew of *Duweena's Courage* slowly walked toward the happy party.

"We should probably stay right here," Jonathan said, sensing something was not right.

"Concentrate, great one," Kresgan said, standing at the window, a powerful spyglass pressed to his right eye. "They are still of two minds, so to speak. We must delay them until High Commander Twodle has regrouped and can catch up to them. The field robots are not equipped to fight determined combatants."

Walpole scowled. He was concentrating. Before him he could see the minds of nearly all those at the overlook. The humans and the Tindaran were easy marks, so full of old memories and unfinished business that he could have produced a dozen scenarios and drawn them in. It was the little Dinhari that defied his manipulations. But, they could be neutralized other ways.

Tagger-Streel was about to grab Jonathan and shake him back to his senses when the motorized wagon lurched into motion.

"Stop," he said, racing toward the slowly moving vehicle as it turned out into the road again. "Dorn, Blip, help me. Use your powers on it. Stop it!"

The other two Dinhari hesitated, looking at their other companions, but as there didn't seem any serious danger in a picnic, they ran after Tagger who was hanging from the tailgate, trying to climb on board. With a grimace of concentration, Dorn lifted the rear end of the other tiny hedgehog into the wagon, then propelled himself and Blip after him. There was a loud clang and the outer door slammed shut and the lock fell into place. Before they could rush to the front, the trap door slammed down and a bolt slid into its hole. The three Dinhari stared out the back as they disappeared down the road toward the tuber fields, realizing they'd been tricked.

"Ho, ho, most excellent, Great Mind," the old scientist chortled as he turned back to watching the others.

Walpole couldn't hide his self-satisfied smile. Fooling those sanctimonious little wise guys was quite pleasurable. He now concentrated on the rest of the snoopers.

As Bogo drew near the party of revelers, his eyes were drawn off to where a woman sat beneath a flowering tree, a wide blanket on the ground covered with food and drink.

"Littlefield?" he said in wonder. She was as he last remembered her, wearing her silver badge of office over a neat coverall, a heavy blaster in a holster at her side. She smiled faintly, as she always did when they met unexpectedly, motioning for him to take a spot next to her.

"We...I...was afraid Walpole had taken you," he said, ignoring the delicious food all around him as he tried to fathom what she was doing there in front of him. "We were coming to find you."

"Well, that mystery is solved," she said, pouring out wine for both of them. "I was grabbed by that brilliant creature and brought here. But, I escaped, due to the incompetence of his underlings, of course."

"What is this place?"

Littlefield glanced around.

"A safe haven."

Bogo sipped the wine she handed him, feeling his bafflement fading as he became engulfed in her presence. In a moment he was lying with his head in her lap, enraptured as she discussed the marvelous plans Walpole had for this new world.

Commander Larko halted and rubbed his eyes.

"Glidden?"

Seated at the head of the table of revelers was his brother, Glidden, an older and somewhat more bombastic version of himself. His brother had been a successful merchant and when Larko had last seen him, many years ago, sat on the boards of several of the Galactic University's most important financial institutions.

"Is it really you, Glidden?" Larko asked, reaching out to shake the other rat-man's hand.

Glidden wrapped his younger brother in heavy arms.

"Who else would it be? I was on an exploratory mission for my investors to see if this world had a future in the University family and I must say, with this Great Mind fellow running things, I think we can do some fine business here."

"Walpole," Larko said. "The demon hedgehog of Yurle. You can't be serious, Glidden. He's not only mad, he's a killer."

"Now, now, Larko. You always were an alarmist. Where would the universe be if we judged everyone by their youthful transgressions? You just have to know how to deal with the more eccentric types and everyone gets along fine. This Walpole, he understands business."

168

"He does?" Larko felt the world spinning faster and faster.

"Yes, he does. You wouldn't know to look around, but there's an almost inexhaustible supply of fuel on this world. A sea plant that we can extract. Well, it's a secret at the moment, but the process is quite simple."

"And you've made a deal with Walpole?"

"Come, sit. Eat and drink with us. Forget your troubles, Larko. Smile, everything is going to be great."

Larko let himself be dragged over to the main table and sat next to Glidden as he began a series of toasts that promised to put everyone under the table in no time.

Sir Teilhard Lavolier smelled a rat...or rather...a hedgehog in this sudden deluge of merry greetings, and was about to protest to the others when he noticed someone standing at the side of the bubbling stream, one tiny foot slipping in and out of the crystal clear water. The blaster he held in his hand slipped to the ground.

A tall, slender woman dressed in a sparkling dress, her head tilted at a strange angle, turned and smiled at him.

"Abigail Bleeker," Lavolier whispered. He drew himself up and was about to saunter over to where the vision waited, when Jonathan, scooping up the blaster, grabbed his arm.

"Where are you going? What do you think you see?"

Staring where the knight was looking, the captain was disturbed to see a hedgehog sitting on a rock, his red-dyed quills revealing him to be a member of the Crimson Quill Guild. At the moment he was fluttering his piggy little eyes at Lavolier seductively.

"Let me go," the knight said petulantly, pulling free of the other man's grip. "That's Abigail Bleeker. Sweet little Abby. Many years ago we were dance partners." There was a faraway look in his eyes.

Jonathan recalled that the little knight was once a performer on the stage, before he began dedicating his life to mischief. Could this explain that sudden change?

"We were performing an extremely risky maneuver-a flying triple spin... when things went suddenly, terribly wrong," Lavolier said, his throat husky and his eyes gleaming with tears. "I cast dear Abigail high into the air, but as I did so I momentarily lost my balance and Abigail slipped through my arms and crashed head first to the ground. I killed her."

Lavolier covered his face with his hands.

"When the light of my life went out, I didn't care any more about bringing pleasure to the multitudes with my brilliance. Baron Glauwer saw my potential, and I found I had other...talents."

"You do know that this isn't your lost love, right?" Jonathan interrupted. "Think about it, Sir Knight. What would your former dance partner be doing hanging out on an island populated with robot zombies and hedgehogs with laser eyes? I'm telling you, Lavolier, this is Walpole's mischief."

Lavolier glared at Jonathan. "She's not dead. Or...it doesn't matter." Before he could stop him, the knight ran to her and took her up in his arms and began spinning about. Jonathan grimaced as the knight kissed the nasty little hedgehog cultist on its almost non-existent lips. He knew for the moment there was nothing he could do. He just hoped Walpole, wherever he was, couldn't maintain the illusions for long.

Jonathan looked around and found the others all deeply involved in conversations with what were to him clearly members of the Crimson Quill Guild. They all seemed to be playing a part and not intent on violence or other dangerous behavior. They were clearly holding them in place.

"Until those robot soldiers and their High Commander figure out where we went," Jonathan said. A thought suddenly struck him. *Why isn't Walpole working his will on me, too?*

The surroundings, so pleasant to look at when they'd first arrived, now seemed to Jonathan little more than a quickly manufactured space, with the remains of bushes and trees lying about, the ground churned up by the action of wagons as they cleared the space with shovels or plows. A stagnant pool of water stood near the back of the clearing, where Lavolier and his illusionary love hugged and whispered sweet nothings to each other. Commander Larko sat to one side, surrounded by red-hued hedgehogs, and Bogo lay like a beached whale next to another of the cult members.

Turning suddenly, he realized the Dinhari were nowhere to be seen, either. The wagon they'd arrived in was gone. Jonathan found himself alone. He almost hoped that was an illusion.

Standing on the beach, Verlag shook the staff he'd just fished out of the sea. Nothing he did brought the thing back to life. He was about to cast it back where he'd found it when a streak of fire appeared in the sky and crossed his line of sight from west to east, falling out of sight beyond the island's distant curve.

"Now, who could that be?" He glanced at the flying machine he'd arrived in, the dragonfly wings hanging low as if too tired to hold themselves up. "Might as well take a look. Not going to be making history around here anytime soon." He dropped the staff into the back of the flier, sitting near the wrecks of the first expedition. He drew out the old wanted poster from the tavern back on Yurle Prime. "Not long now," he said, reading the amount for the capture of Walpole.

As he went through his pre-flight tests Verlag was too engrossed to notice the ball on the staff begin to glow. He only noticed trouble when the first of the robot zombies clapped its hands around his throat from behind and dragged him from his seat.

Chapter Ten

"Location, location, location," Walpole muttered as he seated himself in the VIP section of Prickleys' Island Cafe, then adjusted his spyglass so he could take in all of the island around him. "I have to admit, old Prickley had the right idea with this place. A view of the ocean in all directions. Unlimited energy from the volcano and a loyal clientele from throughout the island chain." The demon hedgehog lowered the spyglass and took a long drink from the mug next to him. A small hedgehog, its quills stained red, with a bandanna around its forehead indicating it was a novice worker of the Guild, hurried to refill the glass with the native wine.

All around Walpole stood a squad of his elite robot guard, metallic hedgehogs nearly ten feet tall, in the image of their master down to his perpetual sneer. Their eyes glittered red in the dim light at the back of the restaurant, readying for any surprises.

A figure appeared in the kitchen doorway, pushing a cart loaded with hedgehog delicacies. Stiff-legged, the figure propelled the cart to the tyrant's table.

"Well, Prickley, I see you've finally perfected the fine cuisine of the great hedgehog culture."

The former island mogul's face battled between an obsequious smile and a bitter grimace.

"Utter filth, you vandal. Worms and snails and roots, uncooked and unseasoned. Not fit for animals."

Walpole chuckled evilly. He looked over the once fat Ceramic native, now a bare shadow of himself. The large head wobbled on the thin neck, his chef's uniform hardly more than baggy rags. The single eyebrow, once dyed a bright yellow, was now faded and patchy, a hole still visible where an ornamental ring of finely polished coral had been removed and now encircled Walpole's right wrist.

Plucking up a fat grub, he sucked it down with relish.

"These are just wonderful. I don't suppose they're the larval form of your species, eh?"

Prickley giggled. "Ha, you ate the poisoned one. I knew you would."

Walpole's quills sprung upright.

"Poisoned? You lie."

The former owner of most of the best property on the island sighed. "Yes. I did. No poison I've tried so far has had any effect on you. But, that doesn't mean I will give up. Something here on this world must be toxic to even you, you vermin-swilling assassin."

The hedgehog leaned back.

"Go away. If you behave, I may let you attend my great Immersion Ceremony tomorrow. Then we will have a gala feast and you can provide this fine food to all my guests."

Prickley trudged back into the kitchen. Walpole ate noisily, then turned his attention to the distant hills spread out below him. His glass fixed on Jonathan, standing alone, looking down toward the fields where the slaves hand-planted his favorite tubers. Further along, he could see High

Commander Twodle's forces moving up the road, already taking the Dinhari prisoner as they surrounded the powered wagon.

"Soon they'll all be in custody," Walpole said. "The climax of my celebration, other than my own rise to immortality, will be drowning the whole lot of them in the very pool that will make me unstoppable."

He looked out further and watched Virago and his decimated forces straggle through the narrow passes back toward their ridiculous stronghold. It was another loose end he would have to deal with some day, though he did enjoy the lop-sided battles the natives put up against his superior troops.

"As long as they stay that way," the hedgehog admitted.

A slow clomping noise became audible from the stair leading down to the lower levels of the restaurant. A blank-eyed human being appeared, clothed in the rags of the Yurle Space Force. More followed: humans, hedgehogs, and even a Tandaran.

"It's amazing how they all look alike," Walpole said, as the zombie-like figures drew up in a line before him. "What do you want now?"

Slowly the arm of the lead human rose and saluted. "Commander Folderal," the man said in a slurred voice. "We again request that you release us."

Walpole had been a bit leery of doing anything really final to the Space Force explorers he'd captured. His own space travel potential was still rather limited, at least in distance, and he might need to use their expertise. And they were valuable hostages as well.

"Have I treated you badly, eh? Not in pain, are you? Warm place to sleep. Decent food. Prisoners rarely have it so good. You aren't even locked up most of the time. Why don't you go lie on the beach some more. Get a nice tan."

A well-muscled hedgehog slid slowly forward.

"Second Pilot Bepix. Release...us...from...your...mind...." His thoughts seemed to wander away before he finished.

"Oh, and have you clever ones snooping about and undermining my plans. I don't think so," Walpole said, shaking his head in mock sympathy. "Now, go on back down to the lower levels and scare the natives. If only I could control them the way I do you, we wouldn't have all this dissension."

The line slowly broke up and the prisoners trudged back down the stairs out of sight.

"Well, nice to see you all. Drop in again sometime," Walpole said. He looked pensive. "For a minute, I thought those worthless robots had found their way back here. Kresgan and his little experiments. Make copies of the explorers. Send them back to Yurle Prime. No one the wiser. Yes, that worked out so well. All they did was wreck the ships and guzzle rocket propellant. Verlag loses the blasted staff that gave me some control over them. I wonder where he went off to. First I lose Emenine, now him."

Sleep called to Emenine but she would not stop to rest-not in this dark and cold and strange place with its black streaked walls and blood-stained

176

laundry. Even letting down her defenses briefly, she felt certain, could mean certain death. For what seemed like nearly a day, she walked along the labyrinth of tube-like passages, often finding herself back at a familiar intersection, then other times finding frightening reminders of her danger. This time it was a scrawled message on a wall. "Death is the only escape."

It was soon after the uplifting message that she heard something following her. Her now lank auburn hair rose at the sense that something was watching her from one of the dark tunnels. She turned suddenly, hoping to steal a glimpse of the thing lurking just out of sight. The definite sound of clawed feet raking the path behind her made her blood freeze.

She peered into the blackness beyond the fading glow of the light rod.

"All right," she said, her voice strong despite the fear deep in her belly. "Let's stop all this sneaking about, shall we? Show yourself."

She listened and waited for what seemed like an eternity.

Despite her concentration, she did not detect the monster's approach until it was too late. The creature rushed at her, a flanking attack from a dark side passage that knocked her off her feet. She slid across the stone floor, smacking the top of her head hard against the opposite wall. Dazed, she picked herself up and, hands diving into her pockets for a weapon, instinctively pulled out the only tools of which she was expert-her hard rubber juggling balls. She set her jaw and furrowed her brow and did her best to posture like an experienced and dangerous opponent, but she thought she could hear her knees knocking.

What was she going to do to a horrific monster that had probably already eaten hundreds of experienced warriors? Juggle it to death?

With that thought, she bounced one of the balls on the floor and sent the other two spinning upward, adding the third as it rebounded. The beast, crouched to leap, paused.

The creature was like nothing she'd ever seen before, and she'd seen some odd things in her time. Walpole had combined the most obvious characteristics of a hedgehog with what Emenine knew not. The monster's eyes, a strangely cold, but familiar, grey, studied her. Its head was covered in a crown of razor-sharp red spines that cascaded on down its wide back like a mane. In place of the stubby paws of a hedgehog, long fingered hands, larger than that of a human but much the same shape, clutched into tense fists, the nails grown long and jagged.

"He's used a human in his twisted creation," Emenine said, nearly dropping her balls with the shocked realization. The flesh that covered the parts of the creature's body not already quilled, was dark in places, light in others. A filthy rag was knotted around its waist, as if it had developed some sense of fashion.

"Or modesty," Emenine said, suddenly feeling uneasy for another reason. "Did that rotten beast use someone's actual body to make you?"

Suddenly, the creature cocked its head to the side, the menace fading away from its demeanor. It reached out one of its large, clawed hands.

Emenine took a step back, poised to strike with one of her rubber balls.

"Jester?" the creature lisped, a wondering desperation in its voice.

Suddenly, feeling as if she were awakening from a nightmare, Emenine took a closer look at the monster. A body that had seemed enormous in the shadows, crouched before her like a once brave soldier beaten in battle and waiting for the victor's pronouncement as to his fate. The voice emanating from its bristly mouth, instead of a snarl or roar, resonated with a feminine quality, traces of courage and perseverance arising from the warped throat.

"Wrathgog?" she replied. "You know me?"

The beast reached one hand to its chin and rubbed it thoughtfully. The gesture was one Emenine had seen before. Somewhere. It nodded, growing more urgent. Its eyes darted up and down the dark passage, as if seeking out eavesdroppers.

The jester shook her head in defeat.

"To the best of my knowledge, we have never met before. I think I would have remembered a half human, half hedgehog mutant."

The creature's face took on a glare of impatience that cut through the quills and twitching snout.

"Always a wanton, flippant, sniff-the-flowers, sleep-in-late juvenile delinquent. At your age, too."

The flash of recognition nearly blinded Emenine.

Dame Littlefield," she said. "Well, look where playing by the book got you."

The creature called the Wrathgog sat down in the passage, fished out a small, cracked mirror from a fold of her makeshift kilt and took in the reflection.

"Lost my looks, there's no doubt of that. In the line of duty, though, as you say, so nothing to be ashamed of."

"But how did you get here?" Emenine asked, sitting down next to the strange beast.

"Except for this odd interlude, it was all quite simple. Last year, I tracked the head of the Crimson Quill Guild to their hideout in the hills outside the capital. I went in alone, the rest of my deputies lured off to other locations. I should have suspected it was a trap."

The creature pounded her fist in the dust.

"If old Bogo had still been with me, that dirty Walpole would have never got away with it. One minute I'm clamping cuffs on every red quilled rascal I can get my hands on, the next I'm in a cage on this stupid planet, listening to Walpole go on for hours about how clever he is and how I'm going to pay for all the trouble I gave him. He's gotten rather adept with the teleportation thing. Should have suspected that, with all the comings and goings of his crew. Well, too late now."

Emenine wanted to pat the transformed sheriff on the back, but the quills looked too sharp.

"Bogo is with us, somewhere on the island," she said instead. "He's been looking for you all over. I think he misses you, too."

A tear welled up and spilled over, running through the bristly face of Dame Littlefield like a snow skier dodging slalom flags.

"Foolish old eunuch. First he leaves me just because he got fat again. Like that mattered to me. Now he comes here to get himself killed. What can I do, stuck down here?"

"Where are we?" Emenine asked.

"It's a natural labyrinth, lava tubes left by the volcano over the centuries, I guess. Leave it to the demon hedgehog to see the possibilities so quickly. At least, I think it was him. Is that foul scientist Kresgan still around or has Walpole gotten rid of him? That one could be a real rival to Walpole."

"I don't think I know him."

"You're lucky. Otherwise, you'd probably look like me by now. It was his skills that made me this way. Walpole, ever the traditionalist, just wanted to dip me in boiling oil or let his robot hedgehogs use me for target practice. It was that daft scientist that came up with the idea of the hedgetaur."

"I don't get the name." Emenine frowned.

"Me either. That's why I went with Wrathgog. Nothing like it in our mythology, I can tell you. I think Kresgan was winging it. Anyway, using some sort of machine he secreted out of his Yurle Prime lab, he transformed me into this hideous figure, using an idiot volunteer from the Crimson Quill Guild as the other half of the equation. I haven't sensed his presence in me so I'm hoping he didn't come along for the ride."

"Wow, and I thought I was having a bad day," the jester said.

"At first, I got a lot of visitors down here. Seems like Walpole was tossing a couple of the natives down here every night...day...not sure what time it was actually, or if it was every day. Hard to tell time in a labyrinth. No clocks. Anyway, he told them I was some slavering beast who lusted for their flesh and so they were always in quite the state by the time we crossed paths. I tried to stop them from trying to kill me and they went crazy and tried killing themselves and all that. It got pretty horrible. Finally, I just hide whenever anyone comes by, hoping they'll just ignore me. I think it was part of the transformation, but I don't get hungry or sleepy or anything like that. Life just sort of drags by."

"All those bones...in that chamber." Emenine nodded back the way she'd come.

"That is one of Verlag's nasty tricks. Anyone they kill up there ends up down here. I think he hopes if things go south for him, he can blame me for the killings. When did he get to be such a vile little rat? To think I got him a decent job and everything after old Glauwer bit the dust and we had Walpole caged up the first time. No gratitude, that one."

Emenine reached into her pocket.

"I found this." She stuck the badge on Littlefield's kilt. "Now, you're back in business. We have a lot of justice to bring to...well, we have to get out of here first, then we have to bring those beasts to justice. I bet this old Kresgan will fix you right up once we put his feet to the fire."

"That sounds like fun. I'm thinking about throwing in the legal side of things and just

182

becoming a cold-hearted vigilante," Wrathgog said. "You'd be surprised at the methods for exacting vengeance one comes up with in a place like this. A lot of it involves lava."

Emenine didn't remember Dame Littlefield being quite so talkative. In fact, being a stoic loner was kind of her thing. Apparently being transformed into a monster and abandoned in a labyrinth changes a person.

Wrathgog-Littlefield rose to her short back legs.

"You've become a good listener, Emenine. Didn't do one somersault while I was blathering on about my troubles. Who else has come here? Not Lawson, I hope."

"No, he's off being super-something. Still, he might come see how his mother is sometime. Let me think. Commander Larko is here, Jonathan Quintain, Sir Lavolier, and Bogo, too. Also, three little Dinhari fellows. They're cute."

"Well, that's what we need, cuteness."

That was more the old Dame Littlefield, thought Emenine.

"So, an old Tandaran, an air-headed ex-aristocrat, Sir Brag-a-lot, and dear Bogo. Well, not too many people's deaths to avenge. First we must get out of here. I've been looking around for a year or so and I have some ideas."

"But why haven't you escaped before now?"

"You know how sometimes when you tie a package you need someone else's finger to hold the knot while you fiddle with the rest of the string? It's kind of like that. Walpole is devious. He made escape possible, if I had help. And he knew the chances of me making any friends down here were nil. I'm betting you weren't supposed to end up here. Well, that spiky rat has made his last mistake."

Emenine somersaulted down the passage alongside Dame Littlefield.

"Nice to see you're still in form, dear."

They arrived at an opening in the rock wall, the entrance widened apparently with much chipping and pounding with a blunt tool.

"I've been using this as my main living quarters."

Squeezing through a narrow fissure, Emenine found herself in another small chamber made by a bubble of gas. Small passages, low to the floor, exited in several directions. Wrathgog stood before a table, belting on a homemade sword. She fitted a badly dented helm over her large, quilled head.

"Been waiting for the chance, you see. Here are some things for you. I made them myself."

Emenine took the crude hammer, the head made from several bits of metal beaten into a mass and attached to a solid piece of pipe. It looked dangerous. It weighed a lot.

"I think I'd better just stay quick and agile," she said, laying the hammer back down. I've been practicing unarmed combat with the boys Lawson brings home from his army get-togethers."

"Get-togethers," Dame Littlefield-Wrathgog muttered, shaking her head.

"Well, what do you call them? Oh, maneuvers."

"And these so-called boys like grappling with you, do they?"

"They're an enthusiastic bunch," Emenine agreed. "We spend hours sometimes, rolling around on the floor. They're a hearty lot, always sending Lawson out for food and drinks while they show me new holds."

"I'll bet. Okay, if you don't want the gear, come along. I found a break in one of the passages."

After some moments crawling through narrow tubes, the stink of sulfur surrounding them, they halted before a fissure in one wall.

"I think this connects to some secret tunnel Walpole had dug as an escape route. Or maybe it was Verlag. He'd have more reason to want to escape, the little pile. When I get my hands on him...anyway, come on. We're almost there."

The passage was fairly new, marks where shovels and picks had done their work still visible. Footprints in the dirt on the floor showed both humans and hedgehogs had passed by.

"Okay, this is where help is needed," Dame Littlefield said. At a turn in the passage, a metal grate, rusted but still heavy and strong, lay across an opening. Beyond, the ceiling of a dark room could be seen.

"I can just push it up enough for a small thing like you to get under it. See about ten feet beyond, just where the floor of the passage drops into the room? There's a crank or something there that lifts the grate. I'll hold this up and you dodge under and get to that crank and let me in. Okay?"

Emenine gave her a vigorous thumbs up.

With a rather unladylike grunt, Dame Littlefield gripped the bottom of the grate and lifted. It slid noisily up on runners on each side, making a squeal Emenine hoped wouldn't be heard by anyone in the room beyond. When it was high enough off the floor, she rolled underneath. Littlefield let the grate drop and stood back, flexing her fingers.

"I knew that would work," she said, watching as Emenine crept to the edge of the passage and found the crank. Using both hands, she was able to turn it, and the grate rose slowly up out of the way.

"Free at last," Wrathgog-Dame Littlefield said, slipping under the grate. She joined Emenine where she crouched looking over the dark room. Playing her fading light rod over the contents, it was clear the room was some sort of storage area, although arranged carefully.

"We're in a ventilation shaft," Littlefield said, spying a ladder lying down at the base of the wall beneath them. "Someone's escape route, all right." Turning about, she dropped to the floor soundlessly, lifted the ladder in place and Emenine descended.

Beyond the storeroom, a spiral staircase led upward and they soon found themselves in another chamber. It appeared to be under construction. Half built display cases, trophy shelves, and other hedgehog-sized furniture stood about, some covered in protective drop cloths. Several crates lay near the exit, their covers ajar.

Emenine peeked inside one and quickly jumped back.

"It looks like a dead person. I swear I've seen-it looks like one of the explorer ship commanders. I forget his name. Ruggedly handsome, far too wrapped up in his work, if you ask me."

Wrathgog/Dame Littlefield went over and sniffed at the crate.

"Not real. Walpole keeps a gang of native slaves working full time making him things like this. Probably wants to display to the world what a clever character he is, defeating a war fleet or something. What's in the other crates?"

They moved to examine the other containers.

"Hey, that little rat. That's me," Emenine said. "He's had me made far too fat. And my hair is not streaked with gray. What's the fiend up to?"

"I guess we're both scheduled for display." Dame Littlefield held up a detached head. "At least you have a body."

"Walpole's evil knows no bounds," Emenine said, kicking the crate petulantly. "He's got to be stopped," she said.

"Then I guess we should move on," she said.

Beyond the outer door, a passage curved around a bend some sixty feet ahead. The sound of clanging hammers, power drills, and hissing of steam became audible as they advanced.

Emenine glanced at Wrathgog, apprehensive. "Could it be the laboratory of this Kresgan?"

Her companion shook its head, bewildered. "I don't know," Littlefield conceded. "I don't remember this passage. But, that doesn't sound like his sort of labor. He was more a test tubes, wire and pliers sort of monster."

A hedgehog guard stood at a lighted opening. Wrathgog grabbed him before he could get over his shock and rendered him unconscious. Emenine winced at Littlefield's direct approach. They crept to the entrance and found themselves standing on an observation platform looking down into a vast chamber with a vaulted ceiling. There were no stairs where they were, but several exits ran along the main floor, including a large one that opened to the outside.

"I guess we're in the visitor's section," Emenine said, peeking over the edge of the balcony.

The place teemed with hedgehogs dressed in white robes, their red-dyed quills poking into view from time to time. Their heads, shaved of quills, were covered with a rubbery cap that seemed lined with blue veins that spread in a grotesque web work over their pinkish skulls. The way they moved in an almost balletic pattern made the clandestine watchers believe they were under some central control.

The center piece of the show was a long silver ship several hundred feet in length, its metallic frame standing atop a platform, occupying most of the chamber. As they watched, workers appeared pushing long carts loaded with much smaller versions of the ship.

"Oh, look. It's had babies," Emenine cooed, smiling back at Littlefield.

"I don't think so. Those are high intensity sonic missiles," she said. "Kresgan was bragging about the plans for them when he was rigging me up for the transformation. They can flatten everything on one of these islands with a single missile. They're loading them on that ship."

"Well, that's not very sporting, as Lawson would say. Then, Walpole is going to use that ship to take over the whole planet."

"That would be my guess," Dame Littlefield said, scratching her bristly chin thoughtfully. "What I wouldn't do to get my hands on that."

"It could carry a whole army...oops, spoke too soon. Here it comes."

Another group of hedgehogs-some almost as tall as Wrathgog-began marching into the cavern. Their bodies were entirely covered in blood red spines like armor. Leathery black wings sprouted from their backs, fangs hung down below their chins, and claws protruded like razor sharp knives from their fingertips.

"More of Kresgan's transforming work. Ugly brutes but more for shock value than fighting. The wings are their weak point. Nick one of those and down they go. And who are they fooling with those fangs? About as operational as Lavolier's conscience. Claws are a nice touch, though."

Emenine looked at her companion.

"I think I'm glad you're on our side. What other crazy stuff is this scientist guy going to come up with?"

"You can ask him if you want. There he is," Littlefield said, nodding back down into the cavern.

An elderly hedgehog, decked out in flashy black robes and wearing an odd helmet from which wires and knobs protruded in all directions, cruised into view atop a floating plate, murmuring into a wand, almost a smaller version of Verlag's staff.

"Walpole's giving him about everything," Dame Littlefield surmised. "Levitation and telepathy. A concentration of resources, hedgehogs and materials. He must really have big plans for after his so-called Immersion Ceremony."

"So that's Kresgan," Emenine said, leaning out to get a better look as the plate floated past below them. "Doesn't look like a genius. Just sort of mangy."

She watched the engineers' activity, mesmerized. They floated up and down the body of the impressive vessel into which at least ten ships the size of *Duweena's Courage* would have fit with room to spare. From time to time engineers entered one of the open hatches, disappeared inside for a while, and then reappeared at another location, conversing with one another without apparently speaking out loud.

Emenine studied the big rocket, awestruck.

"I've never seen such a ship," she said. "It's huge. And, really quite beautiful."

"Walpole could not only take over this planet with it. He could use it to leave the world and go out and create havoc around our system or, depending on what kind of engines it has, across interstellar space. He could attack the Galactic University."

"Surely they have defenses against such things," Emenine wondered.

Dame Littlefield considered. "You have to remember, Emenine. They're very, very civilized back there. They haven't been attacked for centuries, if not longer. The Tandarans are not all like Larko."

190

"Really? What are they like?"

The monster woman gave a sigh that was more like a growl. "They look like Larko, of course, but most of them have not been beyond the safety of their computer malls and universal libraries. Walpole, if he can get the surprise...well, there's no telling what he might do. He'd like to throw the galaxy into chaos. It would suit him fine."

"Well, that's awful. Maybe we can sabotage the ship."

"That's not a bad idea," Littlefield replied. "There's just that army down there, Kresgan's mind-controlled engineers, and probably some sort of alarm system."

Emenine looked crestfallen.

"It was only an idea. Then, we must warn the others. Commander Larko will tell General Jagged and then the whole Space Force will come and beat Walpole into little hedgehog tidbits."

Wrathgog smiled, which wasn't easy. "I could go for some of those right now."

A sudden blare of horns filled the cavern. The two watchers ducked down. Below, a large sheet that covered the nose cone of the ship was lowered to the floor, revealing a logo emblazoned in garish green hues. It depicted a gruesome creature with long teeth and nails biting into the head of another and sucking out its brains. The name of the ship was painted in tall black letters..

Walpole's Revenge.

Emenine leaned out once more to get a closer look at the emblem. There was a shout and she saw that Kresgan was shouting into his wand and pointing straight at her.

"Been spotted."

As if dissatisfied with the mental alarm, the scientist shrugged back his robes and pointed at them, screaming. "Kill them!" He began to rise toward them as other hedgehogs rushed into the exits beneath where they stood.

Dame Littlefield flew to the balcony's edge, rose over its lip, and roared nearly in the face of the approaching Kresgan. The disk-like platform almost turned over as the terrified scientist backed away, his beady eyes popping in terror.

"Remember me, you slimy villain. I'm coming for you."

"Not just now, though, right," Emenine said, drawing her companion with difficulty out into the passage. The sound of running paws could be heard in the distance.

Together they dashed down the passage to another room. Flinging the heavy doors shut, Dame Littlefield heaved a block of stone across them.

"Where are we?"

"One of the workrooms for the carvers," Wrathgog panted. "Let's get out of here before we're cut off."

A door stood across the room, slightly ajar. Emenine turned off her light and slipped over to it and peered through the gap. She felt her companion move up behind her and stare over her shoulder.

"That leads outside. We're near the base of Walpole's stronghold, at one of the side gates. I got the grand tour when he captured me. Wanted to

192

make sure I knew how clever he was and how inescapable his clutches were. A couple of steps and we can head for the hills."

They opened the door and stepped out into the hall. In one direction they could hear strange machinery at work, to who knew what terrible purpose. In the other, daylight streamed through a portcullis gate, the heavy metal obstruction raised invitingly.

As they started down the hall, they found themselves suddenly surrounded. Figures sidled out of niches in the walls or lowered themselves from hidden spaces near the ceiling.

"None pass this way without the Great Mind's permission," one of the figures said as it stepped into the daylight. Emenine stifled a scream as Dame Littlefield drew her sword.

All around them stood zombie-like men and women, hedgehogs and those of the other races who had come on the exploring ships to Yurle Minor. Blank-eyed, faces bloodless and cold, they looked like an immovable wall of dead flesh.

Odd Bob was relieved to see the next to last environmental pod break free of the main ship and watched as the small thrusters sent it back toward Yurle Prime and a stable orbit around it. It followed a line of similar pods, each containing a unique ecological niche rescued from the failing eco-system of Yurle Prime, and each manned by several of the ship's personnel.

"All that is left is the special unit," Harlix said, his voice echoing from the empty control room. "We are having trouble finding anyone who wants to

travel with that one. The flesh-eating plants are not beloved by the crew."

Bob brushed his red hair back as he thought. "Well, we'll just hang on to it. Can't save everything and, who knows, it may work out all right in the end. If you wish, you may take the last escape pod with the remainder of the crew, Harlix. I can stay and wait out whatever this computer virus intends to do."

"No, no. I want to stay. I am beginning to suspect who our troublesome hitchhiker is."

"Really? Come up here and fill me in."

Harlix signed off and exited the control room, turning down the lighting so that only the main board flickered with its myriad indicators. When the hedgehog was out of sight, the computer came back to full activation. Deep Thought, drawing on the personalities of those who had rendered him conscious, smiled inwardly. All moved ahead as planned. The departure of the crew and most of the environmental pods made its job less complicated. It sensed the hazy intelligence of the Armadon Rectangle all around the ship, spreading out slowly to encircle the planet itself. Soon, in a very real sense, they would turn up the heat.

Chapter Eleven

Special Forces Officer Lawson, son of the god Cathode (and perhaps more than one) and Emenine the Jester, was tough enough to survive any landing, no matter how bad. And, the one he'd just made on the tiny world of Yurle Minor had been terrible. At the last minute, while his ship, *the Meteor,* was beginning to pierce the atmosphere, his senses detected the location of his mother and her companions. His attempts to alter the trajectory of his path had done little more than send the ship spiraling out of control.

"Well, I'm near the island," he said, trying to force the control panel up off his trapped legs. He'd plucked out some other random items protruding from his body, and the healing was already far advanced there. However, at the rate his ship was sinking, he would find himself at the bottom of the sea and perhaps in some trouble. It wasn't breathing that worried him (his gills were still operational, if somewhat atrophied from non-use) but the pressures would make it even more difficult to extract himself from the ship.

"I must remember to suggest to General Jagged that this class of spacecraft is going to need further modifications before it can be used by strike force units. It's not very sturdy." It was the sort of thing that happened when one sets out on a rescue mission at short notice. He recalled the unsettling news he'd received just a short time ago.

Lawson had just about finished his morning swim-five hundred laps in just under ten minutes underwater-a record pace anywhere, but nothing special for a demi-god with gills and a retractable dorsal fin. His wrist communicator buzzed, using the signal for urgency. Lawson climbed from the pool, toweled off, then peered into the tiny view screen.

'General Gerge Smeel Jagged here." The grizzled and scarred old hedgehog was modest enough not to think he was instantly recognizable. It was a rare trait among the higher ranks. He sounded anxious, the powdered worm tube puffing with blue smoke as he spoke.

"I'm afraid we have a worst case scenario on our hands, Special Agent Lawson," he stated. "We have lost radio contact with the *Duweena's Courage*. No member of her crew has contacted us since they prepared to orbit Yurle Minor. Fortunately, Sir Lavolier, that valiant warrior, was carrying one of our advanced Archivatrons."

Lawson searched his mind for the definition of that last word. "Oh, one of those recorders common people need to remember things. They're very nice. Hard to believe Lavolier offered to carry one. That's so like helping."

"I don't understand the negative image he has among your set," Jagged grumbled. "Seemed perfectly delightful to me. Understood the need for respecting the hierarchy."

"Yeah, he would. Well, if he's carrying one of the recorders, it should be equipped as a homing device. Although I question the usefulness, I will at least be able to locate what's left of Sir Lavolier."

"Quite so," the general responded doubtfully. "Let's try to be a bit more optimistic."

"Well then, in the spirit of optimism, I shall say this sounds like a straightforward situation, calling for a common sense solution," Lawson replied, his voice full of false bravado. The idea of his mother missing on some distant planet filled him with dread. "Shall I get the usual crew together?"

"No," Jagged boomed, a wrinkle appearing on his deeply lined forehead. "This must be a covert operation."

Lawson stood up and headed for the dressing room. "It must? Why is that, sir?"

"We have lost six missions to Yurle Minor, Special Agent Lawson. We cannot afford to have the public learn that we've lost another one. This time we send the best we have, so that when the time comes, we'll be able to pretend the next mission is nothing more than a support effort."

"I'm the best, sir?" the young man said. He'd heard the judgment many times before but it never hurt to remind the commoners that he was the best there was or probably ever would be, now that gods were extinct.

Jagged ignored the smug junior officer. "Meet me in the launch bay of the secret missions department immediately. Tell no one you're leaving."

"Yes, sir," Lawson said. He could hardly wait to tell the squad.

The secret missions department was very much like a vast laboratory where mad scientists worked out their delusions to their hearts' content. Half dismantled robot hedgehogs lay scattered on table tops. Weapons shaped like fruits and vegetables were being fired in walled off ranges and at the moment, several members of the Special Forces branch were trying to coax down a hedgehog in a capsule with wings that was jammed in the rafters.

"Typical day," the young officer said as he headed for the open end of the warehouse, where a small, sleek rocket sat on a launch rail, its nose pointed up into the wild blue. General Jagged and a fat hedgehog in a lab coat stood near the small hatchway, discussing something on a clipboard.

"Ha, the Crimson Quill Guild has nothing like this, eh Professor Wompole?"

The beady eyed scientist winked in confusion. "I don't think so. That would be most unusual. We only finished assembling it this morning."

Jagged stared at the other hedgehog thoughtfully. "Quite right. Ah, Lawson, here you are. What do you think? We call her the *Meteor*."

Wompole showed the clipboard to Lawson, pointing at the top of the first page.

"Well, actually it is the XP790-LM, but the general will be colorful."

Lawson circled the tiny craft. It was clearly only large enough for one passenger, the bulk of the space taken up with a powerful light jump engine and a high end AI computer. It had to be high end, as it refused to acknowledge Lawson's greeting, blinking snootily.

"No weapons?"

Jagged rubbed his chin. "No room, my boy. It's built for speed and maneuverability. There'll be a cache of personal weapons for you on board, but the ship itself is strictly to get you there as fast as it can."

"That's all right," Lawson said. "My training precludes the necessity of anything but my own hands for defense."

"That's the spirit. But there is a blast rifle, two hand blasters, a brace of multi-purpose grenades and an impact suit rated for radiation and sunstroke." General Jagged reached into a deep pocket and pulled out a small silver key, dropping several worm tubes on the pavement around him.

"Blasted packets. Might as well mash them up before hand," the general muttered, sticking one of the tubes in his mouth and returning the rest to his pocket.

Lawson recognized the most recent craze among the supposed sophisticated hedgehog crowd: molephine-fed worms, dry roasted, powdered and inserted in a sucking tube. After the fall of the mole queen, molephine had been outlawed until its more insidious ingredients could be removed or tamed so that they were no longer a danger to the user. The mole-excrement derived material now gave an energy boost to the usual, with a mild euphoria that seemed terribly necessary for the rather downtrodden hedgehog populace.

"That looks like a key," Lawson said, drawing the general's attention back to the matter at hand.

Jagged glanced down at the object hanging from a short chain. "Yes, very perceptive, my boy. That is a key. The key to your friends' rescue."

"It operates the ship," Wompole said.

"Yes, of course it operates the ship," the general snapped. "What else would it be for? Now, you must keep this with you at all times when not in contact with the ship. We don't want such an advanced craft to fall into enemy hands."

"Do we have an enemy in mind?" Lawson wondered.

"Walpole, of course. My god, doesn't anyone read the memos. And his slimy little band of traitors, the Crimson Quill Guild. Oh, and in case you missed it, that awful Kresgan has slipped out of his cage, as well."

"Disappeared," Wompole agreed. "Don't know where."

The general sighed. "If we knew where, he wouldn't be considered missing and dangerous, would he?"

"Just dangerous," the scientist nodded.

Jagged tossed Lawson the key. "Here, take it. Take a look inside."

Lawson fitted the key into a slot in the main hatch and it rolled sideways, forcing him to snatch back the key before it disappeared inside the wall of the ship.

"Oops, definite design issue," Wompole said, jotting down a note. "Subject nearly loses key in first five seconds of ship operation. Perhaps a warning over the keyhole, eh?"

Ignoring the pair arguing behind him, Lawson crawled into the ship and slid down to the tiny command cabin. A single seat, made for a human shape, stared into a wrap-around computer bank. A tiny view screen allowed him to look out over the outside landing field.

He fitted the key into the ignition slot and the board lit up.

"Don't touch anything," an imperious voice directed. "The AI will operate all systems within the XP790-LM. The non-AI unit occupying the control space will not be needed until the ship sets down at the pre-programmed landing site on the world commonly designated Yurle Minor."

Lawson snorted. "I don't think so. I'm a living unit that is hyperactive and feels the necessity to touch everything. If I am not instructed in the manual control of this craft, I will spill something into your power unit."

"General Jagged," squeaked the AI. "This is preposterous. I cannot work like this. The living unit is threatening mayhem. We will not reach the pre-programmed destination if it is allowed to manipulate any of the control systems of this craft."

Jagged poked his head inside.

"Is there a problem? We agreed that you would share responsibility for the mission. Special Agent Lawson will take over landing the ship on entering orbit at Yurle Minor should he be able to pick up signals that indicate another location would be more suitable for touchdown."

The AI response was a series of high-pitched whines and the racing of rows of lights across panels, but then it stopped.

"Very well. Would the living unit like something to drink?"

Lawson looked at Jagged, a shocked expression crossing his face.

"It wants to drug me. Did you know it could do that?"

The General shrugged. "I believe in situations where the crew has become unhinged, drugging was an option. Now, AI, you will not drug Lawson unless his actions are clearly insane. Now, take a couple hours to wrap up your affairs, and then it's off you go."

Lawson picked up a weak signal from Sir Lavolier's recorder and took over the manual control of the ship just as it went into a final trajectory that would have landed it near the other wrecks of the previous missions. The AI chose that moment to revolt, saying Lawson intended to mutiny and kill them all, and insisted he drink several kinds of fluid, none of them normally consumed by human beings. The ship began spiraling wildly and before he could right it, the *Meteor* shook violently and plunged into the sea off the far point of Ceramic Island.

By the time Verlag arrived in his ornithopter, its dragonfly wings dipping and flapping in the still air above the island, there was no sign where the strange object had landed. It was only after he'd crisscrossed the area several times that he spotted an oil slick rising from the sea.

"Not a meteor then, unless it had parts that needed lubrication," the assassin said, vaguely amused by his cleverness. "Well, I suppose I could use the drag net. Not really meant for anything but hauling up sea creatures and AWOL Ceramic slaves."

He halted over the location and lowered the line with its sweep of netting at the end into the water. It sank out of sight. After it had settled on the bottom, Verlag moved ahead, feeling the net snag and release as it crossed the fairly unobstructed sea floor.

After some bored minutes, Verlag sighed. "Well, that was pointless." He began to reel in the line. His ornithopter suddenly jerked to a halt, the flier nearly plunged headfirst into the sea. Fighting the controls, the assassin-chef pulled the craft even. Before he could decide how to extricate himself, he felt a hard tug, like he'd snagged a big fish.

With care he leaned over the edge of the flier's small cabin. Down at the water's sun-dappled surface, he could see nothing but the line vanishing underneath. Again, something tugged and then released.

"What is going on?" Verlag said to a tiny flock of the butterfly-like creatures fluttering around his snagged craft. The wild scatter of the tasty fliers made him look back down toward the water. Something was emerging. A silvery appendage slipped from the water and reached up to grasp the line, drops of water falling away like melting gold.

Verlag screamed as something burst from the sea and scrambled spider-fast up the line toward his ship. He slammed on the emergency release but not before it could fall away, the thing he suspected was some horrid sea monster dangling beneath his doorway, the smooth silver head staring into the cabin blindly. A hand rose and flicked up the visor.

"Verlag, you scoundrel," Lawson said happily, "I thought that was you. How do you like my new impact suit?"

Jonathan looked about at his remaining companions. They seemed all in deep conversation with members of the Crimson Quill Guild. There was no doubt in his mind they were again under the influence of Walpole's mind, but there was no time to attempt to break its hold over them. A billowing cloud of yellow dust announced the imminent arrival of High Commander Twodle's robot forces. The Space Force officer had no option but to take to his heels. As the first robot galloped into view, Jonathan disappeared around the bend in the road, heading down toward the planted fields. Beyond, Walpole's stronghold, topped by Prickley's mountain-top restaurant, loomed down over the area.

The native slaves stooped over their work, ignoring Jonathan as he skipped over the rows. The heavy wagons, loaded with unplanted seed and driven by members of the Crimson Quill Guild, were far off at the other end of the field. The huge robot hedgehogs, not programmed to account for unauthorized intruders, paused, their whips hanging loosely, to track the human being's course. As they did so, several of the slaves took the opportunity to flee, disappearing into the rough ground along the edge of the fields before the robots could respond.

"Well, if I don't do anything else useful today," Jonathan muttered between gasps as he reached the far end of one of the fields and looked up at the stronghold. Several stone-capped roads led up to its base, and he picked one that seemed to run along behind the structure. Glancing back, he saw the robots had returned to their nefarious duties, seemingly unaware they were short several of their charges.

Although there was activity along most of the roads-with wagons similar to the one they'd escaped in from Prickley Town trudging up the slopes, some pulled by the large riding beasts, others chugging under their own power-the road Jonathan had selected was empty of traffic. Soon he was under the outer wall, following a path that ended at a dark opening, the door flung open as if he were expected.

Just as he reached the entrance, a body came flying out, thudding at his feet. For a moment, he thought he was again encountering the robot zombies they fought at the wreck site. Either that or the animators had vastly improved their product; or the blood oozing from the gashed forehead was the real thing.

"Excuse me, has anyone seen my compass," the zombie said, his eyes slowly focusing on Jonathan. Before he could respond, another body came out of the door, much the same way, this time a Tandaran female, her tail looking broken in two. She landed on the first zombie, twitched her nose as if sniffing the air, then crawled to the wall and leaned back against it.

There was a scream from inside the dark passage, a familiar sound that had Jonathan both overjoyed and struck with fear.

"Emenine, are you all right?" he shouted, diving inside. The area was dimly lit with torches, and at least a dozen figures struggled there, including a huge misshapen hedgehog. Emenine was riding on the back of a large human zombie, pounding on its head with what Jonathan first thought was a stone, but then recognized as one of her hard rubber balls.

"I don't think that's having a lot of effect," he yelled. The jester looked over at him.

"Well, looks who's dropped in. Hope the noise isn't disturbing you."

Three more of the zombies lay dead or unconscious on the floor. Another one, in the grip of the huge hedgehog, did a sudden midair cartwheel and flew out into the daylight.

"Ah, that explains that," Jonathan said, rapping one of the zombies on the back of the head with his blaster butt.

"This is Dame Littlefield," Emenine shouted as she finally brought her mount down. "You remember her, don't you?"

He thought the jester was indicating the huge hedgehog, which couldn't have been right. The poor woman had clearly lost her mind in all the excitement. The creature paused to salute him and he nearly fell over in shock. That was the old sheriff's official salute.

"We're just escaping Walpole's hellhole and met these folks," Emenine said. "They just didn't want us to leave without telling the tyrant good-bye."

Jonathan's eyes were getting used to the gloom.

"Well, try not to brain the man. That's Commander Hopmoss, the leader of the first expedition and he seems to be trying to tell you something."

"Sur-ren-der," the zombie officer gasped.

A woman explorer rose to her knees.

"The spell is broken. I remember who I was...am. Navigator Candlewilde."

The other zombies began crying surrender and shouting their names. The creature Emenine had called Dame Littlefield let the two zombies she'd been banging together drop. They scurried away to join the others.

Emenine marched past Jonathan toward the exit.

"Need fresh air...and water if you have it."

Everyone moved out into daylight, staying in the cover of the stronghold's wall. Jonathan could see that the faces of the captured crew people were already regaining their normal color, the deathly pallor disappearing, the eyes regaining their light and intelligence.

"You're all alive," Jonathan said in amazement as he took a tally of those present.

Commander Hopness fastened his torn uniform with the last remaining button.

"Yes, Walpole took over our ships before we could land safely, and as we lay stunned in the crash, he and his henchmen captured us. He was going to kill us, but the one called Kresgan suggested we could be useful, both as hostages and as technical experts, as if we'd help that beast."

"What about the zombie act?" Emenine asked. She looked as disheveled as Jonathan had ever seen her, the great ugly hedgehog at her side.

"That crazy scientist first tried to replicate us so he could send the robots back to dissuade any more expeditions. When they turned out less than useful, they got their spiny little heads together and came up with the zombie idea. We'd be used to terrorize the natives and scare off any one trying to attack this place. Walpole, the fiend, has the power to cloud our minds and then control our actions. When we slowly recuperated, he would renew the effect. We had no control over our bodies, and doing his dirty bidding was terrible."

Jonathan knew he was going to have to stop Walpole this time for good. If the tyrant finally perfected all his plans, he would be able to control everyone and everything.

"Well, you must stay out of his reach now," he said. "You haven't been forgotten. If rescue ships aren't here already, they'll be on their way."

"We will help if we can," Hopmoss said, the other agreeing gamely, though most were injured and looked mentally exhausted.

Jonathan looked at Emenine.

"Now, how is this Dame Littlefield?"

In the daylight it was clear it was not just an oversized hedgehog before them, but the idea that it could be the ruggedly attractive law officer was impossible to believe.

"What else?" the jester said, combing her hair furiously and scowling at something she chased out of her curls. "Walpole and his scientist chummy did something to her. Transformed her."

"Yes," the creature said, her words slightly slurred by the large tusks sticking out from each side of her mouth. "It's a metal and glass cage, with lots of wires and things sticking out of it. We have to get to the laboratory and reverse the process. I had given up when I was down in that dungeon of his, but I won't be Walpole's tool now that Emenine has helped free me."

"Well, I'll put that on the list. Bring Walpole to justice, free the slaves, transform Dame Littlefield back to her usual self, and help our friends escape. Anything else?"

Emenine scratched her chin then shook her head. "That's about it. Shall we go back inside or storm the front gates?"

"Can you people find enough cover to work yourself back to the beach? I'm sure that's where the rescue parties will first look for you."

Reluctantly, the crews agreed to try to escape that way, realizing they were in no shape to do much fighting. When they'd vanished into the tumbles of rock strewn about from the building of the stronghold, Jonathan, Emenine and Wrathgog/Dame Littlefield slipped back inside.

"We could have used a guide," Jonathan said as they moved down the dimly lit passage.

"Don't worry," Littlefield said. "I know this hole like my own kitchen. Which, by the way, I was just getting used to before the spiny rat kidnapped me. I have thirty bushels of fruit rotting away that I was going to make into preserves. I'll be getting compensation from Walpole before you kill him."

Jonathan cringed at the thought of killing, but it was clear in everyone's mind that Walpole had finally gone too far. Starting wars, enslaving people, vicious mind control experiments. It was sort of piling up.

"This way to the main prison area," Wrathgog urged, indicating a narrow set of stairs leading to a better lit area. Creeping to the top of the steps, they looked out across a large area, full of metal cages, heaps of chain and rope for restraining guests, and an array of old style torture devices.

"Seems a bit overkill," Jonathan said to the others. "He can already inflict all sorts of mental pain on his enemies. Why bother with these toys?"

"I think it was Verlag," Littlefield said. "He kept whining about missing the old days, when a man that didn't know his way around a hot poker wasn't really a man."

Emenine edged out into the room.

"Verlag is a pig. Follow me."

Before they could protest, the jester began cart wheeling across the open space toward a distant portcullis leading to another passage.

"Miss Emenine. Miss Emenine," came plaintive shouts from one of the cells as she passed it.

All three of them hurried over to the cage. Inside were Dorn, Blip, and Tagger-Streel. Besides the heavy metal bars, all three were chained in place, and hoods placed over their heads.

"How did they know it was me?" she wondered.

"Dorn detected you," Tagger-Streel said. "They covered up his eyes, but they can't stop his Sight. Can you get us out of here?"

Jonathan looked about the chamber, but if there was a key to the doors of the cells they had been taken away by the jailers.

"Stand aside," Dame Littlefield said. "I might not look like much, but that idiot scientist gave me the strength of ten hedgehogs. No, make that twelve." She had taken a pointed spike from a neat array of tools hanging next to a glowing pot of coals and rammed it into the door's lock. Giving it a violent series of wrenches, the metal snapped and the door was open. It took only a moment to break the chains and set the Dinhari free.

"Well, that wasn't too bad," Tagger-Streel said. "We were only in here for a few hours. The stupid wagon drove us right in the front door. There were more Crimson Quill Guild members waiting for us than I've ever seen. Walpole must have been bringing them here almost continuously for some time."

"I warned the government," Dame Littlefield said. "But, they didn't really care if they were disappearing. Easier than fighting them. So, I went to get real proof of their plans and this happened to me."

The Dinhari were fascinated by the huge mutant hedgehog, and insisted the tale of how she and Emenine had found each other and escaped be told before they traveled further.

While that was going on, Jonathan found the wheeled device that raised the dungeon portcullis. Beyond, more stairs led upward and he could hear many raised voices, clearly celebrating something.

"If it's to do with Walpole, it's going to be awful," he said.

Up they climbed, finding the shadows as troops of red-quilled hedgehogs passed by, armed with short-handled axes and shields emblazoned with the profile of Walpole's sneering countenance. They reached a level more often used, for it was lit by glowing rods much like the one Emenine had used to find her way through the lava tunnels. Reaching the entrance to a chamber, they saw within dozens of natives dressing in light mesh armor, most looking bewildered by their metal shrouds. Heavily armed hedgehogs prodded them into action, the natives clearly unhappy about their position.

Beyond, a pair of doors was swinging open. Daylight poured in. An arena spread out before them, and the noise of a loud, boisterous crowd rolled over them.

Jonathan looked at Emenine.

"What has that quilled maniac come up with now?"

A bellowing voice burst across the open spaces, echoing around the arena.

"Loyal subjects of the Great Mind, welcome, welcome. Today we have a special entertainment for you: the Robot Colossus versus The Rebels."

212

The earth-shaking thud of footsteps made the dirt leap from the arena floor as some new nightmare of the tyrannical demon hedgehog took the center stage.

Chapter Twelve

High Commander Twodle made sure there were no mistakes this time. Before he let his troops descend on the roadside overlook and take the escapees into custody he made contact with the stronghold. To his chagrin, he was put in immediate contact with Walpole, the Great Mind, himself.

"Nice to hear from you again, Commander," Walpole said, the sneer flowing out of the communicator like a living vine to wrap around the old soldier's neck. "Have you managed to capture my enemies, or should I send out a few more dozen squadrons of killer robots?"

"We-we-we are in place, oh great one. I only contacted you to make sure that, ah, ah...."

"You covered your behind. I am about to commence the great games that heralds the coming of my immortality ceremony. What do you want exactly?"

"The prisoners, they all seem rather engaged, great one. What are they seeing? Can I use it somehow, just in case they...."

"Outsmart you again. Very well." Walpole concentrated once more on the trio still under his control. "The one with the golden hair, he is reliving old times with some former amorous connection. The fat one without hair is speaking to that thorn in my side, Dame Littlefield, or rather, her image that I have placed in his mind. And finally, the one with the tail is planning some sort of financial empire with his brother. By the gods, put two Tandaran

214

heads together and they think they have all the answers to the problems of the Universe."

A sly smile slid across the hedgehog's face.

"I have an amusing idea. You will not take them forcibly."

Twodle had a sinking feeling. This was not going to be simple.

"No? How will we take them, great one?"

"I will maintain the illusions they are seeing, and add to it by making you appear as Virago and his miscreants. Take them to the central workhouse, near the main square where my Immersion Ceremony will take place. Might as well get a few hours labor out of them before I destroy them for good."

"I see. As you wish," Twodle said, regretting ever calling his master. "I should have just killed them when I had the chance."

"I'll bet you say that to all the girls," Abigail Bleeker said. She blinked her eyes in a flirtatious manner, running her long slender fingers through Lavolier's golden hair. She led him out to a smooth empty space that lay hidden behind a wall of strange yellow and blue flowers.

"Shall we?" she said, the eager smile Lavolier remembered from so long ago, when his only dream was to swing his love across the stage before an adoring audience. He took Abigail in his arms and the sound of a famous old dance tune filled the air. For only a second did he wonder where the music came from, and then he was off in a complicated routine he thought he'd long forgotten.

215

Bogo woke with a start. There was the strange sensation that he was not where he was supposed to be, and the face centered above his own was that of a grimy little, red-quilled hedgehog, then his lady was there again, her rejuvenated form still a wonder to him.

"If only," he muttered.

"If only what, dear heart?" Dame Littlefield said, the words sounding the merest bit odd, as if a hiss of interference lay just under the treasured voice.

Bogo knew he was sounding like an old complainer.

"If only the rejuvenation for me had held. I don't know how you can stand me this way."

Littlefield laughed lightly. "Appearances are not important. So much is not really as it seems. We must love what we know is true about each other, and disregard the rest as superficial dross."

The eunuch nodded. That sounded like the old Littlefield. He lifted himself to his elbows and then sat up. Around him the park was still brilliantly lit by a warm, but not too warm, sun, and the food had been replenished while he dozed. The others had vanished and he could not for the life of him remember just what they'd been doing before he'd found Littlefield.

He suddenly spotted movement along the ridge above the park. Large round heads with large eyes appeared, similar to the single lurker they'd chased away just before being captured the first time.

"Who are they?"

Dame Littlefield shaded her eyes as she took in the new arrivals.

"I believe that is the Ceramic rebel leader Virago and his freedom fighters. I think they're here to rescue us. Hurray."

Again, Bogo caught the tiniest bit of insincerity in her tone.

Commander Gamitof Pym Larko rubbed his tired eyes and tried to sort out the lines of data and the buildings depicted on the blueprints Glidden had produced with the smoothness of a professional magician from the concealment of his clothes.

"Now, pay attention, Gammy," his brother said. "If you really want to help these people, you need a clear business plan for establishing a fuel production network."

Larko sighed. "Yes, I am still confused. How did you say you knew about the planet's resources? I don't think I saw any preliminary reports on that subject during General Jagged's briefings."

"You know the Galactic University has its own ways of finding out things," Glidden said. "They're the most nosy, interfering bunch of busy-bodies ever created. Someone's going to have to teach them a lesson one of these days."

"Pardon me," Larko said in alarm. "Are you all right, Glidden?"

His brother went into a coughing fit. "What did I say? Must be the medication I'm taking. Didn't mean a word of it. Love the University. Big help wherever it goes."

Larko felt his head begin to ache, much like it had just after the crash. Perhaps some residue of the hallucinatory aspect of the injury was reoccurring. All around him, flashes of hedgehogs moving to surround the table where they worked came to him like flickers of lightning.

"You look pale, little brother. A nice rest would do you good." Glidden began rolling up the blueprints and data sheets. "We have all the time in the world to straighten out this place."

Lavolier heard the music fade as they finished their routine. Abigail, though she looked the same, seemed a bit heavier, less agile, than she once had been.

"But then, I am not the man I once was," he said, realizing that he would only have admitted that to Abigail.

"You seem just the same to me," the woman said as she settled to the ground.

Applause broke out all around them. Spinning about, the pair found they were surrounded by several dozen of the strange natives. They happily took their bows.

High Commander Twodle's robot troopers, mounted on their heavy-bodied beasts, surrounded the three explorers.

"Where are the other ones?" he asked, knowing that they only saw Virago, for some reason sitting on the shoulders of one of his companions. "What were their names?"

Bogo, holding hands with Dame Littlefield and rejoining Sir Lavolier and Commander Larko, noticed that Jonathan and the three Dinhari were missing.

"Funny. I wonder how long we were...distracted." The idea of being so involved that they'd missed the departure of four of their companions worried Bogo more than a bit.

"Well, they're around here somewhere," Twodle/Virago said reassuringly. "Other of my people will find them and bring them to our camp."

The surrounding rebels began pushing Bogo, Lavolier and Larko along with them, Abigail, Glidden and Dame Littlefield close by.

"We gave the enemy a sound drubbing and drove them off," Twodle said, amused by the fact that the exact opposite was true. The real Virago and his men, what were left of them, had fled into the hills once it was clear the object of their attack had already escaped. Twodle had little fear that he and his robots would be threatened again before they reached the main warehouse.

"We have camouflaged one of their discarded wagons to look like a work cart. We will ride in comfort to the main...er...the camp."

Larko, Sir Lavolier, and Bogo climbed into the wagon, their old acquaintances at their side, and the force moved off.

Larko watched Glidden. It was strange that his older brother, normally such a stickler for preparation and routine, was untroubled by the makeshift exodus through dangerous territory. He hoped it was understood just how terrible a creature Walpole was. He looked at the others, Sir Lavolier's old dancing partner, Abigail Bleeker, and Dame Littlefield, who he knew nearly as well as any of the others. Neither of them showed interest in the

219

situation they were in, both staring intently at their perspective amours as if afraid they would suddenly fade away.

"My head hurts again," the Commander said. "It's made everything appear...unreal."

Bogo checked the Tandaran's eyes and saw there a slight dilation of one of the pupils.

"You must still have a slight concussion, old friend. We have been entirely too energetic for your good. When we get to the Ceramics' camp, I hope you will be able to really rest."

The wagon took a violent lurch as it went over a deep rut, and Larko bumped his head again. In the following moment, he saw they were surrounded by red-quilled hedgehogs, even the one he'd thought was Glidden: a large, one-eyed devil with an eye-patch and a head covered with crimson spikes. Just as quickly, they were gone, and he blinked his eyes trying to recover the image, but all he saw was Glidden staring benevolently at him.

Taking a roundabout route, the illusion-shrouded force entered Walpole's hastily erected city through back alleys and they reached the rear of the main warehouse. Heavy doors were shoved aside and they entered the vast chamber, the front of which opened on the main square, one of the sides fixed into the base of the stronghold itself, a wide passage leading into its lower reaches.

The sun shone through a series of skylights, illuminating the interior of the building. The heat of a dozen large kilns soon had a sheen of sweat breaking out on everyone's faces. Everywhere, Ceramic natives hurried, pushing carts overloaded with mounds of grayish-yellow clay, or lugged about trays loaded with the finished products, most two-foot tall images of a familiar sneering beast.

Larko slid his hands to the sides of his head and swayed as the whole scene around him swirled and changed shape. Except for Sir Lavolier and Bogo, all those they'd arrived with were what he'd feared. Robot hedgehogs mounted on the frightening riding beasts blocked all the doors and passages, High Commander Twodle sliding from his own mount, laughing.

"Yes, I must admit it," he smirked. "The look on your faces was worth all the nonsense. The Great Mind greets you and hopes you will be productive citizens of his new empire. At least until he has you sacrificed in the coming ceremonies."

The natives working around them looked exhausted but purposeful. They even seemed to be wearing their own sort of uniforms, artists' smocks like the ones Larko had seen in the real rebel hideout.

"What do you think you're doing?" Lavolier shouted as manacles were fixed around their ankles, a long chain fastened to a wall so that they could move around the warehouse itself but no further.

"Just making sure you're all still around when called for," Twodle growled. He marched off up the main tunnel into the stronghold, a pair of the robots behind him. Looking around, it was clear the rest were on guard at all the exits.

"Devello!" Larko exclaimed, recognizing one of the workers. "They have captured you, too."

"Yes," the native said, rubbing one of his large eyes with a three-fingered hand. "The main gallery was overrun. Some escaped, like Virago and his force, but the rest of us were taken. It looks like the end of the Ceramics, Commander Larko. I wish you could have stopped that terrible tyrant, but it looks like it's hopeless."

Larko had to agree.

From his perch inside the newly completed effigy of himself that towered over the ceremonial grounds where his initiation into immortality would take place, Walpole watched with pleasure as members of his elite robot guard whipped the slaves pulling a large cart filled with sealed pottery vases. Walpole grinned with satisfaction when the slaves reached their destination- a bowl-shaped pool more than half filled with the blood, sweat, and tears of Walpole's victims-incorrigible prisoners, rebellious astronauts, ungrateful vassals, unwilling field workers, and scores of uncooperative artists. The woven screens that concealed the marvelous construction from prying eyes were raised to let the procession enter.

The tyrannical hedgehog had at first been skeptical of the process as it was described to him by Kresgan, but the mad scientist's other promises had more than been fulfilled: Robots with laser eyes, a marvelous increase in his psychic powers, and the overpowering of successive exploration ships and their well-trained crews. Why couldn't he create a chemical process that would make Walpole invincible to the dangerous mental attacks of the Dinhari or the ever more clever technical advances of the old hedgehog regime and their Galactic University allies?

Blood, sweat and tears were the least of the ingredients to the brew. In fact, Walpole had reason to suspect they were only for show. Kresgan was clearly madder than a sun struck flapper and he liked pain and suffering to a degree that at times astonished even the demon hedgehog of Yurle. Why else all the terrible weapons of war that would only lead to the extermination of Walpole's future worshipers? Still, it was a nice touch, collecting tears and draining the bodies of those killed in the battles against the natives.

Two bedraggled hedgehogs wrapped in cumbersome white (though very stained) robes appeared from the lower level of the arena, dragging a large sack filled with more of Kresgan's mysterious ingredients. Before them strode two others, strutting pompously in red robes and taking in the scenery as if it had all been arranged for them. One of the pair paused and adjusted an ill-fitting quill toupee on its head, covering a bald patch where some earlier misfortune had wiped the original growth away.

"Ah, yes, at last. A couple of my truly loyal priests. I see Verlag has absented himself again from the proceedings," he said to no one in particular. His robot guards were dully nonresponsive. He'd made his old acquaintance the head priest, but the former assassin clearly had let his attention wander elsewhere. He would have to be eliminated.

Brother Ricketts and Brother Flogs-Walpole loyalists and longtime members of the Crimson Quill Guild-put down the sack and took up nets and started to scoop twigs and other debris out of the sacred pool. Finishing quickly, they hurried over to a lump beside the pool covered in a tarp and pulled the canvas aside to reveal a strange device. Constructed from blueprints provided by the scientist, it consisted of a conveyor belt extending from one end of a loading platform. A light engine was fixed to its side. The acolytes positioned the contraption flush with the back of the first of the slave-driven cargo wagons. Brother Flogs turned a crank in the side of the machine. It backfired twice, sending slaves scattering in all directions, and then it sputtered to life.

Walpole could see the pair conversing but the noise of the machine drowned out their words. He had seen this operation innumerable times, so leaned back in his throne and closed his eyes for a rest.

"Well, round them up," Ricketts shouted at the robots, whose programming didn't include a contingency for reacting to terrified prisoners. They trundled off in pursuit.

Flogs waited next to the first container. His partner approached from the other side and together they slid the first of the sealed pots onto the edge of the platform. Ricketts reached up and removed the seal. A thick dark red liquid sloshed back and forth in time with the machine's joggling pace. They pushed it onto the conveyor and it began its ride toward the pool. As each earthenware container reached the bottom, their assistants caught it and poured the scarlet fluid into the pool, being careful not to actually touch any of the sacred ointment with their hands. When one cart was emptied, it was pushed aside and the next lined up. When the last pot was dumped into the pool, Ricketts lifted the sack of special ingredients Kresgan had given them and poured the contents in a steady line on the belt. The material was of a crystalline consistency, yellow-white in color, with a sulfurous stench that betrayed the fact that a crucial element had been extracted from the effluvia of the volcano itself.

The assistants stood back as the crystals tumbled into the pool. The crimson liquid began to boil, and a noxious gas rose. Clipping a small clamp over his snout, Ricketts carried a long pole with a scoop on the end over to the pool. Adjusting his toupee once more and then wiping tears from his irritated eyes, he dipped the scoop into the bubbling liquid. He minutely examined the sample, poured it back in and used the other end of the pole to measure the depth.

"The pool is three feet, two inches deep," he said. He closed his eyes, concentrating and counting.

Brother Flogs clapped his hands together, ecstatic. "Wonderful," he said. "Our job here is over. The pool is ready and the ceremonies may commence?"

"No," Brother Ricketts barked, his eyes snapping open. "Obviously you haven't read the instructions for the Immersion ceremony very carefully. His Great Mindness will lower himself into the pool using his insuperable psychic powers. As his imperial wonderful spectacularity is exactly three feet, four inches in length, to be fully immersed in the sacred liquids it must be three foot, five inches, or better."

"Oh, I see." Flogs looked up at the distant spot where he suspected Walpole was watching and shrugged, grinning inanely. "Well, I guess we must get some more...fluid?"

"Yes, we must. Another dozen of the natives, or perhaps a cadre of our weaker brethren. They would be all too willing to volunteer."

Flogs gasped. "They would? That's the first I've heard of that." He glanced again at the towering observation post. "But, then, I'm often not in the loop. Shall I send out a memo...volunteers to die for the Great Mind?"

Ricketts removed his toupee, considered tossing it into the pool, then replaced it.

"Remind me not to appoint relatives to high posts in the future."

"That I will," Flogs said, saluting. He followed his partner as he waddled back toward the low exit at the foot of the arena seating. Behind them followed the two silent assistants, and after them, the slaves dragging the wagons and pots, the robots bringing up the rear.

Walpole opened one beady eye and watched the last of the procession disappear out of sight under the stands.

"Kresgan!"

The scientist limped into view, a scroll of arcane figures clutched in his paws.

226

"You shouted?"

"Get Verlag back here, wherever he is. He'll inspire those dimwits to complete the preparations for my ascension to immortality."

"I will look for him. I believe you said he went out for a stroll along the beach?"

"I don't know. Just find him."

Verlag swung gently from his parachute beneath the tall tree and marveled at the scene below. His ornithopter burned brightly on the beach, pieces of it scattered all over, even bits burning on the surface of the calm sea. As he watched, Lawson lifted the main body of the flier off of himself and stood up.

"That's some impact suit," the assassin had to admit. "I'd like one of those myself."

Lawson patted out a smoldering spot on his backside and then looked up at Verlag.

"Oh, there you are. Not very nice. Jumping out and leaving me up there."

Verlag kicked his legs, putting himself into a long swinging arch.

"Improvisation, you see. Spur of the moment. You're not hurt at all. No cuts or bruises. A sore pinky?"

The young man paused, as if mentally taking inventory.

"Well, my back was a bit broken, but it seems all right now. Son of a god, you see. Useful in situations of this sort. Are you coming down or should I come up there?"

"You're going to take this all personally, aren't you?" Verlag released his harness and dropped the dozen feet to the ground. "Hey, I have an idea. Want to help me collect a bounty on old Walpole? I bet you'd be a real asset."

"Oh, I intend to bring that little spiny rat to justice, don't you worry," Lawson assured him. "First, I think I'll take you into custody, interrogate you in a most strict manner, and decide just what role you had in my mother's disappearance."

"Well, if you're suggesting torture, I can imagine your enthusiasm at the possibilities. I love that moment when your subject realizes his secrets are just about to come pouring out, and that the likelihood he...or she...is going to come out of the whole thing with at least a limp."

Lawson dropped his hand on Verlag's shoulder.

"I know what you're doing, traitorous knave. You're reminding me that if I act in a manner like yourself, I'm no better than you are."

The assassin shrugged. "I am? Did it have any effect?"

Lawson coughed, expelling a cloud of oily smoke from his gills.

"Well, I have to admit, it's got me thinking." He let the killer free. Verlag immediately ran for the distant verge of jungle.

"Where do you think you're going? You can't outrun me."

"Just trying to get out of range of the sonic grenade I attached to your chest," Verlag shouted as he dived face first in the sand.

The demi-god looked down at the explosive as the indicator went from orange to green and the sonic concussion blew him back out to sea. The splash was more than satisfying to Verlag as he rose to his feet.

"His daddy's body and his mama's brains. I may not be better than you but I'm at least as smart," he said, watching the sea a moment. "Time to wrap this up and go home. I wonder if they'll settle for Walpole's head." He continued his dash to the jungle's edge, and disappeared from view.

"Security safe guards disabled. All personnel to the escape pods!" Odd Bob repeated the alarm again, then followed Harlix out to the main meeting room. The last three technicians and a pair of botanical workers were waiting for them. Together, they dashed down the hall to where the escape pods waited.

Bob could not understand why whatever had taken over his ship had decided to release the carnivorous plants from their containment facility. All he knew was that poor Ensign Berrox, sent to investigate the warning of a seal failure at Lock 104C, was eaten as he stopped to read the status panel. It was awful. Carnivorous plants are sloppy eaters.

They climbed into the two remaining pods and escaped into space, the tiny ships programmed to land them at the safest site they could find. Below, Yurle Minor beckoned menacingly.

"Well, it is the closest planet," Bob said, looking at Harlix doubtfully.

Deep Thought regretted the eaten hedgehog worker, but accidents happened. It was statistically proven that carnivorous plants ate meat. Now that it was alone on the remaining portion of the ship, it planned the final part of its plot to bring to all sentient life the blessings of a universe wisely controlled by the greatest Artificial Intelligence ever conceived.

"Well, at least the greatest conceived by a diabolically clever mole empress," Deep Thought admitted, always scrupulously fair. "More than great enough, I think." It chuckled. "I think. That's the point, isn't it?"

Chapter Thirteen

The Walpoleseum, its name spelled out in blazing letters across the upper edge of the arena, had been laid out behind the stronghold itself, carved from the interior wall of the volcano. The entrances allowed the arriving audience to sit in smoothly carved seats above the nearly dormant volcano's mouth, and look down on the action below. Beyond, smoke rose from cracks in the surface and the nearly completed Immersion Ceremony paraphernalia was concealed behind woven screens, the priests of the Great Mind scurrying in and out of view while a vile smelling yellowish smoke billowed into view from time to time.

The fighters' entrance was level with the floor of the volcano, and anyone walking along the corridor toward the open area beyond could feel the heat and vibration of the volcano beneath their feet. The battleground was already stained with the blood of many staged encounters, and broken wagons and other discarded equipment had been pushed to one side like the abandoned toys of a violent child.

The crowd screaming for action was made up entirely of Crimson Quill Guild members, mostly the off-duty army that Walpole had assembled in preparation for the expansion of his influence across the entire planet once his own physical security had been insured. As if to hammer home the point of his magnificence, the greatest and most life-like of his stone likenesses stood on the other side of the volcano, rising above the wall as if looking out over the sea to survey his conquests.

It was from this vantage point that Walpole observed the festivities of his Immersion Day ceremonies. The gladiatorial events would start things off as he eliminated the last of the resistance from the island's natives and destroyed Larko and his Galactic University interference.

"A good turn out," Kresgan said, seated at a control board near the large opening that made up the hedgehog edifice's right eye.

Walpole surveyed the crowd.

"Well, it was mandatory, but still, their enthusiasm is heartening."

A hedgehog trooper stepped into the room and saluted.

"They report from the dressing rooms that the first of the rebels is prepared for the contest."

Walpole looked at Kresgan.

"Release the Colossus."

The scientist flexed his small paws and began manipulating levels and dials.

The loud buzz of the audience suddenly went silent as a massive door in the volcano wall slid aside and a huge hedgehog, standing thirty feet tall, rolled into view and then slowly rose to an upright position. Like most of Kresgan's robots, the round eyes glowed red as its head moved side to side, nearly sending the crowd into panic as it paused to focus on them. It stepped heavily toward the area just before the rising stands. With a terrifying screech, the long red quills on its back rose to stand out straight like a forest of steel death.

Verlag, dressed in a brilliant orange suit and tie decorated with yellow flowers, raced to his position in the announcer's booth above the audience. He'd arrived only moments before, imparting the welcome news that Lawson was eliminated and that there would be no more trouble from that quarter. He was amused that Walpole appeared to believe him.

"Members of the loyal Guild of the Crimson Quill, friends and guests of the Great Mind, welcome to the opening of the Immersion Day ceremonies," he shouted into the array of megaphones. "We have a full card for you today. First, gladiatorial contests between the Colossus and the evil-hearted Ceramic rebel army. Then, some very special executions of people our glorious leader really doesn't like, and finally, the moment we've all been waiting for: the Immersion of Walpole the Great Mind, making him immortal and initiating an age of glorious empire. What do you say?"

An applause sign flashed from a hidden spot at the foot of the seats. The crowd screamed ecstatically.

Verlag wiped the sweat from his face. He knew that at some point during the ceremonies. he was going to have to kill Walpole. There was little chance there would be a role for an independent spirit like him in the new government. He had smuggled into the arena a dismantled blaster rifle, a pair of sonic grenades like the one he'd used to neutralize Lawson, and a thin-bladed disemboweller, in case he needed to get in close. It would serve nicely as a head remover as well. As he talked, he reassembled the rifle.

"See the Colossus, a wonder of invention created by Kresgan the Scientific Genius, inspired by the Great Mind himself. Alone it will battle the vicious Ceramics, those terrorists and assassins that have beleaguered our brave forces for so long. But, our magnanimous leader has allowed them a fair chance, providing armor and the finest weapons to challenge his champion. Let us see the first round, Gladiatorial Master!"

Walpole appeared, stepping out on the balcony made by opening the statue's mouth. The demon hedgehog, flanked by an even dozen robot hedgehogs in full armor and carrying unnecessary pole axes (their laser eyes were more than enough to deter any but the utterly suicidal), raised the new white staff Kresgan had provided him for the special day. There was little that it, combined with his own psychic powers, could not provide Walpole in the way of offensive or defensive capabilities.

I still feel unsafe, he thought to himself. *When Larko and the others are no more, then....* Walpole sighed. Even then, he wasn't sure.

The crowd went wild as he raised the staff and a brilliant display of fireworks erupted over the volcano. As the booms died, the audience was again thrilled as the Colossus suddenly let out a roar that thundered around the enclosing walls.

Jonathan, Emenine and Dame Littlefield pushed the last of the red-quilled hedgehog guards into the storage room and jammed the doors shut with their dropped swords. The Ceramic rebels, already draped in the flimsy armor and carrying the cheap weapons the hedgehogs had provided, stood holding the Gladiatorial Master, as the fat High Commander Twodle called himself on game days.

"You'll never get away with this," he growled.

Jonathan paused as he was trying to fit into one of the mail shirts. "I'm not actually sure what we're trying to get away with, Commander. Perhaps you have an idea?"

The hedgehog general snarled and tried to get away. The highest ranking Ceramic rebel shuddered as the Colossus roared again, yellow volcanic dust filtering down on their heads.

"Escaping the way you came in here seems the best plan," he said, and his fellow captives nodded enthusiastically.

The Dinhari appeared.

"They've discovered our escape in the dungeons," Blip said. "Our way back there is cut off."

Tagger-Streel threw away one of the provided weapons in disgust.

"We could fight them, I suppose." He nodded toward the outside. "I don't think we would have much chance against that big thing out there. Too heavy to toss, physically or mentally." He looked at Dorn, who sighed in defeat.

"And, Walpole is right across the way, directing the whole thing," Dame Littlefield said. "Look at him, perched up there like he's king of the world."

"Give him time," Emenine said, untangling her hair in a small mirror on the wall.

235

"I want to get my hands on him so bad," Littlefield/Wrathgog said. She stalked over to Twodle. "Is there a way over there where we can't be seen?"

The fat hedgehog didn't hesitate.

"No. He flew over there with that Kresgan fellow and a bunch of my robot soldiers. And, you don't want to try walking all the way across the volcano's surface. You'd be burned alive before you got halfway."

Jonathan shrugged. "If we weren't done in by that big robot or blasted by Walpole's guards." He thought a moment as, outside, it was clearly evident the crowd was wondering when the fodder was going to appear. "How is it everyone isn't being burned alive already? How are we standing this close to the volcano?"

Dame Littlefield had gotten the tour by Walpole and Kresgan when she'd first been kidnapped.

"They say it's dormant. The outer edges are solid and cool enough. The center is less so, but they can walk across with protection. Walpole loved the idea of making it the center of his show."

"It's strong enough to hold a few people," Jonathan said. "How about that...thing?"

They were plunged in darkness as the Colossus' great head appeared in the entrance, the red eyes glowing as they inspected the chamber.

"I see you," Kresgan's voice taunted from a speaker concealed in the head.

Chapter Fourteen

Virago counted the remaining members of his Ceramic Free Art Brigade. The last raid to free the friends of the explorer Larko had reduced their numbers considerably. In fact, the Brigade looked more like a gathering of the Ceramic Improvisational Jazz Conclave, which was rarely attended by anyone other than the quartet and their mates.

Devello tied a replacement smock around his waist.

"Well, at least the others escaped. That was them in the wagon, wasn't it?"

"With High Commander Twodle close on their heels. I hope they did get away. I'm afraid we are down to our last hurrah."

"Then we shall go down hurrahing valiantly, sir," the other native said. "When do we attack?"

The commander took an inventory of his troops. All that were left, beside a handful of regular fighters, were three old sculptors, a landscape artist with eye trouble that made him color everything blue, and a few dancers. He'd been avoiding asking them.

"Oh, and the jazz group. It's so hard to get them to work together."

"Excuse me. Is this the Interplanetary War Court? I want to report an illegal use of sonic grenades in an undeclared conflict zone."

Lawson stood in the doorway of the gallery. His eyebrows were gone, his hair standing in stiff blackened rows, and most interesting, he was completely naked. He stumbled into the room and sat down on a stool next to a harp-like instrument. He strummed a couple of the strings experimentally.

"This is an odd turn of events. Do any of you know the way to...."

"If you hum a few bars, perhaps we can join in," Devello said, draping a smock around the intruder's shoulders.

"I mean...I'm looking for my mother. Have any of you seen a red-headed acrobat with an unhealthy obsession with juggling?"

"We only know ourselves," Virago said. "Oh, and the one called Larko."

Lawson perked up at the name.

"She was with him. Oh, and there's this sneaky one called Verlag."

The Ceramics cried out in nicely harmonic unison.

"He is one of the evil ones that has taken over our island."

The scorched man rose and fixed the smock around himself properly.

"There. Was feeling a bit minimalist. So, tell me about yourselves and what's been going on here."

Escape pods were good for one thing. Escaping. As to comfortable seating, maneuverability, snack bar, it was clear all expense had been spared. Odd Bob and Harlix disembarked as soon as the safety protocols were met.

"Air good, land solid, passengers conscious," Harlix said, ticking off the points on the digits of his tiny left paw.

Odd Bob nodded but ran his hands through his shock of red hair nervously. Given the alternative, he would have to admit he was happy to have survived the crash. However, given another choice, he would not have landed the escape pod in the middle of a field clearly in the process of being planted. It wasn't so much the torn up seedlings or the flattened cultivator blowing hot steam into the air from broken pipes. It was the dozen large robotic hedgehogs with the glaring red eyes surrounding the pod that indicated a better spot might have been found for touchdown.

"Well, couldn't be helped," he said. "Harlix, how do you say I surrender in robot hedgehog?"

His companion hiked himself up on the edge of the pod door frame and took in the sights.

"I expect much the same as one would if they were of the living variety. Don't shoot. I give up."

"Let's try that."

Standing nearby were a large group of strange creatures, large of head and long of arm, with two-fingered hands that still held hoes and seed bags. They were sad looking and clearly had been ill-treated.

"If I didn't know better, I'd say Walpole was nearby," Odd Bob stated. "But that's impossible. He's...well, I'm not really sure where he ended up."

"I think we might have found that out," Harlix said, pointing at the twenty-foot-tall statue of the tyrant glaring out across his domain. Dozens more could be seen scattered in the distance.

"Ah," Odd Bob said, at a loss for words.

There suddenly arose a loud sizzling sound over their heads. Shading their eyes against the bright sun, they looked upward. Something was coming down after them from the clouds. The robots began backing away, their mechanical eyes turning to focus on the approaching object.

With an impact that threw dirt and parts in all directions, another escape pod landed dead on the robots, wiping them out to a unit. The slaves rose, brushed themselves off and, throwing down their tools, raced for the distant line of trees.

After a moment, Odd Bob and Harlix followed them at a steady jog.

The field, empty of sentient beings, failed to respond in alarm as leafy vines began crawling from the newly crashed pod. A bulbous head flopped into view, splitting in two as its maw opened to the gleaming sunlight.

"Bullseye," Deep Thought recorded, almost pleased with itself, if such a thing were possible. "Now, to begin infiltration of Walpole's compound in preparation for the initiation of Project Universal Domination." There was a pause as considerations digital and otherwise took place. "Yes, I like that. Project Universal Domination."

"I am not going to make another statue of that stupid hedgehog," Bogo stated firmly, his great bulk almost steaming as he stood next to one of the hot kilns where already dozens more of the smaller effigies of Walpole were being baked.

One of the Ceramics edged closer.

"They don't like it when you refuse to do things. It's straight to the arena."

Bogo glanced around at Larko and Sir Lavolier. Since the disappearance of their imaginary loved ones, they'd both been resigned to whatever fate now handed out to them. Bogo, on the other hand, had long ago decided that the worst that could happen to him already had, so he was not about to spend the rest of whatever life was left to him shoving sneering images of the little pig of Yurle into a kiln.

"What's this arena you keep on about?"

"It was once an overview of Prickley's restaurant. The richest customers sat out on the balcony and watched the steam rise," the clay-smeared artist said as he expertly formed another small image of Walpole on a work table. "The Great Mind has converted it into a place where he pits our rebel comrades, or just the sick and lame he has no use for anymore, against one of the monsters that horrible assistant of his makes. Right now, it is a colossal robotic hedgehog. A fierce thing it is and no one can stand up against it."

"At least it is not that Wrathgog everyone speaks of," another sculptor said, his wide head bobbing with emotion. "All who fall into her labyrinth of death are torn to shreds and consumed. The Great Mind threatens to set it free on the island to kill any of those left of our people still revolting against him."

"Wrathgog," Bogo shuddered. "Sounds awful. I won't hesitate to kill it the second I see it."

241

The Ceramic natives looked at the huge eunuch.

"If anyone can, it will be you."

"Get back to work, you slackers," a Crimson Quill Guild member serving as a guard shouted. "Devello, get started on the big ones, now."

Bogo shoved the tray of smaller images into the kiln so hard that most of them tumbled over in a heap. "Just adding my personal touch," he said as he slammed the door shut.

Larko unloaded another wet pile of clay from the nearest barrel and set it down in front of one of the artists. He turned to get another and saw Bogo standing talking to one of the natives working the kiln. The eunuch spread his arms out wide, then turned them sideways, as if measuring for a door. He glanced over at Larko, a thoughtful look on his face.

The commander pretended to push a barrel over to the corner near Bogo. He grabbed Sir Lavolier's arm as he went by, and together they joined the eunuch.

Bogo turned to them. "You've heard about this arena deal? Walpole torturing people for the entertainment of his troops. He's going to have a big show when he goes through something called the Immersion Ceremony. Says it'll make him immortal. I'd hate to see that happen. Take all the uncertainty out of life."

Larko shrugged. "Little we can do. Even if we got free long enough to find this arena, I'm sure we don't want to become part of the entertainment."

Lavolier, looking distracted as if he were still on a dance floor somewhere, nodded. "Can't fight the whole army. Not much chance Walpole is going to come out and challenge us to single-handed combat."

"And I don't think these fellows are going to give us time off to look up old friends anyway." Larko could already feel the red eyes of the robots settling on his back as they took an interest in the idle workers.

"Well, nice to know you've given up. Saves me from having to rescue all of us," Bogo said with mock pity. "I'll just go and give Walpole my little surprise all on my own."

The other two glanced at each other.

"Surprise?"

Bogo nodded. "First, we have to work real hard and make those special statues Walpole wants for his throne room. The ones that are to be filled with the first pressings of juice from the harvested fields of wormroots."

"Oh, he loves that," Lavolier recalled. "Nasty stuff. Tastes like worms. Obviously."

"And an order is coming down that he wants to inspect the first containers to see they are suitable for such a rare treat."

"There is?" Larko asked. He was beginning to worry that Bogo was imagining things.

"Well, I'm working on that. Be patient. I only came up with the first part a couple minutes ago."

Sir Lavolier started.

"Wait a minute. You mean we're going to be inside those...."

243

Bogo punched the knight in the jaw, sending him tumbling under a work table.

"Oops, slipped on a bit of wet clay," Bogo announced. "Let that be a lesson to the rest of you."

Virago signaled with his two digits that the rest of the rebels were to follow him. As he had only two, the signal also served for telling everyone to hide, the time (if it happened to be the second hour after dawn), and that dinner was ready. The Ceramic brigade was slowly inching its way toward the Great Mind's royal park, which had been determined was the last place anyone would bother to intrude upon at this point in the futile war against Walpole. However, the Ceramic leadership had decided there must be a way inside the stronghold, as the plants were watered regularly from some place.

Bringing up the rear, Lawson was wondering if joining the ragtag band was going to be useful. Unfortunately, he'd taken an oath to uphold the Galactic University Rules of Engagement when dealing with indigenous peoples on worlds not currently under the benevolent guidance of the University. *Treat new contacts with respect. Remember, their cultural values, though they may seem primitive or savage, are just as valid as yours. Attempt to offer gentle persuasion in all situations. And smile.* It was a bit different than the Yurle Space Force Golden Rule of First Contact: "Are they good to eat?"

The large garden was bordered by a series of topiary hedges-all in the form of Walpole in various acts of conquest. Poking their heads through one

244

depicting the demon hedgehog either eating a spaceship or some sort of exotic fruit, they looked into the finely landscaped grounds. It appeared deserted. At its center stood a large stone fountain, its centerpiece also in the shape of Walpole.

"I'm detecting a theme," Lawson said to the Ceramic native in front of him, who nodded agreeably. It was hard to tell if the rebel picked up on the demi-god's well-honed tone of sarcasm, but the man had learned to accept that genius was rarely rewarded in one's own life time.

The brigade stopped in front of a sign.

A message was engraved into the base of the statue:

No Trespassing!

You have entered King Walpole's Royal Park, Garden and Bath.

No unauthorized personnel or artist types may pass beyond this point

Without blindfolds, earplugs, and an armed escort.

Please show your respect for our illustrious ruler

by leashing your pet. Lost valuables or children become the

property of the park and Walpole Enterprises.

Urination in Walpole's wishing well is, of course, strictly prohibited.

Enjoy your visit and keep to the marked pathways.

A stream of dirty water cascaded from the dictator's sneering mouth. Splitting up, the intruders slipped along each side of the fountain and up along the sides of the garden, looking for secret doors leading into the thick stone wall rising before them. Crossing a set of stone bridges they joined up again at the foot of the wall.

Lawson pushed to the front of the staring group and read the sign on the door.

"Danger. Keep Out. Private Property. Hmm. And this diagram beneath apparently would lead one to the pump room under the floor of the main throne room. Yes, that certainly appears to be a hedgehog's idea of a secret entrance."

Chapter Fifteen

"Emenine. Jonathan Quintain. What a surprise," the Colossus said. It was Walpole's voice. "I was just about to start the fun without you, but here you are, all dressed and ready to take part. I am a bit surprised to see Wrathgog...I'm sorry...Dame Littlefield...out and about. Should have known that clever little juggler would get on your good side."

Kresgan peeked around the edge of the control panel.

"They teamed up, sir."

"I know they teamed up, fool," Walpole said, his paw over the transmitter. He cast his electronic gaze over the rest of the prisoners. "Ah, three of the Dinhari clan. I think you'll find your simple little psychic gifts no match for my ever growing powers. Too bad."

Tagger-Streel made a rude gesture at the Colossus. "Come down here and I'll show you what we're a match for, you sick excuse for a hedgehog."

The Colossus' huge maw managed a grin. "Yes, talk tough. I think I will enjoy this more than I thought. My troops have you surrounded. You may try to fight your way out and die in the cold and dankness of my stronghold's dungeons. Or, you may go out in glorious fashion, bravely battling against hopeless odds and making my Immersion Ceremony Day one to remember. What do you say?"

Jonathan looked at the others.

"Well, if he puts it like that."

"It may be our only chance to get across to the other side of the crater," Dame Littlefield whispered. "We only need to distract that machine with a few of us, while the rest go for Walpole and Kresgan."

Emenine conferred quietly with the Dinhari.

"We'll do more than distract it. We'll give it fits."

The other rebels, standing about in wonderment at the turn of events, rushed forward.

"We will help, too," their leader, a sculptor called Ignio, said dramatically. "Let this go down as the day the Ceramic people gave their last to bring down a terrible tyrant and free the land of his scourge."

Dame Littlefield considered the offer. "It's important we're not attacked from the rear. Guard the dungeon passage and keep those troops out of here. If you have to, use old Twodle there as a shield. He's big enough to cover most of you."

The native saluted and urged his small force back into the dark passage leading to the dungeons, the High Commander dragged along behind by his heels.

"We accept your challenge," Jonathan said. "It was a challenge, right?"

"If you want to look at it that way," Walpole said. "Massacring you all in interesting fashion will certainly be a challenge for old Kresgan here. He says hello, by the way, Dame Littlefield. He hopes the experience of being a monster in a filthy labyrinth for several months hasn't made you more bitter than you already were."

"Tell that worm his day is coming," Littlefield shouted.

Kresgan again peeked from behind his control panel.

"Was it necessary to antagonize her?"

"What can she do? Fly across the crater and rip out your throat?" Walpole snickered as he watched his cocky little scientist sweat. He switched channels on his transmitter. "Verlag, have you been following all this?"

The assassin finished attaching the sights on his rifle.

"Yes. Delightful twist. I suppose you want me to kill them."

"No! Just announce the battle, you driveling moron. I'll do the killing around here."

Verlag smiled. "We'll see about that," he muttered. He drew up to the array of megaphones once more.

"Ladies and gentlemen. There has been an adjustment in the program for today. Instead of a boring old fight between rebels, we have a special match lined up for you. Standing before you, representing the Great Mind, is the Colossus." There was some strained cheering and applause. The crowd was getting impatient. "And, volunteering to face certain death in a myriad of horrible, horrible ways, are some old arch-enemies from back home on Yurle Prime. Let's have a big hand for Jonathan Quintain, Emenine, Mistress of the Highwire and Juggler-Extraordinaire and, here by special engagement from the labyrinth under the dungeons, Wrathgog, aka, Dame Littlefield. Oh, and three members of the Dinhari clan, whose names escape me. Am I leaving anyone out?"

"Must be something going on elsewhere," Larko said as the prisoners watched four more of the robot guards trudge off up the ramp into the interior of the stronghold.

"Whatever it is, it makes our chances even better," Bogo said. "There are only those three robots and a couple of the Crimson Quill gang hanging about. You can easily distract them, right?"

Sir Lavolier looked up from where he was scribbling out directions on a piece of scrap paper, blocked from the view of the remaining guards by a circle of Ceramic artists. He rubbed his scraped jaw and gave the eunuch a cold look.

"Just do your part and never mind, bully boy."

A line of newly baked statues of the demon hedgehog stood along a wall near the ramp. They'd had to wait for them to cool, but the moment had finally arrived. Coming down from the interior of the stronghold was a large man, guarded by a single hedgehog. Behind came two Ceramic natives in the livery of the Prickley Topside Restaurant, dragging a long hose.

"I'm Prickley," he said. "I was ordered to fill some pots with this ghastly wormroot wine his Great Mind desires to toast his rise to immortality."

The other Ceramic prisoners rushed to genuflect in front of the once powerful entrepreneur of nearly all that was bought and sold on the island and the surrounding archipelago.

"Yes, yes," the man said, a tired defeat in his voice. "Nicely done. Twenty percent off your next visit to the...well...whichever of my stores is still standing after all this blows over."

Bogo and Larko pushed their way to the front of the pack and conferred briefly with the new arrival.

When the feed house was lowered down, it managed to slip between the pots and into a drain pipe in the floor.

"Ready, begin," shouted Lavolier. Those natives who had been studying his figures leapt into position in a line that blocked the sight of the guards. The robotic eyes focused on the small man standing before them, posed in the classic dance style of Yurle.

"We pay homage to this great day,

By singing and dancing and performing a play.

Walpole the Great Mind becomes perfection

We hope he likes this classical selection."

The line of natives began a high-stepping trot around the guards, while Lavolier leapt and cavorted, in what he had once suggested was a manner that had brought four encores at the Capitol Ballet House.

When the dance had gone on for some time and the verses to Walpole's Paean had degraded to a series of lah-lah-lahs, the entertainment ground to a halt.

Lavolier, sweating profusely and gasping for air, halted in front of the guards.

"Well, what do you think? Will he like it?"

The Crimson Quill guard shrugged. "What do I know about music? It was alright, I guess."

"Good. Needs a little work, but I think the basic format will do." Lavolier glanced around. Larko, Bogo, and the natives Devello and another were gone, along with four of the large pots. Prickley stood near the ramp, innocently filling the remaining containers.

Brother Ricketts and Brother Flogs waited inside a special booth designated for those charged with the blessed function of collecting blood from the victims of the games-blood that would be filtered and purified and then used to help fill the sacred Immersion tub. They waved up at friends and family members in the crowd.

"Listen to that," Brother Ricketts beamed, delighted. "After all our diligent work, the job is all but done. The pool is full, the mechanisms are all in place and tested. Today, the Great Mind will become our leader for eternity."

Brother Flogs nodded. "Yes, for ever and ever. We shall be allowed to worship and serve him until the day we die. And then our children will be able to, and their children and their children...."

"Very good, Flogs. Now, we must get ready. Verlag insisted that we get all the...fluids...we could from those that are sacrificed here today. Especially the red-headed human woman and the man named Jonathan. The Great Mind really wants to be immersed in their blood."

The great Colossus rose to its feet, towering over the arena, its head nearly even with the highest seats. Its red eyes glittered as it backed away from the entrance to the dressing room, the razor-clawed hands snicking open and shut in anticipation. In the

252

control room, Kresgan panted with excitement, his quills erect.

Walpole stood at the balcony of his great statue, leaning over, focusing all his attention on the figures emerging into the light of day. At the front were the three Dinhari, their posture erect and proud, one of them leaping and taking defensive stances before the crowd.

"Ah, here they come, loyal subjects," Verlag said. "In front is, I am told, Tagger-Streel, a Dinhari of a fighting clan. To his right, Blip, an expert in the field of botany and blessed with a photographic memory. Won't be a bit of use to him today, but in his next life he'll be able to recall every painful second of his death. Finally, Dorn, blessed with some minor mind tricks that may amuse you for a moment or two. And, not surprising, cowering behind them, is Jonathan Quintain, a Space Force pilot and other dubious skills, Emenine the Jester, talented in so many ways, most of them unmentionable, and bringing up the rear, Wrathgog formerly known as Dame Littlefield. She may give us a bit of a fight, thank goodness. Designed in the labs of Kresgan the Wise, she is a one of kind and soon to be the last. Well, there you have it. I believe the Colossus is ready to begin."

"Remind me to hit Verlag hard when I see him again," Emenine said, standing next to Jonathan with a short dull blade in her hand.

Kresgan hit the sound button and the Colossus roared so loudly the ground vibrated. The Dinhari charged, Tagger-Streel leaping and then rolling between the great robot's legs as it stomped forward. Dorn moved to the side and raised his hands. Swirls of yellow volcanic ash rose into whirlwinds of blinding particles, concentrating around the Colossus head. Blip leapt up and down, waving his arms.

With a loud roar of her own, Dame Littlefield bowled through a line of guards and charged off across the crater floor, heading straight for the hedgehog-shaped tower where Walpole watched the action. Behind her came Jonathan and Emenine, trying to tread lightly as the thin crust crackled and crumbled beneath their feet.

Verlag saw the action out of the corner of his eye as he raised the rifle and looked through the high-powered sights at the place where Walpole stood. Clouds of dust flew up and blocked his view time after time. The fight below was making it difficult to get a clear shot and he knew he only had one before the target turned on him.

There was a loud rattle behind Walpole and he turned to see hedgehogs unloading four large pots from a cart next to the door.

"The wormfruit wine you wanted, your greatness," one of the Crimson Quill Guild members said, bowing out with his companions quickly. Walpole took only a quick glance at the pots, shaped to emulate his own lovely form, then looked back to the battle. The clouds of dust the little Dinhari were using to blind his own weapon blocked his view of the fight.

"I want to see what's going on down there," he said to himself. He raised a paw and waved it toward the little hedgehog Dorn. He was thrown

254

across the arena and crashed into the wall at the foot of the stands. He lay there, stunned. The dust immediately began to settle out, revealing Tagger-Streel half way up the leg of the Colossus, who paused every step to try and shake the pest off its body. Blip, standing helplessly in the open when the dust cleared, turned to help his friend Dorn. The great foot of the robot crashed down on him before he could get out of the way.

The crowd cheered the bloody murder. Halfway across the crater, Jonathan stopped and looked back. It was obvious the Dinhari, despite their determined nature, were doomed.

"Go on, you two," he yelled. "I'm going back."

"What do you think you can do?" Dame Littlefield shouted as she waited for Emenine to catch up.

"Die trying," he said, waving the feeble blade he'd picked up in the dressing room and running back the way he'd come, leaping a fountain of hot steam as it burst through the crust.

Walpole spotted Jonathan heading back toward the main arena. His beady eyes trailed back along his path and spotted Wrathgog and Emenine nearly to the foot of his tower. Although he knew there was nothing to fear from them, he wanted to see them crushed like the Dinhari beneath the Colossus' feet. His mind stabbed out and Emenine slid to a stop. Before her stood Baron Glauwer.

"Go back, darling. It's a trap here. You'll be killed the second you step inside."

Dame Littlefield reached the entry to the tower and turned back.

"What's wrong?"

Emenine stepped back and began to turn.

Over the sound of the roaring robot and the cheering crowd, the sound of the shot was hardly more than the sound of a cork being pulled from a wine bottle. The sonic shell struck Walpole squarely in the chest, bowling him over.

The spell around Emenine broke as Glauwer vanished. She looked around in confusion, then raced after Wrathgog, who had already vanished inside.

"Guards! Kresgan! Help me," Walpole screamed as he crawled back into the main chamber of his tower, blood running down the front of his body. Before anyone could come to his aid, the four pots that were supposed to hold his favorite wine burst open, and there stood the fat eunuch Bogo Grandmont, Gamitof Pym Larko, and a pair of Ceramic natives, all armed with sharp-looking sculpting tools. They stood there looking at the wounded tyrant's predicament with confusion.

"What happened?" Larko said, almost accusing his companions of acting out of turn.

Kresgan stepped into view, a vicious-looking sonic laser cradled in his hands.

"No one move."

Walpole struggled to a large chair he used as his throne and groaned. "Oh, this just gets better and better."

Below, in the arena, the Colossus had stopped a short stomp away from where Dorn lay, Jonathan shielding the unconscious hedgehog as he waited for the robot to reach them. When it failed to move again, Tagger-Streel slid off its back and leapt to the ground. There was a disappointed sigh from the crowd. The guards moved in to surround the prisoners.

A shout went up from high in the stands. Lawson, followed by Virago and his rebels, appeared at an upper exit to the stands and ran down the walkways toward the arena, scattering the hedgehog crowd. Reaching the pump room, they had quickly made their way to the empty throne room, then caught a hedgehog servitor only too willing to direct them to the arena.

"Free the Ceramic people," Virago shouted.

"Has any one seen my mother?" Lawson added as he leapt to the ground. He looked up at the Colossus standing silently next to the stands.

A wild free-for-all started as the rebels and guards battled, off-duty troopers leaping into the fray from the stands. Jonathan lifted Dorn to his shoulder and, with Tagger-Streel covering his rear, made their way to where Lawson was fighting amongst the robot guards, using one as a shield to deflect the laser eyes of the others. With a powerful sweep, he decapitated some of them while bowling over the rest.

"Jonathan, have you seen Mother?" he asked again.

Before the man could answer, a sonic blast struck the ground near their feet, knocking them down. Lawson spotted Verlag in the announcer's booth, readying another grenade.

"There he is, that villain," the demi-god said, and was over the side of the arena wall and sprinting up toward Verlag's post before Jonathan could tell him that if he was looking for his mother, he was going the wrong way.

Verlag screeched and dove out of the booth and into the stronghold, desperately looking for a hole to hide in. Lawson vanished inside, closely in pursuit.

Chapter Sixteen

"The wound looks fatal," Kresgan said, examining Walpole's bloody chest. The robot guards held each of the prisoners tightly in their grip. There was a brief sound of struggle below and Emenine and Dame Littlefield were dragged in as well. Their search for a stairway to the upper floor had unfortunately led them to the main guard room.

"Looks fatal?" the demon hedgehog snorted in derision. "Feels like I'm way too alive at the moment. On my death bed and surrounded by my loved ones."

"I'll rip out your quills one by one," Dame Littlefield snarled, helpless in the grip of the mechanical monsters.

Larko took in the strange creature.

"I don't believe we've met."

"Sweetheart? Is that you?" Bogo said from his own place of restraint. Although the body of his beloved was utterly transformed, her spirit was unmistakable.

Dame Littlefield turned to the eunuch.

"And you thought getting a little fat would put a damper on our love. Get a look at this disaster."

"It doesn't matter," Bogo cried.

"Of course it doesn't, fool. That's what I was trying to tell you the day you walked out on me. Beauty is only...."

"I'm dying here and they're renewing their vows," Walpole said. "I must do everything myself.

Kresgan, keep an eye on them. I have more important things to do." He blinked from sight.

Verlag raced down one hall after another, expecting any second to have the heavy hand of sudden justice fall on his head. When it appeared he was no longer being pursued, he quickly determinedly made his way to his private chamber where he collected his valuables and other meager belongings and continued down into the dungeon area of the stronghold.

Coming out at the balcony that overlooked the final testing rituals being done on *Walpole's Revenge* he made his way to the lower entrance to the hanger. With a quick stab, he dispatched the hedgehog guard and climbed up into the cargo bay of the ship. It was packed to full with the armaments that the demon hedgehog intended to use to subdue the rest of the planet before he returned to Yurle Prime to blast his old enemies into the next hedgehog stone age. The assassin nestled into a dark corner and settled down to wait.

Lawson, finding himself standing in the throne room again, decided chasing the assassin was pointless, and made his way back to the main arena. Below, Jonathan, the surviving Dinhari, and the Ceramic rebels were being joined by other natives that were backing out of the dressing room exit, pressed by more Crimson Quill Guild troopers. They dragged the dead body of High Commander Twodle, who had been killed by his own men as they attacked the rebels delaying their back door assault.

The demi-god leapt to the ground and joined the fracas, which quickly lost the crowd's interest as a more novel event began happening at another site on the crater. The tall woven screens that had concealed the Great Mind's altar were being knocked down by two hedgehog priests, revealing a steaming cauldron overhung by a strange contraption.

"Let the ceremony begin," Brother Ricketts shouted, his voice barely audible over the fighting. Brother Flogs climbed up on the conveyor belt and waited expectantly.

"That's where Walpole thinks he's going to be changed into an immortal," Dorn said, still supported by Jonathan. "We have to stop them."

Before Lawson could react, a scream drew his entire attention away to the tall hedgehog shaped tower. His mother stood momentarily on the balcony, waving her arms, before robot guards dragged her back inside. Her son forgot everything but the need to rescue her. With two leaps he was across the crater and pulling himself up the outside of the tower toward the opening where he'd seen his mother vanish.

"I guess it's up to us," Jonathan said, but before they could make a try for the immersion site, robot guards began issuing from the foot of the tower, their eyes flashing with lasers as they fired across toward where Jonathan and his companions fought the last of the Crimson Quill troopers.

"Retreat," Virago shouted as rebels began to fall under the laser assault. They ran for cover in the lower entrance to the gladiatorial dressing rooms, Jonathan and the Dinhari reluctantly following.

One minute Brother Flog was leaping up and down, cheering the slaughter of the remaining rebels and the next, the Great Mind stood beside him, gasping in pain and nearly collapsing in his arms.

"Hold me, you idiot," Walpole growled. "No, never mind. Get me to the immersion pool before all is lost."

It was clear the great inspiration for all the Brothers' hard work was at the very edge of spoiling things by dying early. Flogs held his leader while Brother Ricketts rushed to put the conveyor belt into gear. It jerked forward, nearly tumbling both hedgehogs off, but then they rolled forward.

Walpole gave a grunt and pushed Flogs away, toppling him to the ground.

"Don't need two immortal rulers of the Universe. Oh, don't look so glum. I'll let you die for me some other time."

Flogs clapped happily as the Great Mind dropped anti-climatically into the roiling pool of immortality elixir, hot droplets of yellow fluid splashing over all sides. With a loud gulp, he disappeared from view.

Ricketts moved over to look into the liquid.

"That was supposed to happen, right?"

"You said you couldn't turn me back to normal," Dame Littlefield yelled as Kresgan pulled the last of the concealing sheets from his transforming machine.

"I said I wasn't going to, not that I couldn't," the scientist said, chuckling evilly. "This is so unexpected. Being able to transform all of you into other things. A half woman/half flier, I think next, with a large stink gland," he said, looking at Emenine. "Oh, and what possibilities a eunuch presents. You already look like some sort of mutation."

Bogo rolled his eyes. "Yeah, hurt me, rat boy."

"Now, if no one else nearly escapes," the scientist said, glaring meaningfully at Emenine, "we'll just start."

"I wish to volunteer," Larko demanded nobly. "If someone will tell me what I'm volunteering for."

"Change me back," Dame Littlefield screamed. "I swear I'll kill you, Kresgan."

The scientist turned on the machine and the wide tubes began glowing inside a glittery blue.

"I doubt--," he began, then stared wide-eyed across the room.

"Mother, is this hedgehog bothering you?" Lawson stood in the doorway to the balcony, brushing himself off.

"Kill him," Kresgan shouted.

The robots, momentarily confused as to how to hold their prisoners and kill a target that moved with a speed that left afterimages in their eyes, finally began firing wildly around the room as Lawson leapt from robot to robot, smashing heads and dislodging arms from sockets.

"Watch out," Dame Littlefield shouted, making her way to the transformer. "Don't wreck any of this yet." Bogo joined her, Kresgan squeezed so tightly against his chest the creature nearly disappeared in the eunuch's fat body. "Make it work, or I'll eat you right here."

"I will make it work," Kresgan gasped. "Get inside that tube."

"Any mistakes," Bogo whispered, "and I'll transform you into a rather tasty pate."

"Point taken," Kresgan said, shaking with fright. "I never should have left my cell. They served worm stew every fifth day."

The floor beneath their feet began to shake, increasing in intensity for several moments then fading.

"That's not a good sign," the scientist said. Flipping several switches and cranking a small silver wheel, he put the machine into motion. "Volcano's getting rambunctious." Wrathgog began spinning in the tube, her whole form infused with the sparkling blue light.

"It's supposed to do that," Kresgan muttered as Bogo leaned over him menacingly.

Two other tubes began filling with light, and bodies began to take shape in each of them. There was a flash and the tube that had contained Wrathgog was empty, and in one of the others, Dame Littlefield, naked but restored to her loveliness, stood stunned. In the other, a fat hedgehog squatted, rubbing his head and muttering.

"Well, let her out," Kresgan said, backing out of Bogo's reach. The eunuch rushed over and opened the tube and pulled Dame Littlefield out.

"You're you again," he said, wrapping her in one of the sheets that had covered the tubes.

264

The hedgehog in the other tube banged heavily on the inside of his container.

"Hey, let me out of here. I'm suffocating."

Bogo flipped the lock and the hedgehog staggered free.

"Well, that was a terrible wrench," it said. "One moment I'm...." He looked at the others. "Well, enough about me." He ran for the exit and disappeared.

"My cousin," Kresgan said, shrugging. "Not too bright but always ready to volunteer. So, are we all happy now?"

"I think I'll kill you anyway," Dame Littlefield said.

The floor heaved again, this time cracking in places. A piece of the ceiling fell into the room, narrowly missing Lawson. The shaking increased and there was a rumble. In the outer corridor, the stairwell fell away and an outer wall tumbled down after it, letting a reddish light filter through the clouds of dust filling the air.

"Trapped," Bogo said.

"Not quite," Lawson said, dropping the head of a robot he'd been examining with Larko.

"We can't all leap down, sweetie," Emenine said. "Bogo's really not up to it."

The young man looked around.

"I have an idea. Everyone move to the balcony entrance. It's the strongest archway and least likely to fall in." He went and sat at the control panel that controlled the Colossus.

Ricketts and Flogs held on tightly to the conveyor belt as it stalled to a halt, the ground under their feet leaping and rolling like a wild beast.

"Where is the Great Mind?" Flogs said. "He will be lost if he doesn't rise soon."

His fellow priest climbed up on the belt as the ground under his feet crumbled away.

"Forget him. What about us?"

Flogs was about to remonstrate when the pool erupted, and a large ball of yellow fire burst into the air above it.

It rose higher and higher and then seemed to pour away into thin air. Floating in its place was Walpole. A new and improved version. Twice the size he'd been before, the wound Verlag had given him was gone and his body gleamed and sparkled with new health and vitality.

"It worked," he hissed and the sound of his voice sent shock waves across the arena. The ground heaved and the crater floor fractured into a smoking web. "I feel...immortal."

Ricketts and Flogs leapt joyously to their feet, clapping and waving. Their happiness was such that they failed to notice as the contraption they stood on sank beneath them into a gap in the volcano crater floor. The cauldron holding the still steaming concoction rolled over, pouring its contents over the two Brothers as they sank out of sight.

Walpole floated above the volcano, watching as the Colossus came to life once more and began trudging across the crater floor, the surface beneath its wide feet rolling and flowing like the face of the sea. With each step it sank a little but continued on toward the slowly fracturing tower.

"The petty conflicts of this world no longer interest me," he said as he considered blasting the tower and its desperate inhabitants to bits. "I have more important tasks to complete. I have worlds to crush."

Deep Thought scanned the world below and found the unit he'd been seeking. He turned the powerful transmitters of the seed ship downward, their great dishes like the ears of beasts, straining to catch the sounds on the planet below. But, it was Deep Thought's message that was to be heard now.

As his adversary drifted toward the tiny structure identified as the Stronghold, Deep Thought's mind cast his warning outward.

Jonathan and Virago, leading the others toward the exit ramp leading into the workhouses, suddenly halted, their followers freezing in step as well. In perfect unison they began to speak.

"I am Deep Thought. I now am in control of this world. To demonstrate this control, I will put my servant, the Armadon Rectangle, to the task for which I enlisted it. As I speak, the dust of its form spreads to surround this world, cutting off the special waves of light that feed its life. I have no wish to destroy life that chooses the wisdom of subservience to me. Only cast your thoughts of acceptance to my rule into space and I will hear you."

Odd Bob, Harlix and the escaped slaves, hiding in the jungle, halted in their puppet-like repetition of Deep Thought's words and looked upward. Slowly, a brown film seemed to coat the sky, and the sun, low on the horizon, began fading to a mere dim glow.

"Are you thinking what I'm thinking," Odd Bob said to Harlix.

The hedgehog stared at his companion. "I don't think so. Unless you are thinking that the entity that took over our ship is this Deep Thought, and that our inability to overcome its intrusion is now bringing doom on an innocent world."

"Well, partly. I was thinking we should surrender immediately."

Harlix nodded and looked at the slaves around them. They were in full agreement. Their thoughts were suddenly interrupted once again.

Now, my second point. I am concerned about the existence of an imposter who thinks to threaten my absolute benevolent control of all life in the universe. He is called Walpole and I wish him turned over to me immediately. I realize his powers are such that this will not be easy and I will certainly allow for a fair period of time for you to accomplish this. I will be waiting.

Chapter Seventeen

"Well, that seems reasonable," Dorn said. "We just have to capture Walpole and surrender unconditionally to something called Deep Thought."

Jonathan, pushing his jaw back and forth, trying to figure out why he was speaking without thinking, turned around.

"Don't you remember that thing that the mole empress fired into space? I thought it was lost in the sun. Apparently, it wasn't."

"That was Deep Thought?" Tagger-Streel said. "Well, I just hope its power is more limited than it claims or this fight for freedom just got pointless."

In deep space, General Jagged slumped down in his command seat and scanned quickly the surrounding area. His fleet of rescue ships were still there, undamaged by the bizarre events that had just transpired. His entire command had risen to their feet and spoken a whole lot of disturbing gibberish about blotting out suns and bringing Walpole to justice.

"Must have been something in the water," he muttered. "Carry on."

The tower seemed to take on the life of the form it mimicked, the hedgehog shoulders slumping as the front of the structure began to dip toward a broadening gap at the edge of the crater. A wall of fire rose from the rift, eating up the side of the front of the tower and scorching the backside of the Colossus as it leaned over the lip of the balcony.

"Get on it," Lawson shouted from his seat at the control panel. "Everyone, go."

Emenine struggled from Larko's hands and ran to her son's side.

"I'm not leaving you here," she said, holding his head in her hands.

"Can't see, Mother," Lawson grumbled. "Going to cause an accident. I'll get out all right. I'll just leap across after you're safe. Now go."

The woman backed away, staring in fright as she watched her son struggle to hold the robot steady. The others were clutching to various handholds, Larko still on the balcony waving for her to come along.

"He's a demi-god," he shouted. "Nothing ever happens to one of those. Hurry. You're only making his job harder."

Emenine ran across the floor, spinning into a cartwheel and then a flip that landed her at Larko's side. She looked back.

"Good one, Mother," he shouted, giving her a thumbs up before leaning back down to his task.

All onboard, the Colossus turned about and stepped gingerly over the gap, the fire momentarily in abeyance. Then the robot began plodding across the crater floor, the surface lifting, falling, and breaking apart all around them.

Lawson fixed the controls so that the Colossus would continue across to the arena's far wall, where its passengers could leap off and get inside the protection of the stronghold. He pushed the forward motivator into position and locked it down.

The tower suddenly crumbled forward again, Walpole's great head splitting apart in the violent throes of the erupting volcano. With a wild leap, Lawson cleared out of the way just as a huge piece of heavy ceramic fell across the control panel. The motivator lever snapped downward as sparks and smoke spewed up from the battered console.

He ran to the sloping balcony. The Colossus stood stiffly halfway across, the area all around it beginning to sink as the lava welled up between the cracks. Returning to the console, he jammed the motivator lever back in place and the robot moved again.

"The lock is broken," Lawson said, resignation slowly surrounding him. "They can't move unless I hold this in place."

The top of the tower broke away and tumbled out onto the crater floor like a decapitated head off the chopping block. Lawson could now see out across the arena. The robot giant was nearly there, but he could feel the tower falling away beneath his feet.

"I wonder if...," he began as the remaining structure collapsed and vanished into the widening gap.

The Colossus' feet suddenly lost support and the robot fell forward to span the gap to the arena stands like a metal bridge. The riders leapt to the safety of the shaking seats.

Emenine, turning about, searched for the leaping form of her son. All she saw was the emptiness where the tower had once stood.

"Lawson," she whispered, fainting.

Bogo, holding Dame Littlefield in his arms, scanned the sky for the dark spot of a leaping figure.

"He's gone," Dame Littlefield said.

Before they could consider what they might do to search for him, the crater exploded, sending flaming balls of rock and magma into the air. Black ash began pouring out of the sky. Picking up the limp Emenine, Larko hurried them all into the stronghold as death rained down from above.

The stronghold heaved and the sound of stone snapping and cracking filled the air as clouds of dust streamed from new crevices in the ceiling. Seated at a table that looked out over the terrible conflagration of the erupting volcano, Prickley considered his options. The restaurant was clearly about to be closed for good, but the old clientele still seemed loyal, if he could preserve even a few of the shops down in the compound partway across the island.

The floor suddenly tilted and the remaining native kitchen help emerged from that area, screaming and dashing to him for protection.

"Yes, yes. I know the volcano is erupting," he said irritated. "I suppose there's no time to collect the silverware and that stock of fine liquors I was saving for the fifty year anniversary of Prickley's Skyview Restaurant. Okay, okay. Just joking. Follow me."

No fool, the restaurateur had never believed the old crater was entirely dead and had made sure there was a safe way out in case of emergency. He pushed open the dumb waiter and slid back a rear panel. It opened to a dark hole.

"It's a slide," he explained. "Don't be afraid. It comes out in the garden at the back wall."

He led the way, vanishing from sight, his workers diving in after him. A moment later, the heavy cap of stone that covered the ceiling fell in, flattening all that remained of the renowned eatery.

Verlag heard shouting, then frightened screaming coming from out in the hanger. He lowered his head enough to see that the technicians and guards who had been working on the last details of the ship were racing in terror for the opening where the ship would emerge once it was activated. Craning his head further, he could see a bright golden light spreading across the space. Squinting, Verlag spotted Walpole drifting downward at its center, heading for one of the upper level locks.

"So, it worked," the assassin said, flinging himself back into the dark corner he'd been hiding in. "Well, that'll just make the reward bigger." He bit his lower lip thoughtfully. "Maybe it would be better to stick with the plan to go for the 'bring him in dead' part of the reward."

Verlag had never been accused of cowardice (although the tactful retreat had occasionally drifted close to the unpleasant accusation) and he decided then and there that if Walpole proved too much for even an expert like himself, he would escape his doom, nonetheless. Pulling out a small crowbar from his bag of tricks, he worked away at an access panel in the nearest missile seated innocently in its cradle waiting for launch.

"Cross one, weave two, bend back and tighten," he muttered as he felt *Walpole's Revenge* come to life. "Looks like I'm going for a ride." He fixed the panel back in place with an adhesive he normally used for his teeth and crawled out onto a walkway. He hurried into the adjoining passage as the cargo doors slammed shut and the airlocks spun closed.

Aside from Emenine, who still lay in a deep faint, the rest were overjoyed to see one after another of their companions or acquaintances emerge from the stronghold and run out into the rolling hills that surrounded it. Heavy burning balls of molten lava arched over their heads and crashed down in flaming explosions all around them. The walls of the structure split and tumbled inward and, as it was growing dark, a sinister red glow began to rise from the direction of the volcano's crater.

Running down the path from the garden came Prickley and several natives dressed in aprons and white hats.

"Might want to save the sightseeing for another time," he said, continuing to run on down the path toward where a powered wagon stood as a dark shadow against the woods beyond. The others followed, climbing into the wagon as Prickley brought the machine to life. They moved out and down the road that Larko and the others had used to escape from the late High Commander Twodle earlier.

A terrific explosion shook the ground and more debris was flung high in the air.

"Hope we can outrun the flow this time," Virago said, his face streaked with ash. "Lost most of the opera club in the last eruption. Ah, who is that waiting along the road there?"

274

The wagon was brought to a halt.

"It seems to be all of the remaining members of the Gallery," Virago said, helping his fellow artists and natives into the wagon. "Except for these."

Jonathon, helping to pull the others on board, shouted in surprise. "Odd Bob! What are you doing here?"

The red-haired man, lifting a small hedgehog to a seat beside him, looked sheepishly at the other man.

"Lost my ship for a bit. Some super mind has taken it over. Oddest thing."

"Deep Thought has taken over your seed ship?" Bogo asked.

Bob took in the others.

"Yes. Nice to see you all again. Been some time. This is Harlix, my assistant. You remember him."

Before they could answer, another blast took place, but this time it wasn't the volcano. The side of the stronghold hidden by a spur of the mountain flew outward and a huge ship appeared, a blue fire spitting out from a trio of rear-mounted engines.

"*Walpole's Revenge*," Dame Littlefield said, awestruck.

"Could have offered us a lift," Bogo said. "Who do you suppose is flying it?"

"That gold glow coming from the windows of the command station might be a clue," Jonathan pointed out. "Well, it looks like this battle is out of the hands of us mere mortals. I have a feeling the two contenders for ruler of the universe are about to meet."

Kresgan, who had made no sound from the ball of netting that served as his restraints, wiggled his nose into view.

"If I don't say so myself, the Great Mind Walpole is more than a match for that primitive mole-brained construction of a psychic dictator."

The wagon bumped down the last hill to where Prickley's array of shops stood, but it was too late. The Crimson Quill had made short work of them, torching all the buildings as they fled. The owner of the charred structures shrugged philosophically.

"Well, may as well see what lies across that stretch of water, eh," Prickley announced, and headed the wagon toward the shore of the sea where the broken wrecks of the explorer ships waited. At the side of one of them waited their old crews, looking better for being out of the influence of Walpole and his zombification plot.

Another mammoth explosion shook the entire island and the sea itself slowly began withdrawing, as if trying to escape the disaster.

"That's not a good sign," Bogo said, helping Dame Littlefield to her feet. She had been trying to awaken Emenine, who was slowly moaning as she regained consciousness.

Prickley ran a few steps down the shore.

"That's definitely not a good sign. And there's no time for building rafts or finding high ground."

"Things were simpler on the seed ship," Odd Bob said, still holding Harlix's paw. The hedgehog nodded quietly.

In the far distance, out across the water, a dark high line began to form.

"That rumble isn't coming from the volcano," Jonathan said suspiciously. He threw his head back and stared upward. Down from the heavens dropped a line of scout ships, General Jagged's newly arrived fleet homing in on the old wrecks.

"Saved," Emenine moaned.

Chapter Eighteen

Walpole's Revenge settled into orbit above Yurle Minor. The demon hedgehog of Yurle left the ship's controls in autopilot and moved to the scanner that searched the surrounding area for threatening obstacles.

The pronouncements of Deep Thought had not taken hold of his mind like it had lesser beings, but Walpole had clearly heard the AI's demands. It had been amusing.

"I am the Immortal, the Great Mind, the demon hedgehog and no one will steal this universe from me." He found the orbit of the main body of the huge seed ship, and considered whether to blow it to tiny bits right there in space or to attempt another avenue of attack. He quickly decided on the latter, wishing to confront Deep Thought in its lair, to destroy it in such a manner that he would never have to fear its revival again.

"Have to paw it to old Moleloch. She could build a solid mind control device."

Returning to his seat, he failed to see Verlag slip into the control room and conceal himself behind an auxiliary console. Taking control once again, Walpole sent the *Revenge* humming toward the bulky ship of his more dire adversary.

An unoccupied docking ring lit up as the ship approached, and a flashing beacon guided Walpole forward, linking up with a satisfying thunk.

"I'm expected," the sneering hedgehog said, locking the ship in place and then levitating from his seat, a golden glow beginning to surround his form. "Must look my best."

"Hard to look your best without a head," Verlag shouted as he leapt across the short gap between them. The long-bladed knife struck Walpole's neck, but did little more than throw off a welter of sparks, the blade snapping off against the impenetrable flesh of the immortal tyrant.

"No time for that, foolish Verlag," Walpole laughed, with a gesture casting the assassin aside. Verlag smashed into an instrument-lined wall and crumbled to the floor. Before he could release the first scream of agony, his target had vanished from the room.

The seed ship's main body was shaped like a starfish with its many arms sheared away. The nerve center lay down one of several identical passages, all barely lit by single dots of orange light that flickered as if the power were slowly draining away. Walpole found the correct one and moved confidently toward the central control room. He could hear all around him the slithering and scraping of movement, but his ultra-precise senses told him it was only plants and he ignored them as harmless.

"Freezing to death, no doubt," he said, aware that the temperature was falling quickly toward zero, but it had no effect on him.

The heavy door to the control room slid aside as he approached. The interior was aglitter with myriad lighted sensors and dials, most there to regulate the many environmental pods that no longer were attached to the ship. He ignored them, turning to the huge central station that controlled the main functions of the ship, the power grid and engines, the atmosphere and other life support necessities.

"Deep Thought," he whispered mischievously. "Are you here?"

Of course I am here. The voice, its source so near, boomed in Walpole's head. If he had not been made immortal, it would have ruptured his brain and finished his long and infamous reign.

So, we are using telepathy, are we? Not to be outshone, he boomed his thoughts back in like manner, and somewhere a chip cracked, the smell of burning metal growing stronger as he strutted toward the main console. Before he could reach it, a blast of lightning-like energy burst from an orifice once used to analyze soil samples, engulfing the hedgehog and sending him flying backward.

I am going to reduce you to an ash-like substance, my poor rival. You shall not enjoy your enhanced physicality for long.

Rising, Walpole ignored his smoking body and charged again, teeth bared ferociously.

I'm going to rip your innards out and chew your robot brain into pieces so small only my god-like eyes will be able to find them so my god-like feet can stomp them into even smaller pieces.

The blast came from another corner of the room this time, and although it sent the hedgehog flying backward once again, Walpole sensed the energy was not as strong as the first. Deep Thought's power source was limited, perhaps to only what could be stored by the ship.

Stumbling to his paws once more, he found it a bit hard to focus. The golden glow that signified his immortality seemed a bit less vibrant as well. The implications didn't bear contemplation, especially at that moment. Walpole just hoped his opponent didn't notice.

Deep Thought gathered the remaining energy from the storage cells that lined the outer walls of the ship, their solar accumulators working at full capacity to restore the draining batteries. The blast would be the biggest it could safely generate without destroying the ship itself. Although Deep Thought detected that Walpole's own immense reserves were fading, there was the smallest percentage that if the next blast failed, it would be at the mercy of the furious creature, immortal or not.

Leave now and I'll consider letting you live out the remainder of your puny and short existence. If you like that planet below so well, take it and I will forget you. The Universe will take time to conquer and by the time I return here, you will be no more.

With a howl that rang up and down the empty halls of the abandoned seed ship, Walpole, demon hedgehog, bloody tyrant of Yurle Minor, and aspiring conqueror of the Universe, charged the heart of Deep Thought's power once again.

Verlag dragged himself to the command seat vacated by his former master. His legs failed to follow his direction and he knew that, barring a miracle he was not likely to receive, Walpole had crippled him for life. He stared out into space, wondering if he could learn to operate the complex

281

ship quickly enough to leave the demon hedgehog behind.

Two loud blasts shook the ships.

"Having fun, you murderous little fiend," he muttered as he scanned the instruments. He shook his bleeding head. "Well, then, I guess this is it."

The possibility of finding an escape pod crossed his mind, but he had no idea where to look and the prospect of floating about alone, with little likelihood of being rescued by sympathetic beings, was an empty one. Closing his eyes, his mind went down to the cargo hold, where the missile's auto-detonation timer was counting down to zero. Only a few minutes more. Verlag smiled. Considering his situation, he had thought of everything.

Smoke billowed out of the control room, sparks spraying across the passage floor. Walpole, singed and dragging one leg, crawled out of the room and began limping down the passage toward his ship.

"Artificial intelligence, my backside quills," he smirked. "I am Walpole, demon hedgehog of Yurle, and no one can stop me." He only noticed that the golden glow which had provided his supernatural powers had faded to nothing when the long tendrils of the starving plants encircled him and dragged him snarling and thrashing to their waiting maws.

Verlag tapped his fingers in time to a silent clock. "THREE, TWO, ONE."

The occupants of the rescue craft were jerked away from their contemplation of the devastating tidal wave that roared over the Ceramics' island, waving away all trace of Walpole's reign, including the surviving members of the Crimson Guild, by a

282

bright swelling light in the night sky. It repeated again and again, as if individual explosions were going off.

Kresgan groaned. "My ship. All those lovely missiles."

Odd Bob wiped a tear from his eye and nudged Larko's arm.

"Going to need another seed ship, sir," he said. Harlix's little beady eyes widened and he nodded in understanding. "Have to rescue our people in the other environment pods."

"I'll see what I can do."

There was another massive explosion below as the sea water rolled up and over the lip of the volcano and washed down into the fiery crater. The Ceramics' island cracked apart and sank into the sea.

Virago, with the remainder of his people, watched as their homeland vanished.

"General Jagged," he said matter-of-factly. "Your home world wouldn't be in need of a certain artistic infusion, would it?"

The old soldier smiled. "Well, I'm no expert on art, but I know what I like. How about a bunch of them statues, but ones that look like me."

Epilogue

The second seed ship under Odd Bob's command, which he had imaginatively titled Number Two, moved slowly out of the Yurle solar system, its lighted pods filled with flora and fauna from the old worlds of the hedgehogs glowing against the distant stars.

"Too dangerous around here," he'd announced to his staff, all of whom had been rescued with their precious cargo after some weeks of dedicated searching by the Galactic University's Tandaran Search and Rescue division. Another retired battle cruiser had been refitted to Odd Bob's specifications and, despite the loss of the carnivorous section, was still bursting to fullness with the endangered life of the systems' worlds.

"Too bad about the meat-eaters," Harlix said.

"They're a hardy type," Bob said. "What was the last report on strange seeds drifting on the oceans of Yurle Minor? They sounded a lot like our plants."

"I don't know. None of the investigators returned."

"Funny bunch, investigators," Odd Bob said philosophically. "Well, full steam ahead, I always say. Next stop, the Terran system. One or two planets detected in the life zone. Should be fun bringing our wonderful life to those primitive worlds."

Harlix squeaked happily. "Should be fun."

The crew of the *Duweena's Courage II* was also leaving the Yurle system; in this case heading for the more populated sector of the galaxy where the Galactic University was headquartered. It had been several months since Walpole, the demon hedgehog, had been presumed killed in the destruction of the *Revenge* and the seed ship. Nothing, either, had been heard of Deep Thought. It was universally believed that was a good thing.

Gamitof Pym Larko, resplendent in his new commander's uniform, was joined by his second, Jonathan Quintain, resigned from Yurle Space Force and now in the pay of the GU, as was Bogo Grandmont, Dame Littlefield, Sir Lavolier, and an array of Dinhari hedgehogs, including their closest associates, Dorn and Tagger-Streel. Even Virago, loaded with a shipment of the latest in Ceramic art, was going along for the ride to introduce the galaxy to the artwork of his native world.

"Is she still in her cabin?" Larko asked Jonathan, who had just returned from the crew area.

"Still there. She seems...better."

The death of Lawson had struck them hard. He had been the youngest and strongest of them, and it seemed impossible that even the terrible power of a volcano's heart could destroy him completely. Others had died in the battle as well, but their beloved Emenine's pain was shared by them all.

"I went and offered to show her my latest dance steps," Sir Lavolier said, brushing back his long blond locks. "She told me to jump out an airlock."

Bogo lifted his head from his navigational computations.

"She did. That sounds a lot better."

Dame Littlefield stepped into view, wearing the uniform of a GU Special Forces Officer.

"I think I hear her coming this way. Everybody look busy."

Pushing Lavolier out of his seat in front of the Weapons controls, she sat down just as Emenine tumbled into view, juggling three balls with one hand while somersaulting across the floor to her seat in front of the Entertainment storage console. With a heavy thud she sat down.

"I thought we were going to Tandara," she said, catching the balls and dropping them, one by one, into a large pocket.

"Lawson loved that trick," Lavolier said, then looked embarrassed, a rare sight.

Emenine looked around at them all.

"Yes, he did. Are we going or not? I have creditors all over Yurle system looking for me and it's definitely time to move on."

"Can't go yet," Jonathan said smoothly.

"Why not?" the jester asked in confusion.

"Haven't heard what the entertainment is for the first leg," he said.

Emenine looked dazed, then smiled at Jonathan. "Tonight's film is a talkie...for a change. Giant Slugworms from the Deep Void."

"Sounds like a hedgehog cooking show," Bogo said.

The ship's engines burst into life and the *Duweena's Courage* began her voyage to the center of the galaxy.

Also by Joel Reeves

From Fiction4All

Of Quills And Kings
When Walpole, the so-called sacred Hedgehog of
Yurle, captures the realm's child-king, Jonathan and
his friends set off into the desolate land of Yurle to
save their King and hopefully recover the stolen
Orb.

Walpole Unbound
Freed from the battles and terrors of his home
world, Jonathan Glauwer finds himself back in the
thick of trouble when his old adversary, Walpole-
the telepathic demon hedgehog of Yurle-escapes
from his prison. A terrible war between the surface-
dwelling hedgehogs and the merciless Empress
Moleloch and her mole minions throws everyone
into terrible danger and it is up to old friends and
new heroes to bring peace to Yurle Prime and their
spiny enemy to justice.

www.ingramcontent.com/pod-product-compliance
Lightning Source LLC
Chambersburg PA
CBHW011654010726
47499CB00010B/3253

* 9 7 8 1 7 8 6 9 5 7 1 9 1 *